SISTERS

SUN VALLEY SERIES - BOOK ONE

KELLIE COATES GILBERT

Dedicated to my parents, Elwin and Arlene Coates. This sheep rancher and his wife taught me the meaning of family and the value of being loved unconditionally. I am proud to be their daughter.

WELCOME TO THE SUN VALLEY SERIES!

Set in America's original ski resort, Sun Valley, Idaho—SISTERS offers a thought-provoking look at three women...and the choices they make when they realize their lives aren't exactly what they expected.

For more information on this series, and to sign up for notifications of future releases, please visit Kellie's website:

www.kelliecoatesgilbert.com

1

Karyn Macadam slowed her car as the sign to the Hemingway Memorial came into view. She turned off Sun Valley Road into the parking area, not bothering to signal. There was no need, not at this early hour.

Cutting the engine, she sat quietly for a few moments, the radio blaring in the background.

And we expect another warm summer day here in the Wood River Valley as residents in this popular resort area prepare to commemorate one of its own, nearly a year and a half after the tragic accident that took the life of—

Karyn shut off the radio, her heart thudding painfully.

Squeezing the steering wheel, she refused to look at the seat next to her—at the small wooden box intricately carved with falling snowflakes over a set of crossed skis.

Deep breath in. Deep breath out.

Five more minutes she sat there, putting off what was ahead.

Finally, she scooped the box into her hands and climbed out of the car.

She'd made a promise. One she fully intended to keep, even if she'd made it a bit tongue-in-cheek at the time.

Gravel crunched beneath her feet as she traversed the walkway toward the memorial. Even in the faint morning light she could make out wild poppies and blue flax, delicate against the pungent skunk cabbage jutting from the pebbled ground lining the trail.

The sound of water bubbling across a rocky streambed pulled her toward the monument nested against a stand of aspen trees, their tiny dollar-shaped leaves barely moving in the still air.

It was understandable why the famous novelist had loved Idaho, why he'd spent his last days living here. Ernest Hemingway was only one of many celebrities who had traded big city tangled traffic for cool mountain mornings and alpine vistas and made Sun Valley their residence.

Olympic hopeful Dean Macadam was another.

Karyn stood at the water's edge and looked past the pile of flat stones with its stately column rising from the middle, beyond the trees to the golf course in the distance. A deer standing in the middle of one of the greens lifted its head and stared back at her in mutual regard.

A voice in her head rang out as clear as if Dean were standing next to her.

"What is your fascination with Hemingway anyway?"

She closed her eyes, remembered gazing up from the pages of *For Whom the Bell Tolls*. "Are you crazy? He was only the best American novelist of all time," she'd so flippantly reminded her husband.

Dean playfully tugged at the sheet tucked around her bare waist. "Is that so?"

She quickly snatched the covering from his hands and secured it more tightly. "Yes, that's so. In fact, Ernest Hemingway is known for his mastery of theme and imagery.

Take this story for example." She held up the heavy volume borrowed from her dad, its cover worn from repeated readings. "The entire narrative is punctuated with a preoccupation with death and dying, which is so poignant given his eventual suicide."

Dean ran broad fingers through his sleep-tousled hair. "Yeah, you see—that's what I don't get. Why is so many people's imagination captured with a guy who spent an inordinate amount of time writing about life instead of living it? I mean, in my view, that's likely what led to him offing himself in the end."

She raised her gaze in horror and slammed the book against her new husband's chest. "Don't say that."

He laughed. "Okay, okay—look, I get it. Ernest Hemingway is your book boyfriend. I'm not jealous. Really I'm not." His eyes nearly sparkled when he'd said that. "Tell you what. When I die, you just take my ashes and toss them in that little creek that runs in front of his memorial. That way, when I'm gone, you can visit both of us at the same time."

Before she could protest the macabre suggestion, he pulled the novel from her and tossed it to the floor, while at the same time lifting the sheet with his other hand.

She'd giggled as he buried his head against her skin. "Promise me. Even if my mother protests and wants otherwise," he said, in a muffled voice. "Now. Promise. Or, I'll—" His fingers dug into her sides and he tickled, sending her entire torso into a fit of squirming. "Promise," he repeated.

"I promise. I promise," she shouted, laughing uncontrollably.

He immediately stopped tickling. "Okay, that's better." Her new husband looked at her then, his eyes boring into her soul. "And promise you'll always remember I love you."

The sound of his voice still seemed so real, even after all these months. She sunk to the curved stone bench. Tears collected in her eyes and spilled over, making their way down her cheeks. She fingered the familiar lid on the box.

I'm sorry, Dean. I can't do it.

No matter that she'd gotten out of her bed while it was still dark outside with the best intentions. She still wasn't ready to let him go.

Not now—and maybe never.

GRAYSON CHANDLER WRANGLED his way past a bunch of willow branches, taking care not to break his fly rod, then headed south crossing into a clearing.

That's when he saw her.

Early thirties. Coffee-colored long hair. Sitting quietly on the stone bench at the Hemingway Memorial.

Not really understanding why, he quieted his steps as he approached.

She held something in her hands, a little box. Her head was tucked. Was she—?

Holding his breath, he moved closer.

Yes, she was crying.

He crouched behind a clump of thick brush and watched, knowing he was encroaching, but unable to help himself.

She was a pretty gal. Frankly, she reminded him a whole lot of that royal lady in England. What was her name? Not Princess Diana, but her son's wife.

Unable to remember, he shook his head. Didn't matter.

What mattered was that she was openly weeping now.

He wavered. Should he step forward? Offer her assistance? He shook his head. Naw—probably not. It wasn't like he carried a handkerchief in his pocket like his dad used to. Likely she just needed some time to get whatever was bothering her out of her system. Women were like that.

Still, he couldn't help but think whatever she was spilling about was not the least bit inconsequential. Clearly, she was torn up.

Ignoring the reprimanding voice inside that warned him he was being voyeuristic, he rested his fly pole on the ground and continued to watch.

Even crying, she was beautiful, what with her thick lashes sweeping across ivory cheeks that looked as soft as a rose petal. He knotted his hand and pressed it against his lips, imagining brushing his thumb across her skin.

He hadn't thought about a woman in that way for a really long time. Not since—well, since Robin. A subject he didn't care to think about.

The woman on the bench wiped her face with the back of her hand and looked up toward the sky. A few seconds later, she fingered the top of the little wooden box in her lap, chewing at her lip.

Finally, she stood and gazed into the trees, tears still rimming her lashes.

He battled a surge of protectiveness, yet remained still. Under different circumstances he might take a chance, go introduce himself. But he knew better this time.

She turned and saw him. Frowning, she pulled the little box close to her chest.

Face flushed, he reached for his pole and stood. "Hey, I'm sorry. I didn't mean to—what I meant is, I just didn't want to interrupt—" He shook his head. "Look, I'm sorry."

Judging from the way she fidgeted, she too was embarrassed. She tucked a strand of hair behind her ear. "I—I thought I was alone."

"I wasn't really watching. I was doing a little fly fishing." He pointed back at the creek. "I saw you and—"

She rubbed at the place between her eyebrows, then

dropped her hand. "Look, I really need to go." She turned and starting walking toward the parking lot.

He wanted to say something more, maybe get her name, but thought better of it.

Upon reaching her car, she glanced back.

In an awkward attempt to apologize again for his intrusion on her private moments, he nodded and gave her a faint smile.

Inside, he wanted to kick himself.

2

There were rumors, you know. There were always rumors. Rumors of who owned the lear jets parked at Friedman Memorial Airport. Speculation as to who purchased the three million dollar listing on Dollar Mountain Road. Talk swirling in the local eateries about how snow packs on Baldy would affect next year's U.S. Alpine Championships and whether or not Bill and Melinda Gates would vacation at the resort again this year.

Since the late thirties, the area known as Sun Valley, which included the neighboring communities of Ketchum and Elkhorn, and extended as far south as Hailey and Bellevue, enjoyed a reputation as a world-class ski resort and summer-time outdoor mecca.

The quaint community also served as host to a myriad of festivals and fundraisers—most of which were run, at least in part, by an outspoken member of the local tourism council, Leigh Ann Blackburn, an impeccably dressed woman wielding a clipboard loaded with checked-off lists. Evidence she had a cachet for organizing such events, even if on a volunteer basis.

"Make sure we have proper wattage to the speakers. I want

everyone to be able to hear the cellist. And don't forget to test the microphones." Leigh Ann turned from the electrician to the men crossing the lawn toting large baskets of miniature pink azaleas and white dendrobium orchids. "Thanks guys. Let's place those so that they line the stage at the front of the tent."

Her cell phone broke through the noisy preparations. "Leigh Ann here."

"Hey, Leigh Ann. Ben over at Atkinson's Market. Our wholesaler mixed up the order. We may not have enough of the cheese you ordered. They sent Camembert instead."

She scowled and slapped the clipboard on a bar table. "Camembert? We can't substitute. I selected the Taleggio because it perfectly compliments the Sauvignon Blanc I'll be serving."

"Okay, let me see what I can do. No promises, but I might be able to call over to the lodge and see if they have any in their inventory we can use and then replace next week."

She waved at a girl carrying a rack of stemware and pointed her to the other side of the tent. The girl pivoted and headed that way. "Thanks, Ben. You're the best."

Satisfied, she pocketed her phone and reached for her clipboard.

The inaugural Macadam Memorial needed to be perfect. The funds raised would benefit a new adaptive sports program and provide ski lessons for people with disabilities. A noble cause, certainly. And one worthy of her brother-in-law's memory.

Hearing her name, she looked up. Her father crossed the sprawling lawn making his way toward where she stood under the massive white tent awning.

She waved. "Hi, Dad." She pointed to the pie in his hands. "What do you have there?"

"Hey there, Sis. Can you use a rhubarb?"

She leaned and kissed his sun-weathered cheek before taking the pie from his hands. "Sure. Who this time?"

A grin spread across his face. "Bernice Grant."

Leigh Ann laughed. "She does know she's one of many?"

Her father had a number of female suitors—older women who hoped to snag the affections of a widowed sheep rancher of financial means. In a private joke, she and her sisters had collectively dubbed them the Bo Peeps.

"Well, don't worry. We'll find use for it." She clasped her father's elbow and guided him past linen draped tables to an area in the back where the caterers were setting up. "Here we go." She handed off the pie to one of the volunteers passing by. "Could you find room on the dessert table please?"

She looped her arm in her father's. "So, what do you think?"

He looked all around. "Nice. Quite the production. A lot of work, I imagine."

That was an understatement. "You don't even know the half of it. Luckily, we have a lot of people who volunteered to help out on this one."

Her father nodded. "I'm not surprised. Dean was much loved in this town."

"So . . . have you seen her yet?"

"Karyn?"

She gave him a pointed look. "Uh-huh. You think she'll be okay today? This whole memorial fundraiser thing isn't exactly going to be easy for her. I mean, seems she's been making real progress towards being happy again and—well, I was thinking that maybe after the ceremony, we could—"

Her dad placed his arm around her shoulders. "Look, sweetheart. I want to make everything better for her too. But, some things just aren't for us to fix."

"I know, but—"

He cupped her cheek with his calloused hand. "Your sister

is going to have to move through this journey at her own pace. In time, she'll make it out the other side. You'll see."

She opened her mouth to argue, but the look on her father's face stopped her. "Well, what about Joie? I hope you reminded her she needed to show up no later than two?"

"I did." Her father jammed his hands in his front pockets and grinned. "But we both know with that one there are no guarantees."

THE KING AIR engine roared outside the open airplane cabin. Joie shifted her goggles and looked out over the flawless vista, then tucked her head and dove.

She thrust her arms back, and bulleted in the direction of the other skydivers already heading into formation. As she neared, she flung her arms wide sending her body into a full spread, her jumpsuit flapping against rushing air.

Her eyes darted left, then right. She eased her body forward and positioned into place, then grabbed the grip on the leg of Mike's jumpsuit. A pull at her own left ankle and she knew Phil had glided into his spot.

Across the horizon, the sun streaked against the azure sky. Joie counted off the seconds, and waited until she felt the expected tug at the leg of her suit. She reciprocated by tugging at Mike's leg, signaling the need to break in sync with the others.

Tipping slightly to the right, she spiraled making a perfect one eighty. On the count of two, she tipped the opposite direction and circled back, this time stopping in place and grabbing hands with Dennis.

She smiled. Big.

The wind whipped her cheeks and within seconds she

knew they'd done it. Pulled off a successful sixteen-man. With ease, she might add.

No doubt next spring the scraggly team would hold their own when joining in the fifty-man in Perris, California. After that, who knew? Maybe they'd go and join in for the all time record in Australia next year. If she could get away without inciting a national incident, that is. She loved her family, but her sisters tended to be drama queens. Leigh Ann especially.

Another tug and Joie released her grip, preparing for the runaway. On the break, she shifted her arms and waved off her fellow divers. Her altimeter read nine thousand feet and just over one hundred miles per hour.

She glanced at the patchwork landscape below, knowing she'd milk every ounce of flying fun from this party. She pulled into a perfect barrel roll, then tucked her head and maneuvered into a forward flip, reveling in the open freedom of air.

Five thousand feet.

Feeling adventurous, she thrust her knees forward, head back and went into a reverse loop, a rare move she'd mastered last summer that left her heart pounding with adrenalin.

Top that, boys.

Despite her petite frame, no one could fly like Joie Abbott. Her no-fear attitude whipped even the most seasoned divers out here. Even Mike, and he had thousands of jumps logged.

Before she could repeat the maneuver, her altimeter beeped loud enough that even in the rushing wind, the sound caught her attention. She fought the urge to go for one more trick, but gave in to safety and pulled her body into a stable position. After checking for clearance, her hand grabbed the hackey and she deployed.

Instantly, a lifting jolt left her tummy several feet below. Her canopy unfurled and snapped open, and in less than three seconds, her descent slowed from nearly a hundred miles per hour to just over fourteen. Buildings and roads came into view beneath her dangling feet.

Glancing up at the familiar orange underbelly of her canopy, she drew a deep breath and pulled at her right toggle, guiding her flight pattern directly toward the drop zone located at the north end of the River Run parking area at the base of Bald Mountain. The wind whistled, even through her helmet, as she made her descent.

The ground rushed up, the treetops grew bigger. She placed her parachute into a full stall and tapped her feet down on black pavement only feet from the packing house door. As her canopy drifted to the ground, her co-jumpers walked in from an adjacent grassy area.

"Hey Chill, you're crazy. You know that?" Her middle-aged friend with a t-shirt that read *Only Skydivers Know Why Birds Sing* shook his head.

Joie grinned. Dick Cloudt had never called her by her real name. Not after a particularly wild night where he'd drunk too much and sloppily tried to get her to go home with him. Feigning hurt feelings when she'd turned him down—twice—he'd teased she was an ice queen and nicknamed her Chill. The name stuck. Now everybody at the drop zone used his term of endearment.

Frankly, to Joie, the name was a badge of honor. She wasn't like some of those wanna-be females who hung out at the DZ in tight t-shirts hoping for a little guy action to spice up their lives.

Joie didn't require a man to make her feel complete. She'd already proven that.

Convinced a celebration was in order, the group straggled into Crusty's, a local bar located in a historic red brick building on Main Street now named for the owner with a no sunshine attitude, but a heart made of pure gold.

"Beers all around," Joie called out, slapping her credit card on the well-worn counter. "Except for me. I'm going with a club soda and lime."

"You got it. But's what with you and the club soda?" The balding proprietor with shoulder length gray hair pulled three pitchers from a shelf behind where he stood.

She shrugged. "I don't need to go down that bumpy road again today."

Crusty smiled back at her. "Yeah, I hear you." He positioned the glass containers beneath a tap, tilting each until a perfect inch of foam covered the amber liquid, then slid the pitchers down the counter with precision to his waiting patrons. Next, he pulled frosted mugs from a small refrigerator next to the cash register and clunked them down. "So, you're looking a bit bright today. No high like the sky, huh?"

She moved onto a stool. "Nothing like it."

Crusty pushed Joie's credit card back at her. "Your money's no good today."

She shook her head. "How are you going to stay in business, Crusty, if you keep giving all the beer away?"

Grinning, he loaded a tall glass with ice, filled it with club soda and squeezed a lime wedge over top. He plopped the glass down in front of her. "I only charge the ugly ones." He winked. "And there's plenty of 'em around here."

Joie nodded. "Gotcha." She lifted the glass in a toast. "Go high, or go home." She smiled before tossing her head back and draining the cold carbonated drink. Finished, she planted the glass back on the counter.

"C'mon, Crusty. Hit her with a tequila chaser," hollered Phil from at the end of the bar.

She held up her hand. "No way."

Crusty's face broke into a crooked-toothed smile. Ignoring her, he grabbed a bottle from behind the counter and held it up to her with a hopeful look.

She shook her head. "Nope. Like I said, none of that for me. I'm on the wagon."

Mike bellowed from across the noisy bar. "Oh c'mon, Chill. It's not every day someone pulls off an FS-16 and a reverse loop in the same jump."

Terrance Cameron, a retired professor who used to teach African American Studies at Berkeley, slid into the barstool beside her. "Twenty bucks says you'll change your mind before the day's out."

Joie shook her head. "No . . . huh-uh. Not a repeat of last weekend. Besides, it's barely noon."

With wavering determination, she leaned over the counter and grabbed the soda gun and refilled her glass, then dug deep in her front jeans pocket and fished out a quarter. "Who's up for a game of pool?"

Mike downed his beer and headed for the table. "I'm in." He grabbed a cue from the rack on the wall and chalked the tip. "Loser buys the winner lunch."

"You're on." Joie racked the balls. "But I have to warn you, I'm pretty hungry."

After winning the coin toss, Mike leaned over, drew the cue back and shoved it forward. A loud crack followed and balls scattered across the table.

They took turns sinking balls. She was stripes. Mike solids.

At the end of the fourth round, Joie was up by two. She called the eight ball in the right side pocket, then walked around the table, assessing how best to approach the key shot.

After deciding a bank shot might be the best course of action, she looked up, noticing for the first time a guy leaning casually against the jukebox across the room. She couldn't help but stare. His simple white t-shirt accented bulging tanned biceps. He wore jeans. Wranglers. And boots.

He caught her looking and smiled. A casual grin that pushed through his neatly stubbled chin.

Her face flushed and she quickly glanced away, then positioned herself at the table and leaned over.

A green bill slapped down on the edge of the far side of the pool table. "A hundred says you don't make this shot."

Joie looked across at the guy's forearm, tattooed with bear claws winding themselves across his tan skin. She slowly raised her head. Her eyebrows lifted and she stared into the challenge dancing in the stranger's eyes.

Sauntering slowly in his direction, she responded with confidence. "You're on."

She repositioned and swallowed against her dry throat, aware his eyes followed her every move. She drew her cue back, paused and then hit the eight ball right on the sweet spot, sending it into the side pocket. Just like she'd called.

Relishing her shot, she straightened. A satisfied smile of victory spread across her face.

Her friend, Mike, groaned. "Did I just lose a lot of man points?"

Joie moved toward the stranger's side of the table. "You sure did," she teased. She picked up the stranger's hundred dollar bill and slowly slid it into her back pocket.

"Did I tell you I own a Harley?" Mike countered.

Joie shook her head, laughing. "See, that's like 40,000 man points right there."

The guy in the white t-shirt thrust his chiseled hand in Joie's direction. "Name's Clint. Can I buy you a drink?"

She slowly looked him over, noticing the gleam of his perfectly straight teeth, the way his dark brown hair hung careless around his ears. She patted her back pocket.

"I believe you just did."

Laughing, she moved for the bar. "Crusty, hit us all up again. Include the new guy. My treat." She placed the bill on the counter.

The bar owner grinned. "Hey, isn't today that big shindig in memory of your sister's husband?"

Joie's hand flew to her mouth. "Oh crap! I nearly forgot!" She slipped Mike's mug out of his hand and chugged the remainder of the beer, then slammed it back down on the counter. "Look, I gotta go."

She scrambled off the barstool.

Wrapping a stray curl around her finger, she inclined her head toward the new guy and hesitated.

Then, shrugging off disappointment, she raced for the door.

3

Sun Valley prided itself in a long list of Olympic champions. First there'd been Gretchen Fraser, then Christin Cooper and Picabo Street. All honored with named runs on Sun Valley's famed Bald Mountain.

Dean Macadam was next in line to garner the local ski hero designation and was projected to make a name for himself at the upcoming winter Olympics. That was, before the accident.

In the short thirteen months she'd been Dean's wife, Karyn had ample opportunity to hobnob with Sun Valley's elite. He slipped that ring on her finger and she'd become one of them by association. But like so much, that changed after Dean was gone. Almost immediately, the embossed invites quit showing up in the mail and her star power dimmed.

She took a deep breath, grabbed her purse from the passenger seat of her car and opened the door. In the distance, a massive white tent beckoned—the site of the first annual Dean Macadam Memorial. She was honored to be part of the tribute to her late husband, yet at the same time what lay ahead seemed daunting.

As she reached the tent, Dee Dee Hamilton poked

through the crowd and sidled up to her. "Oh, honey, are you nervous? I mean, I just spotted Peter Cetera. Over there." The older thin-framed woman with short spiky white hair and red glasses unabashedly waved in his direction. She leaned in. "Don't tell Andre I said so. Even though Cetera is aging, in my humble opinion he's still one hot apple—juicy to the core." She winked and gave her a shoulder hug. "And don't look so shocked. I'm not picking any fruit, only strolling the orchard."

Dee Dee and her husband owned the Hamilton Garden Center and had generously donated pots of red geraniums tied with raffia for all the tables. She patted Karyn's arm. "Just look at this crowd. What a wonderful way to honor Dean's memory."

Karyn tucked a strand of hair behind her ear, feeling a bad case of nerves bubble up in her gut. "I think he'd have been pleased to see all these people."

"Yes, you are absolutely right." Dee Dee pointed across the lawn. "Oh, look! There's Jamie Lee Curtis."

Karyn grinned at the woman's thrilled reaction to another "sighting" as the locals called it. "Thank you for coming, Dee Dee. We—I really appreciate it."

"Oh, honey, you know I wouldn't have missed this charity event for the world. Andre and I donated a generous check." The woman leaned and air-kissed Karyn's cheek as a large black town car pulled into the parking lot, just yards away from where they were standing. "Must be somebody important. I'm going to go check it out. See you, sweets," Dee Dee hollered over her shoulder as she hurried in that direction.

Karyn nodded and smiled to herself, determined to embrace that kind of enthusiasm—no matter how difficult the day ahead might prove to be.

She stepped to the bar and ordered a glass of Ste. Chappelle Sauvignon Blanc, a crisp white variety from a local Idaho winery her sister bragged had garnered *Best of Class* in an international competition sponsored by Sunset Magazine. Leigh Ann was into that kind of trivia.

With glass in hand, she decided to mingle. She was the hostess, after all.

Among the familiar faces she spotted three friends from high school and moved in their direction. Their lively chatter died as she approached.

"Oh, honey. How are you?" Lydia Blankenship pulled her sunglasses from her face. "Today has to be so hard for you."

Ginny Rush nodded. "But just look at you. Aren't you the cutest thing in that blue shift. Vera Wang?"

She shook her head. "QVC."

The trio looked at her like she'd grown an extra head.

"The television shopping network," she explained. "They carry a lot of designer apparel."

The women exchanged worried glances.

"Oh? I didn't know that. I—we'll have to check that out, won't we girls?" Lydia patted her arm before slipping her glasses back in place.

Karyn gave the group a half-smile. "I wanted to thank you all for coming out today. Means the world to me."

Ginny's expression grew sympathetic. "Oh, honey. We wouldn't think of skipping this chance to support such a good cause. And you, of course. We're so happy we could be here for you." The girls all bobbed their heads in agreement.

Lydia pointed over Karyn's shoulder. "Hey, I think someone is looking for you."

She turned to see her in-laws, Bert and Aggie, heading her way. She stifled a groan. Not that she didn't have affection for Dean's parents, but no one would necessarily describe the power couple in terms of warm and loving. More like privileged, aloof and full of expectations.

Still, they'd been very good to her since Dean's passing. Mutual loss often creates an unexpected bond.

"Karyn, darling!" Aggie extended diamond laden hands and pulled her into a light embrace. "How are you, honey?"

Without waiting for an answer, she turned to her husband. "Bert, find me a glass of wine. And not that syrupy dredge from Ste. Chappelle. And nothing from Argentina."

"In the event I find nothing acceptable, I suppose you would have me send the lear to Napa Valley?" Bert asked, teasing his wife. He grinned at the group of women, then leaned and brushed Karyn's cheek with a kiss.

Aggie waved off his sarcasm and turned to the girls. "You'll have to excuse my husband. His sense of humor is severely lacking."

Ginny grinned and swirled her wine glass while Lydia held out her hand. "Hello, Mrs. Macadam. I believe we met at the wedding." Her friend skipped the fact they'd met a second time at Dean's funeral.

Aggie took Lydia's extended hand. "Oh, yes. I remember. Thank you for coming today." She looked around. "Such a crowd assembling. Of course, that's to be expected. Dean was, of course—" She fingered her throat, her voice now choked. "I'm sorry. It's just that this is all so very hard. Even after all these months, it still feels so fresh."

Her friends nodded emphatically in agreement. "Yes—yes, of course." They looked to her as if not knowing what else to say. And while at some level she wholeheartedly understood her mother-in-law's emotion, Aggie tended to be a bit of a drama queen. Agatha Macadam shined a spotlight on this loss in nearly every situation, which seemed to heighten after several glasses of wine.

Aggie rested her hand on Karyn's arm, leaned in, and confided, "I don't know how you are able to part with all his things." She sniffed loudly, shook her head and stood a bit taller in her gold lamé jacket. "I'm sorry. I know you are only following what our Dean would want. He had such a generous heart."

Bert appeared by her side and handed his wife a stemmed glass filled to the brim. "Yes, we've been through this Aggie," he reminded her. "Dean's mementos aren't doing anyone any good sitting around in boxes."

"But a museum might've—" Aggie tried to argue, but Bert cut her off.

"Point taken. We donated several items to be showcased up at Roundhouse, his medals, for example. But the rest of it, well —" He turned to her. "You are doing the right thing, Karyn. Dean would approve."

For the umpteenth time, she second-guessed her decision. She knew what Bert said was the truth, but she hated disappointing Aggie. Again.

After Dean's death, her in-laws had been very generous with her, even let her remain in the house they'd purchased for she and Dean's wedding gift. Leigh Ann had exploded when she learned the deed was also in their name, but Karyn calmed her by arguing there was nothing malicious going on.

Leigh Ann wasn't so easily convinced. "Mark tells me Bertrand and Agatha Macadam didn't get rich by being nice. Rumors are, they bilked a lot of people in the Salinas Valley while building that little artichoke empire. Now they own half of Elkhorn."

Karyn had laughed. She couldn't help it. "Just because my in-laws are wealthy doesn't mean they're monsters." What her sister didn't know is that Bert had recently been voted out by his board, a big blow to anyone and certainly to the Macadams.

Her sister rolled her eyes. "Even so, there's no reason on this earth why that house can't be turned over to you. Just, be careful."

She'd nodded. But inside, she handily dismissed the warning.

Both Leigh Ann and Aggie wanted to be helpful, but often the advice in their delicately wagging fingers felt more like gruel forced upon her by thick-fisted men with hairy knuckles.

Despite what those two believed, she was capable of making her own decisions now and then.

As the crowd in the tent and on the surrounding lawn grew, Karyn played hostess, sharing her role with Aggie. She submitted to surface conversations, each time nodding as attendees expressed sentiments meant to honor Dean's memory and acknowledge the loss many still felt. Though the effort wore on her, she politely thanked everyone for coming and for supporting the charity.

Eventually, and frankly not soon enough, the cellist's final notes faded into the din of the crowd's chatter. Leigh Ann climbed up the small dais at the front of the massive white tent awning and moved to the microphone. "Could I have everyone's attention?"

The crowd quieted.

"Thank you for coming out this afternoon and showing your support. As you already know, monies raised at this afternoon's Dean Macadam Memorial will benefit sports enthusiasts with disabilities, a cause my brother-in-law cared very much about. Now without further delay, let me bring up the chairman of this wonderful event." Leigh Ann motioned. "Karyn Macadam."

On cue, Karyn moved forward and joined her at the podium. With all the Jacqueline Kennedy poise she could muster, she leaned into the microphone. "Thank you all for gathering today to support this amazing inaugural event."

"As you know, my husb—" She cleared her throat. "— Dean's love for downhill skiing and for his beloved Sun Valley home went unsurpassed. He would be so honored to see all of you here today and to know his legacy lives on.

"Many of you have donated items for today's auction and as

you can see, several of Dean's personal items and sports memorabilia are also included. I trust you'll find something that warrants your bid.

"As honorary chair, I join with Bertram and Agatha Macadam in expressing our appreciation for your generous support. We look forward to seeing you again next year!"

A lump formed in her throat as she stepped from the podium. She struggled for control while fingering the pearls at her neck. Her wedding day pearls.

"Honey, you did great." Leigh Ann's arm went around her waist and Karyn found herself being guided the short distance toward where her father and Joie stood. "Didn't she do great, Dad?"

Joie huffed. "You're treating her like a child, Leigh Ann."

Leigh Ann didn't even blanch. "Hush, or I'll give *you* a time out."

Their younger sister shrugged. "I thought I already lost recess privileges for showing up two minutes late. I'm sure Karyn didn't even think twice about it."

Leigh Ann rolled her eyes. "Nonsense! Even Karyn agrees that—"

Karyn gently stepped free of her older sister's arm. "Hey, you two. In case you've forgotten, I'm right here."

A smile nipped at the corners of their father's mouth. "Do I need to send you girls to your rooms until you can be nice to one another?"

Leigh Ann grinned and bumped against his shoulder. "No, we'll behave."

A server came by and offered up a silver tray.

"Speak for yourself," Joie teased, reaching for a wine glass.

Out of the corner of her eye, Karyn vaguely noticed a man step from the crowd. He wore black jeans, boots, a crisp white button-down and a nervous smile that accentuated his chiseled jawline.

It was *him*—the guy she'd seen that morning. The one from the Hemingway Memorial. And he was moving toward them.

He looked apologetically at her. "I hope I'm not interrupting, but I just wanted to tell you how nice all of this is and express again how sorry I am about this morning."

Karyn glanced quickly at her sisters and their visibly raised eyebrows. "Don't worry about it," she said, hoping he wouldn't say much more. Details would only invite a bevy of questions about her reasons for being at the Hemingway Memorial that morning. Contrary to common belief, not everything in her life was for family consumption.

He ran a hand through his short brown hair. "Yeah, well—that's all. I mean, this is a really nice event and I think it's immensely great what you're doing. Raising funds for such a wonderful cause, and all."

Her father reached out his hand. "I'm afraid I didn't catch your name."

"Grayson Chandler." He firmly grasped her dad's hand and shook.

Leigh Ann's eyes lit up. "And how do you two know each other? You and Karyn?"

Oh, here it comes.

Joie rolled her eyes in solidarity.

"I mean, you two are friends?" Her oldest sister was anything but subtle.

Karyn quickly tried to clarify. "No—"

Grayson coughed. "We—uh—our paths crossed this morning while we were both out—"

"—walking." Karyn added, quickly finishing his sentence.

Their eyes met.

"Yes, walking." His mouth slipped into a slight grin. He studied her for a moment, his dark blue eyes leaving her feeling a bit undone. She didn't know whether to blush or be annoyed.

Finally, he nodded. "Well, nice to see you again." Watching her, he slowly backed into the crowd and was gone.

Her eyes lingered for a brief moment before she turned to find her sisters staring, their eyes filled with questions.

Joie cocked her head. "Okay, Vanna. Fill in the puzzle blanks."

Karyn held up her palm. "Look, we'll have to talk later. Right now, I need to mingle."

She leaned and kissed her dad's cheek. "We still on for dinner next weekend?"

He gave her a light squeeze and glanced over at her sisters, both still standing with their mouths open. "You bet. I wouldn't miss it—"

4

Late afternoon sun heaped through the windows of Grayson Chandler's pickup as he made his way down Fourth Street and parked. He climbed out and headed for the front steps of Bistro on Fourth, a trendy little coffee shop he'd been told was the best in town.

A slight breeze whipped tiny green leaves on a nearby aspen, the kind of breeze that carried the smell of the surrounding mountains. He bent and rubbed behind the ears of a golden retriever lying on the steps. "Hey friend, you're looking pretty comfortable in the sunshine."

"That's Chelsey."

Grayson glanced up. In the open doorway stood a man wearing a white apron over a flannel shirt and jeans. A long gray braid dangled beneath the back of a well-worn ascot cap. "You'll find the 'ole girl there most days. Except in the winter, of course. Then she moves inside by the fire."

Grayson stood and extended his hand. "Oh, hey."

"Nash Billingsley." The guy lifted a towel off his shoulder and wiped his hands before shaking. "I'm the owner of this joint."

"Grayson Chandler. Just moved here from Fairbanks."

"Alaska, huh? Well, welcome to town. C'mon inside." The guy motioned him through the door flanked with pots of brightly colored blooms and pointed him to an empty table. "What can I get you?"

He slid into a chair. "Uh, cup of coffee will do. Black."

"You got it." Nash headed for the counter.

Grayson looked around. A young couple in running gear sat near the window. At the table next to them, a balding man in wire-rimmed glasses read a Stephen King novel.

"Here you go." Nash planted a massive blue mug on the checkered tablecloth. "I use a specialty roaster. This blend is one of my favorites."

Grayson reached for the steaming mug and took a sip, then nodded. "Yeah, it's good."

Nash positioned himself in the chair to his right. "Alaska? That's a far ways off. How'd you find your way to Sun Valley?"

Grayson explained he was a backcountry pilot. Despite loving Alaska winters, he'd grown tired of the cold endless seasons without sun. He'd flown with a friend to central Idaho and spent a few weeks in the Sawtooth primitive area losing his heart to the jagged mountainous area known as the Frank Church River of No Return. Outside of Alaska, few places in America could provide a wilderness experience to match—a land of clear rivers, deep canyons, and rugged mountains.

He didn't mention the move also allowed him to escape a rugged relationship.

"Well, you'll fit in just fine around here. Despite the seasonal influx of tourists, we're just a small mountain community. One big extended family."

Nash patted his shoulder and motioned to the gal behind the counter. "Hey, Lucy. Our friend here needs topped off."

The young woman with blonde hair and a bit too much lipstick nodded and quickly appeared tableside with a carafe.

She boldly gave him an appreciative once-over, checking him out. "You're new around here." Her voice drifted across the table like the smoke from a cigarette.

"Uh, yeah. Grayson Chandler."

A flirtatious smile lifted the corners of her red lips. "Well, welcome to the area."

Feeling awkward, he simply nodded.

She gave him a hopeful look as she filled his mug. "Hey, let me know if you need anything. Like the song says, all you have to do is call." She winked and sauntered back in the direction of the kitchen, glancing back at him over her shoulder.

Nash hesitated, waited until she was out of earshot, before he leaned close. "Good help and a nice gal at heart, but Lucy's one of those firecrackers who wears her jeans entirely too tight. Know what I mean?"

Grayson managed a smile. "Got it."

Outside the open doorway, a woman with long dark hair crouched and petted Chelsey. "You soaking up the sunshine, girl?" She gave the golden retriever a final pat on the head before making her way inside.

His throat went dry.

It was her—Karyn Macadam.

He couldn't seem to look away as she moved to the counter and ordered, unaware she was being watched. "I'll have a large coffee to go."

Nash lowered his voice to barely a whisper. "On the other hand, some women wear their pants just right."

From across the room, Karyn turned and their eyes met. She surprised him with a hesitant smile.

He smiled back, feeling her gaze clean down to his socks and shoes. She had the prettiest smile he'd ever seen.

Nash slid the towel from his shoulder and wiped a spot from the table. "So, you know Karyn?"

"We've met briefly." Grayson watched her carry her coffee out the door and down the sidewalk to her car.

Nash shook his head. "Such a sad thing. They were the *it* couple, know what I mean. Few people were made for one another more than Dean and Karyn Macadam."

Grayson stared into his cup. After the morning at the memorial, he'd googled and learned all about the accident that took Dean's life. "Must've been really hard on her."

"Sure was. The entire town was worried about her. Especially Edwin, her dad."

"Yeah, I met him too. Seems like a nice guy."

"Oh, that he is. A third generation owner of a large sheep ranch south of town. Lost his wife to cancer years ago. Raised those three daughters all on his own. And they were young, Leigh Ann was barely a teenager and I think Joie was only about six. Or maybe a bit younger, I don't remember for sure." Nash shrugged and flipped the towel back on his shoulder. He pushed his chair back. "Well, the lunch crowd will be heading in soon and I suppose I best get back to the kitchen."

He shook the gray-haired man's hand. "Enjoyed the chat."

Grayson finished up his coffee thinking he was going to like living here. He'd moved to Sun Valley in order to leave his old life behind—the one Robin had pushed to the curb with one swift kick and her good-looking stock brokerage business partner.

Here in this resort town at the base of the Sawtooth Mountains, he planned to start over. Clean slate. No entanglements.

Odd thing was, every time he encountered Karyn Macadam, a vague yearning sprouted in his gut.

It would be too simple to say he admired her casual beauty, looks that couldn't come from some drugstore bottle, or that she had a classy sweetness about her. While he barely knew her, her eyes held a deepness of soul he found captivating.

Every encounter left him feeling like a schoolboy with a crush on the prettiest girl in class.

Still, he had to remind himself it was likely too soon. For him, and certainly for her. He probably should just stay clear.

Even if she had the perfect smile.

5

K aryn nested her cup in the holder and started the engine, thinking about Grayson Chandler, the way he'd looked at her and smiled. It reminded her of the way Dean looked at her, like she was the only person in the room.

She missed that.

Fact was, she missed a lot of things. Everyday things. The way he'd bring her coffee in bed before he jumped in the shower. How he'd let her place her cold feet on his warm legs when they'd climb in bed on cold winter evenings with a bowl of buttery popcorn and Star Trek reruns on television. Or, that he didn't mind that she read while he watched.

She'd expected to have thousands more times to enjoy the way he layered thick peanut butter on both slices of bread before globbing two kinds of jelly on top. "You ain't lived until you've eaten a Dean Macadam special," he'd told her, handing her the fattest peanut butter and jelly sandwich she'd ever seen.

On that fateful day in February, he'd promised to be home in plenty of time for dinner, adding that he wanted to eat light in the coming days. Her husband had gained a couple of pounds and needed to be at proper weight for the Olympic trials. No doubt a result of those sandwiches, which were his favorite.

She smiled and squeezed his hand. "I'll pick up some shrimp at Atkinson's on my way home. We can throw them on the grill brushed with a roasted garlic cilantro marinade."

Dean grinned back at her. Said he loved garlic.

And, he loved her.

She put her SUV in gear and pulled out, driving past a row of shops, their entries decorated with brightly-colored banners and pots of flowers. She headed south of town, glancing occasionally over at the container of coffee she no longer wanted.

Karyn stopped behind a line of cars at the light at the end of Fourth and Main. Summer traffic was picking up as tourists flocked to the area to enjoy a few weeks in the Idaho mountains, bringing with them a certain energy that chased away the doldrums of the resort's down season between the last snow on the mountainside and the first blooms of leafy blue larkspur.

When the stoplight turned green, she turned south toward the town of Hailey, driving about a half hour before slowing for the turn off that led to the ranch.

Vigorous stands of aspens and willows lined the east fork of the Big Wood, the meadow grasses now tall and dotted with wildflowers and occasional sagebrush. There was no place better to enjoy the changing scenery than here. Nature's showcase, according to her dad, where occasionally you'd even spot deer or elk.

Soon, she passed under a large hand carved wooden sign that read *ABBOTT RANCH* and into the graveled yard surrounded by buildings, all made of rough-hewn logs.

To the right was the cookhouse. Past that, the barn and the bunkhouse, the riding arena and the small guesthouse where

Joie now lived. Up the canyon, she could see the lambing sheds and the corrals in the distance.

The main house was on the left, an inviting log structure with an expansive lawn surrounding the building and a wrap-around porch complete with a railing and rocking chairs. Tall windows lined both the front and back provided an unobstructed view of the stunning mountainous landscape with large white cumulous clouds peeking over the pine stands. A river rock fireplace jutted from the southern end. Nearby, a wood shed filled to the brim promised warm fires to come.

Her father stood on the front porch. She waved, then switched off the engine and reached into the seat next to her for a plate of oatmeal raisin cookies, still warm.

She climbed from her car and greeted her dad's border collie. "Hey, Riley. How are you girl?" Karyn bent and patted the dog's head with one hand, while juggling the plate of cookies with the other.

"Sweetheart, can I give you a hand?" Her dad ambled across the freshly cut grass and kissed her forehead. "What's this?"

She handed off the cookies into his large calloused hands, enjoying his smile as he lifted the cellophane wrap. He picked a cookie off the plate and took a bite, then nodded, his mouth full. "My favorite," he managed to say through the crumbs.

"Yes, I know." She grinned, loving how easy he was to please. Nothing ever seemed to ruffle him. He just took life as it came, and found a way to find joy through all of it, even the occasional bad parts.

Not a bad way to live and an attitude she tried to mimic even though she found it difficult at times.

Her dad helped himself to another cookie as they headed for the house. "You're early."

They both knew it was her practice to beat her sisters to their weekly family meals. She loved having time alone with her dad. A middle child thing, she supposed.

He opened the front door and motioned her inside.

Karyn knew every square inch of that house, from the stair that creaked no matter how many times her father tried to fix it, to the hairline crack in the upstairs window where Joie had once thrown stones in the middle of the night to wake her, hoping to gain entrance before Leigh Ann noticed she'd missed curfew.

An exercise in futility, of course. Nothing got past their oldest sister.

She pulled off her fleece vest and draped it on the coat tree. "Did I see Sebastian heading up the draw?"

Her dad nodded. "We got reports that a wolf was spotted at the crest of Gray's Peak. He rode up to warn the herders." He led her past the fireplace, the hearth lined with family photos. "We already have our hands full with the coyote population. I don't need to tell you a wolf sighting so close to the sheep has me worried."

"Goodness, Dad. I hate to hear that."

She crossed the knotted pine floors to the kitchen and spotted two pies on the counter next to the refrigerator. "What's this?"

The corners of her father's eyes crinkled as his face broke into a smile. "Pies."

"I know they're pies, Dad. Who made them?"

"One's apple and the other is huckleberry," he said, deftly skirting her question. "You thirsty? Want some iced tea?"

She lifted a brow. "Dad—"

He slid her plate of cookies next to the pies. "Elda Vaughn," he admitted, sheepishly rubbing his neck with one hand.

She slid into a barstool. "Elda Vaughn? Didn't her husband pass on only last month?"

"Yes, the obituary was in the paper. According to the announcement he was her third husband to die, poor thing."

Karyn couldn't imagine losing multiple husbands, or being ready to start a new relationship again so soon.

Or, ever—

But, this wasn't the time to dwell on the widowhood she shared with this new Bo Peep. "Well regardless, baking the pies for you was really sweet." She let a grin form. "Does Elda know she already has a lot of competition?"

The door opened and Leigh Ann moved inside, her arms loaded with shopping bags. "What's this I hear? Is Daddy breaking hearts again?"

"Hi, sweetheart." Their dad crossed and gave his oldest daughter a hug. "What's all this?" He pulled the bags from her and carried them to the kitchen.

"Just a few groceries. I had coupons." Leigh Ann glanced around. "Where's Joie? I didn't see her truck over at the guesthouse."

"She had to make a quick trip into the stables." Their dad moved to the cupboard and retrieved three tall glasses. He placed them on the counter. "I expect her back anytime."

Leigh Ann flung her purse onto a barstool. "I swear, Joie reminds me of a hummingbird flitting from flower to flower, never staying in one place long enough to even taste the nectar." She placed her hands on her hips. "She seems to have lost herself. I only hope she doesn't waste all that time and money she spent on school and returns to the real world at some point. Sooner, the better."

"Our Joie was born at high noon in a fierce thunderstorm," their dad reminded. "I suspect she won't be tethered until she finds a way to shift the atmosphere."

Leigh Ann almost smiled. "No doubt. In the meantime, I need you two to come outside and help me. I brought tomatoes."

Confusion creased Karyn's forehead. "Tomatoes?"

"Yes, tomatoes. Mark had to make an emergency run to

Boise on business yesterday and I went with him. On the way home, I made him swing through Hagerman. Melon season is gearing up, and the u-pick farm had some early batches of these gorgeous beefsteaks ready for harvest."

Dad chuckled. "You picked tomatoes? And Mark helped?"

Karyn and her father exchanged amused glances. Leigh Ann's husband wasn't always the most—well, let's just say his focus was rarely strayed from his business endeavors. He hadn't even shown up to Dean's fundraiser.

When the subject came up, Leigh Ann had been quick to remind he'd sent a large check.

Her sister turned for the door. "I admit, Mark had to be talked into making a quick stop. But I can be pretty persuasive."

Karyn chuckled and leaned close to her father. "She's right you know. Leigh Ann's a Picasso in the art of compelling others into her way of thinking."

He grinned in agreement.

At the doorway, Leigh Ann turned back. "Well, don't just stand there making fun of me. We have work to do." She motioned for them to join her before heading out into the sunshine.

Dad wiped his hands on a towel. "C'mon, Karyn. Not likely we're going to get out of this." He trailed her sister out the door and she followed.

Outside, Leigh Ann opened the trunk of her car.

Karyn peered over her sister's shoulder. "Oh my goodness! You've got to be kidding! There must be over a hundred pounds of tomatoes in those crates. What are you planning to do with all that?"

Leigh Ann looked at her like she had two heads. "Well little sister, *we* are going to do some canning."

Their dad lifted one of the boxes from the trunk. "Honey, I'm afraid I got rid of all your mother's canning supplies a long time ago."

Leigh Ann's face remained bright. "No worries, I brought everything we need."

It was then that she noticed her sister's back seat was piled high with more boxes filled with mason jars. She groaned. "Where in the world did you get all those?"

"They're mine." Her sister lifted a second box from the trunk and passed it off to her.

Riley barked and drew their attention to the lane where a plume of dust trailed behind Joie's blue truck in the distance.

Leigh Ann scowled. "My goodness! Dad, you need to talk with her. Does she always have to go that fast?"

Karyn climbed the steps loaded with a box of tomatoes and called back over her shoulder. "Is that a rhetorical question, Leigh Ann?"

By the time they'd finished carrying the first load inside and had returned for a second, Joie was climbing from her truck. "Hey, sorry I'm late," she hollered from across the yard.

Leigh Ann motioned her over. "Hurry, Joie. We could use your help."

Ignoring the urgency in Leigh Ann's voice, their little sister bent and petted Riley before moving to join them. "What's all this?"

With a wry smile, Karyn handed her a box of jars. "Apparently, we're going to can tomatoes."

"You're kidding, right? I mean, can't we just buy cans of tomatoes when we need them?" Joie looked to their dad for support.

He winked in solidarity and shrugged. "Guess not." He leaned into the trunk and grabbed another box.

Leigh Ann reached into the back seat of her car. "Dear loved ones, you're completely missing the point. The flavor is entirely different when you can fresh tomatoes. You'll see. Besides, this will give us a chance to be together and catch up.

Karyn, grab that cooler, will you? I also brought a yummy pasta salad to go with Daddy's steaks."

Karyn frowned. "What do you mean? We talk every day. And just a suggestion, but maybe we should eat first, before starting this—uh, project," She was starving, and knew Leigh Ann's projects often morphed into much more than first let on.

"I'm with Karyn," Joie piped in. "Frankly, I'm not really into all this canning business anyway."

"Oh, c'mon you two. It'll be fun. Besides, these tomatoes need done up and I can't possibly do all this myself."

Karyn opened her mouth to argue, then thought better of it. She'd learned it was a rare person who could stand in Leigh Ann's way and not get bulldozed when her sister was set on plowing forward.

Resigned, she rolled up her sleeves and stepped to the sink to wash her hands. She squeezed some soap into her palm and turned on the faucet. "Well, let's get going then so we can get this done."

Leigh Ann reached into the cupboard and retrieved a large bowl. "Now, that's the spirit."

Joie glared at Karyn. "Traitor," she mouthed.

Leigh Ann pulled out several jars from the box and lined them up on the counter before turning to Joie and Dad. "First, we need to sterilize the jars."

Their father kissed his oldest daughter on the forehead. "Sweetheart, as much fun as all this looks, I'm afraid you're going to have to count me out. If we're not going to eat for a while, I'm going to go check on the situation up there with Sebastian."

Leigh Ann frowned. "What situation?"

He told her about the wolf sighting.

Joie hastened to his side. "I'll go with you."

Leigh Ann placed her hands on her hips. "Oh no, little

sister. You're staying. We need your help. Besides, it wouldn't kill you to learn a domestic skill."

Karyn reached for her younger sister's elbow. "I agree. I'm starving and without your help this could take all day."

"Here, Joie. You get a pot and fill it with water for the lids. Karyn, you grab another pot. We'll boil the tomatoes, then dip them in ice water which will make the skins slide right off."

Over the next several hours, they reluctantly worked side-by-side while Leigh Ann's instructions fired at the swift velocity of a loaded AK Bossy Rifle.

"No, no. Joie, you have to slide the butter knife around the entire jar or you won't get all the bubbles out."

Joie rolled her eyes. "And that would be worse than an ISIS attack apparently."

Leigh Ann scowled. "Oh, quit. You know I like things done right."

"Really? Because you hide it beautifully."

Karyn held up her palms. "Okay, stop. If you two keep bickering, we'll never get done."

Finally, the last of the freshly filled jars were safely tucked inside a boiling water bath on the stove. Leigh Ann set the timer and motioned them to sit. "See? That didn't take so long. Now, who wants ice tea?"

"I'll have some." Karyn spread a red and white checked tablecloth on the large wooden trundle table and smoothed the wrinkles out with her hands, anxious to rid her mind of anything red with skin and seeds.

Leigh Ann grabbed some glasses from the cupboard. "Can I ask you guys a question?"

Joie plopped into a chair at the table. "Yes, I'd date Steven Tyler."

"Who?"

Joie rolled her eyes. "You amaze me. The lead singer in the rock band Aerosmith. He just released a music video for his very first country song. I saw it on Facebook and surprisingly, he's pretty good."

Karyn nodded. "I saw it too. I agree—he has a lot of talent. But isn't Steven Tyler a bit old for someone your age? I mean, he's got to be climbing on seventy by now."

Joie drew her head back in shock. "Are you kidding me? Rock-n-rollers like Tyler are ageless."

Leigh Ann filled the glasses with ice and turned for the refrigerator. "Okay, you two—focus. I wanted you both to weigh in on the fundraiser. I think the event came off pretty well, don't you?"

"Yeah, it was really nice," Karyn answered her, knowing her sister had a penchant for affirmation. "Don't you agree, Joie?"

"Sure. If you like that kind of thing," Joie murmured while picking a piece of lint from the tablecloth.

Leigh Ann lifted her eyebrows. "Well, you were certainly enamored with my little crab puffs."

"What? You mean those snooty little balls of attitude?"

"And now I need a helpful comment." Leigh Ann pulled the tea pitcher out and walked it to the table, before handing the glasses off to Karyn.

Joie reached for the pitcher. "Oh, lighten up Leigh Ann. I was just giving you a hard time. The event was just as Karyn said. Very nice." She filled her glass.

The back door opened and their father entered carrying his hat in his hand. "So, you girls get all done with your chores?" He surveyed the counter filled with tomato jars. "Looks like no one will go hungry this winter."

Joie grunted. "Yeah, eighty-four quarts should do us, don't you think?"

Their dad rolled up his sleeves and moved for the sink. "Well, just let me wash up and I'll fire up the grill."

When the steaks were done, they all took their places for

dinner, the same spots each had occupied since they were little girls gathered at this table.

After blessing the food, their father rubbed his hands together. "Okay, pass the ketchup." He grinned at his oldest daughter. "Unless Leigh Ann has left over tomatoes and wants to make us some. I hear homemade always tastes better."

Karyn laughed and picked up the platter loaded with grilled meat and slid a steak onto her plate. "Good one, Dad."

Leigh Ann huffed. "We'll see who's laughing when we tap into the fruits of our labor this winter."

Karyn passed the steaks to her younger sister. "So, Joie. How's work?"

Her sister paused before breaking into a bright smile. "The stables are great. We've had a steady stream of tourists booking trail rides over the summer. They say profits are way up." Joie grabbed for her fork and knife and cut into her steak. "Dan just bought two new geldings. Fresca, the one I'm training, is well started. He does great under saddle and is light on his feet with really expressive gaits. He's young and going to take a lot of work, but he's already beginning to clear a few of the lower jumps."

Their father scooped some pasta salad onto his plate. "I heard the Albertsons are contemplating retirement soon and Sun Valley Company plans to put a new stable manager on."

Leigh Ann looked across the table. " Well, I'm sure Cindy wants to be free to travel a bit more now that they have grand-babies. I know when Colby has children, and that's certainly a long way off, I plan to be in their lives as much as possible."

Karyn fought a smile.

It was well known to everyone but his mother that Colby elected to go to an out-of-state college because he needed to escape the blades of his helicopter mom.

Leigh Ann reached for another roll. "Perhaps the new

stable manager hire could lead to extra opportunity for you, Joie."

Joie again turned hesitant. "Okay, sure."

Leigh Ann's face brightened. "All I'm saying is that maybe you could take on more responsibility—even garner a raise in pay." She turned to their father. "That could allow her to move out of the guest house."

"There's no hurry on that front," he assured. He lifted the bowl of pasta salad. "Anyone?"

Joie now scowled. "Looks like the judgment express has pulled into town, and right on time."

Leigh Ann buttered her roll. "No judgment. Just helpful prodding."

Joie squared her shoulders. In a thinly veiled attempt to divert the attention off the fact she was nearly thirty and had recently moved back home, she turned to Karyn. "By the way, who was that hottie at the fundraiser?"

"Yes, who was that?" Leigh Ann chimed in, willing to let the prior subject go in lieu of a more interesting topic.

Even her father stopped eating and looked in her direction.

Karyn weighed her words carefully. "Like I told you all earlier, I was—um, walking. Our paths crossed. He said hello. I said hi back. That's the big news story."

"And so he—Grayson Chandler—wasn't that his name? He said he wanted to apologize to you. Why was that?" Joie looked across the table and waited.

In a perfect world, she could talk to her sisters without every word and connotation being examined. "Oh, stop you two. Dad, you could help me out here, you know."

He reached for his iced tea. "And miss out on the enter-tainment?"

She let out an exaggerated sigh. "Okay, okay. I was having a bit of a bad day. You know, the memorial fundraiser and knowing what was ahead." She leaned back in her chair. "I got up early and—uh, went for a walk."

"You said that," Leigh Ann reminded.

"Well, I did. And unfortunately I was having a bit of an emotional moment, believing I was entirely alone."

Joie stopped chewing. "Oh, and he saw."

She nodded. Not the entire truth, but close enough.

"Well, he seems really nice," Joie offered.

Leigh Ann took a final bite and pushed her plate back. "I have to agree. Granted, I'm a married woman. But Grayson Chandler isn't exactly hard to look at."

Karyn quietly dropped her fork to her plate. "What is this? Junior high?"

Dad cleared his throat. "Sweetheart, your sisters mean well. True, you may not be quite ready," he told her, still smiling. "But it won't be long and you'll be apt to take a few baby steps." He winked. "Maybe even let someone bake you a pie or two."

6

If you were to ask Karyn if she was happy, she'd quickly assure you she was. Despite the pain of suddenly losing her husband, without warning or even having an opportunity to say goodbye, she knew she had a choice—she could move forward as a Tigger or an Eeyore. Since whining wasn't her style, she'd chosen to believe things would get better and live accordingly.

Early on, she could barely pull herself out of bed and find the will to fight the overwhelming notion that she was a widow at the age of only thirty-four—and that Dean was really gone. Close friends and family worried she'd slipped into depression. Looking back, perhaps she had.

It seemed she'd lost herself, and couldn't find her way back.

In those early months, she'd tried going to a therapist, a woman with kind eyes who had pushed a cup of steaming coffee into her hands.

"Karyn, tell me who you were before the day Dean died. What was true of you?"

"I—I'm not sure what you mean?"

"You weren't always Dean's wife, or his girlfriend. Who were you before?"

Karyn thought for a bit. Tears came faster than words. "Well, I—I loved to read. And shop. I loved being around people." She tried swallowing her emotion. "I was confident and brave."

The therapist leaned close and took both of her hands in her own. "You'll be all those things again. I promise."

Karyn wanted to believe that was true. A little less than two years ago she'd lost the love of her life. But a lot of people cared about her, including her family and many friends. Continuing to lean on them would have to be enough.

Besides, it was getting easier to pretend it was getting easier, so easier must be right around the corner. Somehow, she would find her way back to being truly happy again.

Karyn closed her Debbie Macomber novel and placed the paperback on the table next to her glass of tea, now diluted with melted ice. She stood, stretched her cramped muscles, then turned and gazed out from the patio of her craftsman-styled home—a lovely structure made of natural wood and river rock perched on a bluff overlooking the golf course with a backdrop of distant hills covered with pines and pungent sage-brush, the odor made even more sharp in the warmth of the sunshine.

Often, the only sound to interrupt her early morning coffee while sitting out here on the patio was the occasional trill of a prairie falcon flying overhead.

In those early months after the accident, the quiet solitude served to cauterize her bleeding emotions. But now, that same stillness choked her.

Karyn bent and flicked a spider from the cushion on the chaise lounge. Spiders freaked both her sisters out, but not her. The only thing she feared was getting out of bed each morning to another empty day.

Her heart would forever remain connected to Dean. There would always be times of sadness. But the truth was, she was tired of—well, of being a *widow*.

The subject of healthy living was written about in all the magazines, how when facing hard times, you needed to avoid isolation at all costs, spend time with people who lifted you up. And you needed to exercise and eat healthy.

Those magazines were absolutely right.

She wandered back inside the house and got a can of La Croix water from the refrigerator, pulled her phone from her jeans pocket and dialed her father. He picked up on the second ring. "Hi, sweetheart. What's up?"

"Oh, nothing really," she said, hating that her voice sounded a bit warbly with emotion. "I felt a bit loose-ended is all. Thought maybe I'd come out to the ranch for a while."

"Ah, honey. That sounds nice. But I'm on my way to Twin Falls."

"Oh? What's in Twin Falls?"

"I'm going to pick up some gadgets called Nite Guards. The manufacturers promise the flashing lights and high frequency sounds will ward off the wolves and protect the herd. I figure it's at least worth a try."

She nodded. "Sounds reasonable."

"Hey, I'm sorry. If I'd known you were a bit restless, I'd have invited you to come along."

She rubbed at her temple, not wanting to admit even a long drive in her dad's pickup sounded preferable to sitting in this house one more day with no one to talk to. "No worries. I should have phoned earlier."

"Call your sisters?"

"Yeah, I'll do that. Drive safely. And I hope those contraptions work for you, Dad."

They clicked off and she tried Leigh Ann.

"Ah . . . sorry, honey. I'm neck deep in meetings all day.

We're only weeks away from the Wine and Arts Festival. I didn't know how much work I was signing up for when I volunteered to be on the managing committee."

She fared no better with Joie. After the third ring, her call went to voicemail. "Hi, you've reached Joie Abbott. I'm leading a trail ride up Dollar Mountain this afternoon and will be out of cell range, but leave a message and I'll catch you later."

So much for spending time with people she could count on to buoy her spirits. Disappointed, she headed into the living room and slumped onto the sofa, trying to ignore the dust particles that dared to collect not only on the shelves next to the fireplace, but the tables and Dean's trophies displayed on the mantel—despite the fact she'd dusted only yesterday.

What now? A girlfriend, perhaps?

The idea set her teeth on edge.

Most of her gal pals worked during the day. Besides, conversations typically turned to discussions about husbands and babies—topics that did little to lift her spirits.

Karyn's gaze drifted to the opposite wall and a framed photo of Dean and her standing by a pair of mountain bikes. Hers, a Christmas gift from her husband.

That's what she needed—some exercise!

Spurred on with renewed enthusiasm, Karyn hunted down her biking gear, filled her water bottle and headed for the garage.

It took no small effort to get her bike down from the rack mounted on the ceiling. Winded from the effort, she fastened on her headgear and mounted her bike trying not to think how she'd not ridden since losing Dean.

There were a lot of things she'd never done without him, but if that stopped her, she'd face more days staring at the walls.

Committed to see this through, she peddled across her driveway and glided onto Elkhorn Way heading in the direction of Dollar Road, while enjoying the way the warm air felt against her face.

"This is exactly what I needed," she told herself as she wheeled past the Community School.

Dean would be appalled at how stuck she'd become. No doubt, he'd make a point of telling her to get over it already—which was good advice.

Despite the fact she'd been knocked off her bike—metaphorically speaking—she had no choice but to keep on pedaling.

She hit the stoplight at the road that led into Ketchum and stopped, took a minute to catch her breath, already feeling much better.

A couple with two young kids crossed a few feet in front of her leading a beautiful golden retriever on a leash. They waved. She smiled and waved back.

She and Dean had taken this route many times, and it was always here that he—

No, it was time to push those thoughts from her head. How could she possibly move on if she stayed mired in memories? Memories that often speared her, caused her to take a deep breath to keep on.

Deciding to soldier on with resolve, she climbed back on the bike and peddled the final distance into Ketchum, slowing only to maneuver past a couple taking photographs of the iconic Brass Ranch red barn.

Minutes later, Karyn pulled into the parking lot of Giacobbi Square, a quaint little shopping center with gabled rooflines and window boxes filled with orange day lilies, mums and scrubby little daisies.

Trudy Dilworth stood in the open doorway of a storefront beneath a sign that read *Painted Lady*. She wore a purple caftan, her wrists loaded with chunky bracelets. "Don't be bashful,

Karyn honey. C'mon in." She wiggled dimpled fingers and beckoned her inside.

"Sorry, Miss Trudy. Can't today—I've got my bike."

The woman parked her hands on ample hips. "Nonsense," she argued, her voice a Mae West drawl. "Bring your bike inside. We're about to start a new watercolor class. Join us," she urged.

Karyn hesitated, but only briefly. Hadn't she vowed to live with bold spontaneity?

She squared her shoulders and took a deep breath. "Well, sure. I mean, why not?"

Miss Trudy's face brightened. "Atta girl. It'll be fun." She waved her inside.

After helping her wheel her bike through the doorway, the over-cologned painting instructor led her past a small group of people deep in discussion and standing near a wall covered with shelving with clear bins of color-coded paint tubes and labeled baskets of artist pencils, markers and paintbrushes.

They reached a circle of wooden easels loaded with paper, and little cups of paints. Larger cups filled with water had brushes soaking inside. "Everything you'll need is right here," she said, pointing to her designated spot. She then turned and clapped her hands. While only five-three, Miss Trudy somehow managed to tower over those mingling in the room. "Okay, everyone. Take your seats. We're ready to begin."

Karyn slid into her appointed seat next to Buck Randles, the former high school janitor who had retired last spring. They nodded at each other.

He rubbed his balding head. "My daughter thought I needed a new hobby," he explained, looking as uncomfortable with this new venture as she.

Miss Trudy's sister occupied the seat on her other side, a brush poised in her hand and ready to begin.

Karyn lifted her own brush from the water. "Hey there, Ruby."

"How are you, dear?" Ruby leaned close and shot her a knowing wink. "I hear your father went to Twin Falls today. Do you know what time he'll get back?"

Karyn forced a weak smile. "Sorry, I don't."

The woman fingered her tight red curls. "Well, I was thinking of dropping off some strawberry shortcake this evening—or maybe a pie."

"I'm sure he'd like that, Ruby."

Ignoring Karyn's thinly masked amusement, the woman's face brightened. "Well, I hope you enjoy learning to paint. May the force be with you!"

Ruby managed the Opera House, had for years, and often spoke in movie phrases, which could be annoying. Yet everyone knew she had a heart of gold.

For example, she insisted on showing the 1941 movie *Sun Valley Serenade* free of charge every day at five o'clock. Everyone urged her to at least charge for the popcorn, but she gave that away too. And free sodas. Heaven only knew what that did to her profit statement.

Both Trudy and Ruby shared a reputation for supporting the community. Well that, and a proclivity for gossip. The Idaho Mountain Express reported the news, but the real scoop was often delivered by the Dilworth sisters.

From the front of the room, Miss Trudy held up a tube of paint. "Okay, everyone. Squeeze tiny dollops of color into your trays, then dip your brushes into your water cup and dilute by mixing."

Karyn stared at the blank canvas in front of her and swallowed. She had never tried her hand as an artist, but how hard could it be?

She carefully followed Miss Trudy's instructions. In an

extra measure of caution, she compared her mixture to Ruby's just to make certain she'd gotten the proper ratio.

"Okay, take your brush and dip into the blue and run your brush across the top of your paper. Big strokes. The paint may drip, but that's fine." Miss Trudy clasped her hands in front of her generous bosom. "Great art often comes from letting messy morph into beauty."

Ruby swept her brush across the paper with abandon. "If you build it, it will come," she claimed with a satisfied smile.

The janitor looked over top his glasses and made several short strokes. He noticed Ruby scowling in his direction. "What?"

"It's not a broom, Bill."

With a bit more careful precision than either of her neighbors, Karyn grasped the smooth spindle of her paint brush and rolled the tip in the paint mixture. Next, she carefully placed a layer of blue at the top of her paper. Back and forth.

She leaned back and smiled. The watercolor looked like blue sky. Perhaps the stiff aroma from the paint solvents was making her a bit heady, but this was fun.

"Now, using the same shade of blue, we're going to place another layer a little more than half way down the paper. These will be our mountains." Miss Trudy wandered the room, pausing at each of her students' easels. "Good. That's excellent."

Ruby filled her brush again. "So, did you hear about the goings on over at the Sun Valley Lodge?"

Bill paused his painting. "No, what's up over there?"

Ruby set her brush in her water. She cupped the side of her mouth and leaned over. "I heard Sandra Miller ran off with the head chef."

Karyn thought of Sandra's husband and four little boys. How awful they must feel. "Oh no. That's terrible."

Ruby shook her head. "Oh, I know. Life ain't always a box of chocolates."

"No," she agreed. "It certainly isn't."

Bill's eyebrows came together in a frown. "That'll sure put everything in a tailspin over there. I think Sandra pretty much ran the entire hotel operation. She'd been working at the lodge for what—ten years or so?"

Ruby nodded. "At least. With the grand re-opening looming, the Sun Valley Lodge folks are really scrambling to figure out what to do." She placed her hand on Karyn's arm. "Hey, you should apply."

"You're not serious! Why would I do that?"

"Honey, think about it. I'm sure Dean left you fine financially, but at some point you're going to have to admit you're not in Kansas anymore. You need purpose, something to put a smile on your face. Oz is waiting. Know what I mean?"

She shot an incredulous look in Ruby's direction. "And you think I need to run the Sun Valley Lodge? I'm not sure I'm cut out to do anything like that. I'm not sure they would want a literary arts major making a mess of things."

Ruby looked at her like she was crazy. "Have you forgotten all the occasions where you traveled with Dean, the times you had to interact with important people and make nice? You'd be perfect!"

Miss Trudy joined them. "Perfect for what?" She looked over the top of her glasses at Buck's work. "Long, smooth strokes, Buck." She looked back at her sister. "Karyn's perfect for what? What am I missing?"

Buck swiveled in his seat, nearly knocking over his paint tray. "Karyn's going to apply for the opening over at the Sun Valley Lodge."

She held up an open hand. "Wait—I never said that."

Miss Trudy nodded solemnly. "No doubt they'll need someone of your caliber. You're good with people and reliable.

All qualities I'm sure they are looking for." She sighed. "I hear Sandra's husband never saw it coming. What would make a woman take off and leave her family like that?"

Ruby huffed in response. "Elementary, dear Watson. Two people simply got twitterpated and ET forgot to call home."

Buck shrugged his shoulders. "Maybe that's not the entire story."

Ruby's eyes grew wide. "Why? What've you heard?"

Karyn leaned back in her chair, pondering what Ruby had proposed while the others chattered on.

She'd worked for the Sun Valley Lodge in high school, in housekeeping. Even made Ted Brokaw's bed, a piece of trivia Dean enjoyed sharing at parties.

Besides, her literary arts degree wasn't doing any good stuffed in a desk drawer. She'd hoped to be an editor for a big publishing house, but moving to New York wasn't something she was anxious to do anytime soon.

No matter how careful she'd been to fake it—getting up each morning, fixing breakfast, showering and dressing, putting on makeup and doing her hair, even going to social events when invited—the truth was, she wasn't fooling anyone. Least of all, herself.

Her life lacked purpose—a reason to quit drifting through her days.

She rubbed the back of her neck wearily, not daring to look over at the Dilworth sisters, afraid the two astute women would examine her with those keen eyes and might read her mind.

Somehow the vague belief she still had the ability to change course now led her to drive off the cliff.

She drew a long breath and heard herself say, "Who would I need to talk to? About the job, I mean?"

The three of them stopped talking and exchanged surprised glances.

Miss Trudy's arm circled her shoulders and she squeezed. "Oh, honey. You're going to apply. That's wonderful!"

"Atta girl!" Ruby beamed. "Time for you to boldly go where you have never gone before!"

Karyn gave the cheering squad a weak smile.

Yes, it was true.

In a jarring turn of events, she'd decided to gather her nerve, press the horn and make a life-changing u-turn.

She only hoped she wouldn't wreck in the process.

7

J oie wasn't sure which made her more relaxed, the warm afternoon sun on her back or the horse's hooves clopping to the rhythm of the swaying saddle as she led the Wilson family back down the trail in the direction of the stables.

"Cara, I'm not going to say it again. Put the phone away. We've spent a lot of money taking you kids on vacation and I don't want your nose buried in a tiny screen. Besides, I don't even think there's cell reception up here and you're missing the scenery." Mr. Wilson turned back to his wife. "And no, I'm not going to lighten up," he said, warning off a possible comment from his wife.

"Don't give me that look, Jeffrey. I didn't say a word."

The youngest daughter, who looked to be about six, grinned. "Look at me, Daddy. I'm enjoying the scenery."

Joie pressed her heels into the horse, urging the mare to go a bit faster. Time to get this troop back before World War III broke out.

This scene had played out a thousand times. Guilt-ridden fathers who spent fortunes on family vacations, prompted by wives who insisted on them taking time away from work to reconnect with their bored children.

She knew the type, had even worked alongside some of them at the law firm.

From the lead, she turned to face her riding companions. "Hey, what say we take a short-cut?"

The little girl's face brightened. "A shortcut?"

"Follow me!" Joie clasped the reins and tugged to the right. "Careful, don't stray from behind me."

She led her guests off the well-worn path onto a smaller trail leading through sagebrush and a few scattered pines. "Watch for low hanging limbs," she warned.

Up ahead, just out of sight, was a creek bed. While small in size, the sparkling clear stream ran directly from the trailhead to about a quarter mile from the stables where it dumped into the larger, and much better known, Trail Creek. Except for a few locals, few even knew the tiny waterway existed.

A small clearing broke and she motioned for the family to continue following.

A tiny red fox darted across in front of them and sprinted for a dense clump of willows.

"Look at that!" Mr. Wilson shouted. "Did you see it?"

His little daughter squealed. "I did. I did."

Joie smiled. "Keep your eyes peeled. You might also catch sight of a bald eagle."

Minutes later, at the creek bed, she loosened hold on the reins and let her horse tuck his head to the water.

"Okay, everyone. Give the reins some slack and let the horses drink. This is a good time for all of us to do likewise." She lifted her aluminum water bottle from the saddlebag. "We'll be back at the stables in about twenty minutes or so."

The oldest girl nervously tucked her phone in her pocket. "I didn't know there were wild animals up here. We won't see any bears, will we?"

Joie assured her bears were a very rare sighting. "Idaho's grizzly bear population stays in much higher elevations. We do have a few black bears that wander close to town, but they're afraid of people and tend to stay out of our way. Occasionally, one will rummage through someone's garbage. But not often."

She dug into her duffel and pulled out a bag of chocolate snack bars. "Anyone hungry and need a snack for the rest of the way?"

They all nodded enthusiastically, especially the six-year-old.

"Okay," she said, after passing out the bars. "Everyone ready to move on?"

As she'd projected, less than a half hour later they reached the spot where they'd cross Trail Creek. "Careful," she warned again as her horse stepped into the water and picked its way across the creek bed lined with rocks worn smooth from moving water.

"Do you see the rainbows in the water?" She pointed the youngest daughter to where she could catch the sun's reflections. "There at the water's edge?"

"Yes, I see it!"

At the barns, she helped her guests dismount. "Thank you so much," Mrs. Wilson smiled at her, then turned to her teenaged daughter. "Wasn't that fun?"

The girl rolled her eyes and gathered her hair into a knot at the back of her neck.

Mr. Wilson removed his wallet from his back pocket and took out a wad of bills and pressed them into Joie's hand. "Here, a little something to thank you for . . . well, for putting up with us." He smiled and placed his hand on his wife's upper back.

She returned the smile. "Thank you for coming on the ride. I hope you'll book with us again soon."

Mrs. Wilson removed her bandana and dabbed at her brow. "I understand you do sleigh rides in the winter." She turned to her husband. "Jeffrey, we should consider making a trip for the holidays."

The six-year-old jumped up and down with excitement. "Oh, yes. I want to!"

The Wilsons thanked her again and headed for the office, trailed by their daughters.

Patty crossed the pen and handed her a couple of lead ropes. "Successful ride?"

"Always," Joie confirmed as she clicked the ropes in place and handed off two of the horses to her fellow stable employee, who helped her lead the horses into the barn. Together, they removed the saddles and tack and brushed the horses down.

Joie hung up the bridles. "I've got to tell you, I'm glad that's the last run of the day," She wiped her palms on the front of her jeans. "I'm ready for a cold one. Want to join me at Crusty's?"

Patty looked up from the bucket she was filling with water. "Didn't you read your email?"

"What email?" Joie brushed her forearm across her flushed face and slipped a cap from a wall peg and positioned it onto her head.

"Meeting at five o'clock. Dan's office."

"A meeting? For all of us?"

"Yup." Patty checked the latches on the stalls. "Sounds important." The young girl dragged her fingers through her short dark hair and headed for the door. "Well, see you at the meeting."

"Yeah, see you there."

Joie checked her watch. If she hurried, she could race over to the Bistro and grab a diet coke at least, with lots of ice. Last time she'd checked, the vending machine was on the blink again and failed to keep the soda cans cold. There was nothing worse than a lukewarm pop.

Without a second thought, she sprinted to her pickup.

Ten minutes later, with cold drink in hand, she headed back to the stables in order to make the meeting on time.

Unfortunately, she didn't count on Sun Valley Road being backed up with traffic.

Frantic at the notion she'd be late, Joie hollered out her car window at a teenaged boy she used to babysit. "Hey, Campbell. Can I borrow your bike? I'm late to an important meeting." She scrambled out and handed off her keys, mentally kicking herself for thinking she could leave work and get back in time. "When all this clears, you can switch out my truck for your Harley. It'll be in the parking lot at the stables."

The kid nodded and passed her his helmet. "She's a bit touchy in third gear."

Joie nodded and climbed on. After barely securing the helmet, she pulled the clutch, dropped the throttle, and shifted into gear. The motorcycle lurched forward. She leaned hard to the right and quickly diverted around the traffic and blasted toward the stables, praying she'd get there in time.

She didn't.

Joie slipped into the back door five minutes past the start time and snuck into Dan's office, trying not to make a scene.

"You're late," her boss noted.

"I—I'm sorry. Traffic jam out on Sun Valley Road."

Mike, who was in charge of feeding, turned around. "Heard old Mrs. Carter got her hands on some car keys and rear-ended somebody."

Joie nodded, but only slightly. Wanting to make amends, she trained her undivided attention up front.

Dan cleared his throat. "Look, we're all busy, so let's get right down to it. As you all know, we've had a good year. Business has really picked up."

"That's a good thing," Cindy added. "Sun Valley Company is delighted with what we've accomplished this year."

Dan nodded at his wife. "Yes, they've been extraordinarily

pleased with the P&Ls, especially this quarter. And much of this success is thanks to the hard work of everyone here."

Her eyes darted the room. Why didn't he just get on with it? She hated the unknown. And she hated meetings.

"The increase in business, coupled with the fact Cindy and I want to have a little more freedom—"

Joie's heart suddenly clawed up her throat and stayed there. Dan wasn't making the big announcement today was he? She'd hoped to be in line for the stable manager opening she'd heard might be coming, with an increase in salary that might allow her to get back on her feet after making the decision to leave her old life behind. Clearly, he hadn't talked with her about that possibility, so this announcement didn't bode well.

That's when she caught sight of someone she didn't recognize—or, at least the back of a head she couldn't quite place.

Longer dark hair. Not quite shoulder length. Broad shoulders.

Tattooed bear claws running up his arm.

"So without further delay, I'd like to introduce you to our new stable manager, Clint Ladner."

Joie's world slowed to a crawl as she watched the guy stand to face the employees.

He grinned. "Hey y'all. Glad to be here."

Oh no! It couldn't be.

The guy from the bar.

He was shaking hands now, listening as everyone gushed about how happy they were that he was here. A bunch of kiss-ups.

Patty leaned close. "He's gorgeous," she whispered. "And younger than I would have expected."

Joie scowled. "Hadn't noticed."

"What do you mean, you hadn't noticed? Are you blind? I mean, look at him. That hair. Those eyes. He reminds me of that guy who played Tim Riggins on Friday Night Lights."

"Who?"

"Tim Riggins." Patty waved her off. "Oh, never mind. I don't care what anybody says, he's definitely eye candy."

Joie felt her neck go hot as her mind drifted to how she'd played him in the bar that day.

Stupid. Stupid. When would she ever learn? Leigh Ann was right. She needed to quit giving in to her impulses and grow up.

He looked her way, studied her until she was forced to glance away.

Dan suddenly stepped to her side, took her elbow and forced her forward. "Clint, I'd like you to meet Joie Abbott. She's one of our best trainers, the one I told you about earlier."

"I believe we've met." His words hung there like a spotlight, illuminating her humiliation.

She made herself boldly meet his gaze. "Yes, we did meet."

What did she care what he thought of her? Like Dan said, she was a dang good horseman. In time, this new guy would discover that for himself.

Her independent streak forced her hand out with feigned confidence. "Welcome to Sun Valley."

Despite her dauntless demeanor, it occurred to her that no matter what she did from here on out, regardless how hard she worked, or how knowledgeable she was—in his eyes she'd likely only be a pair of tight jeans leaning over a pool table.

For the second time in her life, she wished she could turn the clock back and have a redo, another chance to do her life differently.

Unfortunately, she knew better than anyone second chances were a myth.

8

Karyn paused in front of the Sun Valley Lodge and straightened her jacket. She'd entered through these doors hundreds of times, but never in a professional capacity. And never this nervous.

Ignoring the way her stomach jittered, she compelled her feet to move inside.

Despite the rustic images normally conjured in people's minds when they hear the term lodge, the Sun Valley Lodge was anything but unrefined, or simple.

Even with the recent renovations, the lobby remained much as it had appeared since the establishment first opened in 1936. Wood pillars and floors graced with thick plush rugs. Classy European décor. Local art and massive windows overlooking the iconic skating rink. *"Roughing it in Luxury"* as claimed in travel brochures.

She and Dean had their wedding reception here. They'd danced for the first time as husband and wife out on that deck overlooking the ice skating rink, under strings of lights and the watchful eyes of a crowd of loved ones.

Before she could lose her emotional balance, she chased

the memory from her head. It wouldn't take much to talk her out of going through with this interview. Of course, then all she'd have to look forward to was more days inside her house waiting for life to begin again.

That, and painting classes with the Dilworth sisters.

Even after coming to the rather hasty decision, it took her a whole week to get up the nerve to call the resort director to inquire about the position. When he'd expressed what seemed like genuine interest, her gut went a bit queasy. She'd immediately second-guessed her plan and fought the urge to simply apologize and tell him she'd changed her mind.

Something inside her crumpled at the thought of trying to convince anyone that she was more capable than she felt. Serving in a high-profile hospitality position was a far cry from editing metaphors, tightening prose and arguing themes.

As time grew closer for her big interview, the pit of her stomach grew tighter. Last night, she woke at two o'clock unable to sleep, her mind whizzing. A repeat of several nights prior.

She'd worked endlessly updating her resume, highlighting the few aspects of her degree that might translate, and mentally rehearsing how to best explain why she'd placed a career on hold to support her husband's ski competition aspirations.

Now here she stood in the lobby, armed with nothing more than her sincere intentions and the well wishes of her sisters. There was no turning back.

Two women passed by the registration desk, wearing tennis clothes with rackets slung casually over their shoulders. One wore enthusiastic eyeliner and the other a cloud of unnaturally yellow hair. They smiled in her direction as they headed for the elevator.

"Karyn, you're right on time."

Startled, she turned toward the voice. A silver-haired man wearing a blue and white checked button-down shirt tucked inside a navy sports jacket headed in her direction, his hand extended.

She forced a confident smile. "Hello, Jon."

"Thanks for coming in. I've been looking forward to our meeting." He guided her across the lobby and down a short hallway. "How's your dad? Your sisters?"

She assured him her family members were all doing well as she followed him past frames filled with magazine covers featuring the lodge, some dating back to the fifties and sixties.

In contrast to the lobby décor, his office was decorated with stark chrome and glass furniture. The walls were also covered with framed photographs—images of Jon with Ted Kennedy, with Steve Jobs, with Angelina Jolie. Others up at Roundhouse, skis in hand. Against the wall, his credenza was filled with photos of his wife and adult children.

"Nice office," she commented. She'd encountered the resort director on several occasions, but Karyn couldn't claim to know Jon personally. From the photos, she could tell he was well suited to his position, and was a family man.

Too bad those photos couldn't reveal what he was thinking about her right now.

"Have a seat." He motioned to his guest chair. "Can I get you something to drink? Coffee?"

She shook her head. "Jon, the lodge renovations turned out great. I love how the company updated the amenities while maintaining the historic feel."

"We're certainly pleased." He grinned with satisfaction. "There was a time or two we wondered if we could pull off a project of this magnitude in less than ten months, but somehow it all came together."

He slipped behind his desk and picked up her resume. She noted he'd written in the margins and her stomach churned.

"I have to tell you how happy I was to see your application

cross my desk. Your husband had many fans, and I was certainly one of them."

She'd been a widow for months, yet her role as Dean's wife was still opening doors.

As if reading her mind, he hurried to add, "Your resume is impressive. The director of hospitality is a key position here at the lodge and a special skill set is required." His comments stayed suspended in midair as he slipped a pair of reading glasses in place. "There are several areas here on your resume I'm interested in knowing more about."

Over the next half hour, he quizzed her about her education and work experience. He nodded at all the appropriate times, raised his eyebrows in interest at her answers to his questions, took notes when she highlighted her ability to communicate effectively and juggle multiple priorities.

She looked across the desk at him and did her best to provide a snapshot of a confident, well-trained woman who had plenty of skill and work ethic to fill the job.

For a splinter of a second, she felt like the woman she used to be—one who knew where to find her smile without having to rummage for it.

Jon explained how the position would include overseeing the operations for not only the Sun Valley Lodge, but would include the Sun Valley Inn located on the other side of the pedestrian mall and all the company-owned condominiums. An overwhelming responsibility.

Finally, he closed the folder.

"Well, Karyn. Your resume is impressive." He opened his desk drawer and pulled out a sealed envelope. "The job is yours provided this offer is acceptable." He handed her the envelope and stood. "You can let me know by morning."

Her eyes widened and her hand went to her chest. "Really? I mean, thank you."

"If the employment terms are acceptable, let's plan on you starting next Monday."

She leaned across the desk and shook his hand. "Yes, that sounds fine. And thank you again."

They both stood and Jon showed her to the door. "I'll call you tomorrow and you can relay your decision then."

A smile nipped at the corners of her mouth as she moved down the hall, absolutely elated. She—Karyn Macadam—was the new director of hospitality for the Sun Valley Lodge.

One short meeting and it was as if someone had magically ripped away a tattered page from her life-worn calendar. It was a new day!

On the way out, she exchanged pleasantries with the desk clerk then clipped toward the gift shop, delightfully tangled in the knowledge that for the first time in a long while she had something to look forward to.

Dean would be proud.

GRAYSON CHANDLER REACHED inside the cooler for a bottle of water then moved for the counter to pay. In doing so, he nearly bumped into a woman also moving toward the clerk and the register.

He quickly stepped back. "Oh, pardon me."

"No problem, I—"

Their eyes met.

"Hey." Something deep inside his belly flittered. "Nice to see you again, Karyn."

Her smile was rich and genuine, hinting she no longer considered him a freak stalker.

He reached in his back jeans pocket for his wallet. "Go ahead." He motioned her to the counter.

"Oh no, you were in line first."

"No really, I don't mind. You go ahead."

The clerk raised her eyebrows and smiled. "Well, who's it going to be folks?"

Grayson laughed. "I have the perfect solution." He pushed his credit card across the counter. "I'll get her—" He glanced at her hand. "—granola bar. Add her purchase to mine, please."

He half expected she might argue. Instead, she aimed a full smile at him, and he felt its impact.

"Thank you," she said. "You didn't have to do that."

He fumbled as he tried to press the appropriate buttons on the point-of-sale machine. "No problem."

The transaction cleared and the clerk handed him a receipt.

He tucked his wallet back in his pants pocket and turned. She had really pretty hair, especially when the light hit the long strands. He especially liked the little laugh lines around her eyes. Unlike other times their paths had crossed, she seemed genuinely happy.

Without breaking eye contact, she backed toward the door and gave him a little wave. "Well, see you around."

He nodded. "Yeah, see you." He grabbed his water from the counter when an idea hit. "Hey wait! If you're headed out to the parking lot, I'll walk with you." It was a bold move that seemed to come out of nowhere. Not that he had any particular intentions. The fact was, he didn't have a lot of friends in Sun Valley, and he hoped she might agree to be one—a friend, that is.

"I mean, if that's okay," he quickly added. His pulse thumped against his chest as he waited for her response.

"Sure, I'd like that."

Delight spread over him. "Great."

She turned for the door and he scrambled after her, out the gift shop and into the lobby, which was now filled with people and stacked luggage. A tour bus was parked outside under the porte cochere, its engine at a low rumble that filtered through the open doors adding to the loud chatter inside.

Over the noise, he attempted small talk. "The travel brochures don't even begin to do this place justice."

She nodded in agreement. "I think so too. But then, I'm a bit biased."

"How's that?" He followed her outside and together they moved along the walkway that circled the nicely landscaped pond out front. A white swan glided across the water toward a small waterfall crafted of carefully placed boulders with bright-colored flowers strategically placed.

She grinned. "Can you keep a secret? Because I'm dying to tell someone my news."

"You bet."

She stopped walking and looked at him, her face beaming. "I just came from an interview and was offered a job as the director of hospitality."

"Here? At the lodge?"

She nodded enthusiastically. "Yes. I have the offer in my purse. All I have to do is call in the morning and accept."

"Karyn, that is great news! No wonder you seemed so happy."

"Look what you had to compare it against," she teased. "Admittedly, I still find some days difficult."

He shrugged. "Understandable."

"Yes, but at some point you have to move on or you risk staying stuck forever." She gave him a timid smile. "At least that's what I'm often told." She pointed across the lot. "I'm parked over there."

They headed for her car and she glanced over at him. "Look, I wasn't exactly cordial the first time we met—or even the second. Thanks for being so nice anyway."

"Not a problem," he told her. He opened her car door and she slid inside. "By the way, I'm staying here at the lodge temporarily until I find a permanent place. So, we may run into one another on occasion."

She grinned up at him. "I'd like that."

He reluctantly closed her door and gave her a little wave.

She wiggled her fingers back at him, started her engine and eased from her spot. He watched as she slowly pulled away, pleased that she glanced in her rearview mirror.

He waved again.

While he didn't often admit the fact, not even to himself, the woman in that SUV wasn't the only one mired in the past.

His ex-wife had stolen his past—not his future. Relocating to Sun Valley was his fresh start. He needed to believe he could risk and put it all out there again. Even if his heart took a second hit.

If the way his gut flipped whenever he saw Karyn Macadam was any indication—it might just be time.

9

"Mark, what are your plans today?" Leigh Ann tossed a carefully folded afghan over the back of the sofa. "I was thinking that maybe after lunch we could go golfing, or maybe play a set of tennis. It's been a while since we've had any real time together."

Her husband barely looked up. "Sorry, babe. I have too much work."

Leigh Ann frowned, pulled in a deep breath. "Oh, okay." She bent and freed her aching feet from the ridiculously high heels she'd worn to the tourism council meeting that morning, then moved to where he was sitting, leaning over a coffee table filled with stacks of papers. "Well, maybe we can plan a nice dinner together."

He reached for his cocktail.

She glanced up at the clock, wanting to say something about the early hour, then thought better of it.

"It's my first."

Leigh Ann lifted her chin and decided to press her agenda. "It'd do you good to take a break from all of this. Are you sure you won't reconsider?"

"I did take a break. We took a trip to Boise only last week."

"True. But, that was still work related. I just tagged along."

He rubbed his forehead. "Look, I'm sorry Leigh Ann. I don't mean to be so short—" He let his apology fade. "Hey, do we have any aspirin?"

Leigh Ann took a deep breath and swallowed the argument taking form in her mind. Instead, she headed for her beautiful kitchen, the one they'd recently remodeled. "Sure. I'll get you some."

On her way to the drawer that held the bottle of Advil, she stopped to wipe a spot from the new Thermador induction stovetop. For weeks, her mind had been set on a Miele from Germany, but ultimately a blogger she followed altered her commitment when she read that far fewer service vendors were familiar with the brand.

Mark had complained about the price, of course. But she'd pointed out he had a Harley in the garage that had cost double.

She tipped the bottle and let two tablets drop into her palm, replaced the lid and shoved the drawer closed with her hip, then returned to the living area. "Here you go," she said, holding out the tablets in her hand as a peace offering.

He tossed the pills in his mouth and washed them down with the last of his gin and tonic. He set the empty glass on the coffee table, looked over and motioned for her to sit next to him. "Hey, sorry. What can I say? I'm a jerk. Now, why don't you tell me all about your big meeting this morning?"

Leigh Ann's spirits lifted and she plopped down beside him, folding her legs underneath her. She leaned and rubbed his shoulder with one hand. "Well, the upcoming Wine and Arts Festival was primary on the agenda, and we've already started to make plans for the Trailing of the Sheep Festival this fall."

"Oh?"

The brevity of his response disappointed her, but she went on.

"Yes, the retailers are really enthusiastic about the boost in tourism these events always bring to the area. And we have lots of deep pocket sponsors being extremely generous this year. I'm always surprised at how this community rallies around philanthropic efforts." She gave her husband's back a final pat. "I think you're going to enjoy everything we have planned."

Her husband normally took advantage of any opportunity to hang with the beautiful people. His phrase, not hers.

"Oh, and I wrote them a check."

His head bolted up. "How much?"

She stiffened. "It was only five hundred. Is that a problem?"

Mark was quick to shake his head. "No, not a problem. You just need to tell me."

She raised her eyebrows. "I thought I just did."

"You know what I mean." He shuffled the papers into a stack and slipped them inside his briefcase laying open at the end of the sofa. "Look, I've got to get going."

She fingered the hair at the nape of her neck, disappointed their chat was short-lived. "To the office?"

He looked at her like she had two heads. "That's my first stop, yes. I'm afraid I'm not likely going to be home for dinner."

She thought of the spaghetti sauce simmering on the stove and sighed. She hated eating alone, which was happening far too often lately. Maybe she could call her sisters and invite them over.

"Guess I'll just leave you to your work then." She lifted from the sofa and headed into their bedroom to change into a pair of jeans and tee shirt.

Her marriage hadn't always been like this.

Over the time they'd been married, and especially in their early years, she never had to compete with his work or vie for his affection. Truth was, Mark often raced home from the office for what he fondly liked to call his *nooner*.

In the evenings, they'd cook together and talk about everything—and nothing at all.

When Colby arrived on the scene, her husband's adoration seemed to increase. She remembered one particular time when they were all on the floor playing Tonka Trucks and her husband looked over at her with a sappy expression. Clearly, he considered himself the luckiest man alive.

She too felt fortunate. Especially when she'd walk into a crowded room on his arm and women's heads would turn.

She was Mrs. Mark Blackburn, and proud of it.

When Colby left for college, everything seemed to change. Mark's real estate business took more and more of his time. She had no choice but to fill her hours with additional community service projects.

Don't misunderstand. She loved her volunteer work, and thoroughly enjoyed planning big events on those occasions when she got the opportunity. She was really good at it. Everyone said so.

Still, she sensed she and Mark were drifting apart. They needed to get away and make time to enjoy themselves—to get to know each other again.

Which is why she intended to surprise him with a trip for his birthday. His forty-fifth was just around the corner and she wanted his big day to be extra special.

Last week, she'd booked several nights at Hotel Vintage in downtown Seattle, a quaint boutique-like place that hosted a wine tasting every evening for guests. She and Mark could enjoy some time away, maybe slip over and nab Colby from his dorm and have dinner as a family one of the nights. Then perhaps they could catch a dinner cruise across Puget Sound another evening.

Thinking about her plans quickly lifted her spirits. That, and the thought of the gorgeous sunshine waiting for her beyond their front door.

On the way outside, she was surprised to find Mark still on the sofa. "I thought you were leaving?"

"I am," he said, pointing to his phone on the table. "Had to take a call is all."

She shrugged. "Well, I'm going out to plant the front yard."

"I thought you did that weeks ago," he said, gathering his papers into a briefcase.

"I did. But the beds need a bit more color."

The Hamilton Garden Center had delivered her flats of geraniums, impatiens and lobelia earlier that morning, and while Dee Dee offered to plant them for a nominal amount, she enjoyed doing these chores herself, despite her husband suggesting the neighbors might think they couldn't afford a landscaper.

Outside, Leigh Ann rummaged in her tiny tool shed for her kneepad and planting trowel. She carried them to the lengthy planting beds that bordered the front of their home determined to have a good day despite Mark's rebuff.

The bright summer day did its trick and lifted her spirits. Brilliant shafts of sunlight broke through tree limbs filled with leaves in various shades of green and the smell of freshly mown grass mingled with the slight pine aroma wafting in the air.

She'd barely sent her hand trowel deep into the rich, brown earth when the door opened and Mark stepped onto the front stoop, grumbling as he sidestepped her porch decorations. "Leigh Ann, why on earth do we need all these flower pots blocking our entrance?" Without waiting for her to respond, he headed for his car. "See you when I see you. Don't wait up."

Leigh Ann stabbed the ground with her trowel. "Don't worry dear. I won't." She forced a smile. "Have a good day."

❧

KARYN DROVE straight over to Leigh Ann's to share her good news and found her sister busy planting flowers in the beds lining her driveway. Leigh Ann's home was a showplace fit for a magazine cover and she worked hard to keep it that way.

"Hey, isn't it time you hire a gardener?" she asked, while crossing the portico.

Leigh Ann lifted slowly, her hand rubbing at the small of her back. "Now you sound like Mark." She stepped back and admired her work. "So, what do you think? Aren't the geraniums pretty?"

Karyn nodded. Her sister definitely had a knack for all things domestic. "Really great, Leigh Ann."

"Besides, gardening is my stress reliever. Did I tell you about the recent tourism council meeting? The Wine and Arts Festival is right around the corner, with all the details that needed decided, and all the council members wanted to talk about was that development rumored to be going in up at Triumph."

Karyn looked puzzled. "I thought the old mining site was off limits."

Her sister huffed. "Exactly, which is why we needed to address more urgent matters at hand."

Karyn slipped her sunglasses up on her head. "I have news."

"Oh?" Her sister put her tools away and headed for the house, motioning for Karyn to follow. "What's up? By the way, have you eaten?"

"Not since a granola bar this morning, and I'm starved."

They entered Leigh Ann's gourmet kitchen. Karyn lifted her nose and breathed deeply. "Mmm—smells good."

Leigh Ann pointed to several empty jars on the counter. "Spaghetti sauce from our canned tomatoes. If you want to hang out and go to the nursery with me later, I'd love to have you stay for dinner. Mark's not going to be here tonight and I could use some company."

"Sure." She slid into a barstool, sensing her sister was a bit distracted. "Hey, are you okay?"

"Of course. I want to hear all about your news. Just let me get out of these clothes and then you'll have my full attention."

While Karyn waited for her sister to change, she let her mind drift back to how she'd sat across the desk from Jon Sebring earlier. The questions he posed replayed in her head, and the way she'd been able to respond with confidence, despite her nerves. The interview actually ended up being a bit fun.

In an amazing turn of events, she'd landed a fabulous job with an offer that was far more than what she'd hoped, both financially and in terms of perks. She couldn't help but feel a sense of anticipation at what lay ahead.

Leigh Ann returned and headed for her refrigerator. She pulled out a pitcher of iced tea. "Okay, start at the beginning."

Karyn drew a deep breath. "Well, I've been doing a lot of thinking since the day of Dean's fundraiser." She tucked a strand of hair behind her ear.

Her sister grabbed glasses from the cupboard. "And?"

"And the thought has really been weighing on me that I'm tired of being a widow." She quickly moved to clarify. "I mean, I can't change the fact my husband died and left me alone, but I no longer want to sit around like an old dowager."

Leigh Ann brightened. She poured the tea, filling up the glasses. "That's great news. You're making real progress." She pushed a glass across the counter. "You want lemon?"

Karyn shook her head. "No thanks. Anyway, I was at Giacobbi Square a few days ago and the Dilworth sisters shared that Sandra Miller—"

"Oh my goodness, I heard! In fact, rumor has it—"

"Leigh Ann, I love you. But could we focus, please?"

A sheepish grin formed on her sister's face. "Oh, right. Your news. Sorry."

"Thank you." Karyn reached for her tea. "Sandra's self-imposed sabbatical—or whatever you call what she did—created a vacancy at the Sun Valley Lodge. Long story made short—but you are now looking at the new director of hospitality."

Leigh Ann's eyes widened. "What?" She placed her glass back on the counter. "Are you serious?"

Karyn beamed. "Yes, dead serious."

Leigh Ann circled the kitchen island and drew her into a hug. "Why didn't you say it was something this big? That's not just news. It's a headline!"

She nodded. "I know. I keep pinching myself."

Leigh Ann slid into the barstool next to her. "Spill and tell me everything. Jon Sebring is amazing. He attends the tourism council meetings, when warranted. He's always thoughtful and well-informed."

"Yes, I think I'm really going to like working with him."

"What will you be doing exactly?"

"Well, I'll have overall responsibility for reservations, sales, bell service, the front desk and concierge operations, and housekeeping—primarily I'll be running the entire lodge with the exception of strategic corporate planning and oversight, which is Jon's deal."

A concerned expression sprouted on Leigh Ann's face. "I hope I won't be taking on too much. I mean, that's a tremendous lot of responsibility. Are you even ready for that?"

Karyn had to work to keep from rolling her eyes. "Look, Miss Worry Wart of America—can you give me a little credit here?"

Her older sister relented with a smile. "Oh, of course. You're right. In all truth, I'm sincerely happy for you, Karyn. You deserve this." Her sister stood and went for a spoon. "Have you told Dad?"

"Not yet. You're the first."

Leigh Ann nodded. "Well, I feel privileged. I only wish Joie's story was as upbeat as yours."

"What do you mean?"

Leigh Ann let out a heavy sigh. "Well, not to detract from your good news, but I learned Dan Albertson hired a new stable manager—and it wasn't Joie."

"Oh dear! That's awful."

Leigh Ann nodded. "I know. Joie tried not to let on the other day, but I could sense she was really counting on that promotion. Goodness knows, she needs the money. And she's too stubborn to let any of us help her."

"Do you think Joie's been told already?"

Leigh Ann's face grew even more somber. "Oh goodness, I would hope she learned before the entire town got the news."

Karyn nodded her agreement. "Joie's going to take this really hard, regardless of how or when she hears about it."

Leigh Ann wiped moisture from the bottom of the tea pitcher with a towel. "Well, we're going to have to be there for her, that's all. Find a way to fix this."

"Fix it, huh?" Karyn jiggled the ice cubes in her tea glass. "Do they make a wrench for broken dreams?"

10

J oie entered Crusty's with purpose, and a bit of attitude.

"Hit me up," she hollered toward the gray-haired owner, surprised she was the only patron. Of course, it was early in the day.

Crusty looked up at her from where he labored over a mop and bucket at the end of the bar. "Be with you in a sec, Chill. The keg leaked and left a mess here." He continued swiping the wooden floor. "If you're in a hurry, you know where I keep the goods."

"Got it." Joie climbed on the stool and leaned far over the counter. She grabbed the loose beer spigot and pointed it at an empty glass. With her other hand, she gave the tap several pumps. Despite the effort, the tiny black hose sputtered and spit out only foam.

Frustrated, she held it up. "Seems everything's against me today."

Crusty dipped his mop back in the bucket. "Oh, sorry. The coupling must be out. Probably what caused the leak."

She jumped off her barstool and headed his way. "Never mind." On her way past him, she leaned and brushed his leathery cheek with a kiss. "I think I need something stronger anyway."

The older man rubbed at his cheek and smiled. "Always the tease."

She laughed. "You know it."

With determination, she moved behind the bar and headed for the shelf of liquor bottles. "Got any Cozedores? Or did the boys drink all the good tequila up during their poker game last night?"

Crusty winked. "Under the bar. Second cabinet from the right."

She smiled. "Ah, you're a good man, Crusty."

The owner cocked his head. "So, what's up, Chill? It ain't even noon yet. And aren't you supposed to be down at the stables?"

She pulled the bottle from its hiding place and unscrewed the top. "I decided to take some vacation time."

"Ah—" He nodded.

She closed her eyes for just a second. Some might argue she was running away again. She didn't care. The way she figured, the new guy could handle things without her just fine. At least until she had to tuck her tail between her legs and return for that much-needed paycheck.

Why did life always dish out such impossible choices?

She poured a generous amount of the amber liquid into a glass and grabbed several lime wedges. Her hand gave one a slight squeeze, then rubbed the juice onto her left hand in that place between her thumb and forefinger. Next, she sprinkled the moist spot with salt and licked.

Before she could change her mind, Joie took a deep breath and upended the glass in her mouth, draining the entire amount. The immediate burn caused her to wince. She reached for the bottle again.

Crusty leaned the mop against the back wall and headed her way. "So, want to talk about it?"

She could tell from his eyes he knew.

Likely, everyone in town had already learned she'd been passed over. Despite what her father claimed about the Albertsons being fair people—smart business folks—they'd hired an outsider, someone barely known, over giving her the opportunity and promotion.

What exactly did *that* say?

Her life was still a series of bad patterns—that's what it said.

She squared her shoulders and took a deep breath. "So, Crusty. What have you heard about him?"

"Who?"

"The guy the Albertsons hired to be the new stable manager."

Crusty paused. "The one you were making crow with in here the other day?"

"Correction. I wasn't making crow with anybody," Joie argued. "Especially not Clint Ladner."

Crusty's eyes turned sympathic. He shrugged. "Well, he seems nice enough. I hear he's a good horseman. Not as fine as you, of course," he quickly added. "He's living south of town, not far from your dad's place."

She pulled another lime wedge from her little pile. "South of town, huh?"

"Near Gimlet."

She rubbed her hand with the lime. "What else did you hear about Wonder Boy?"

"He's single."

"Well, no doubt. Everybody in the bar that day could tell he was a hound dog. He has that look."

Crusty lifted his eyebrows. "That look?"

"Yeah, the look." She sprinkled salt, licked, and shot

another glass of tequila, letting the heat of the alcohol erase the fact she'd been dealt a chilling blow.

Wasn't the first time she'd been blindsided.

Joie reached for the tequila bottle, fresh resolve churning in her gut. One thing you could count on.

This would be the last time.

11

L eigh Ann lifted a pot from the nursery shelf. "Here, these are perfect!"

Karyn fingered a ceramic garden gnome with strange eyes. "What did you find?"

"The miniature daisies I wanted." She turned to Dee Dee Hamilton standing over at the register and held up the pot. "How many do you have?"

Dee Dee wedged a pen above her ear and joined them. "You're in luck. The Sun Valley Lodge ordered several pallets and we have extra. I'm sure we could divert a few your way. How many do you need?"

Leigh Ann looked over at her. "What do you think, Karyn? Ten flats maybe?"

She shrugged. "Yeah, I guess." Her answer didn't seem to make her sister happy, so she quickly added, "Or, maybe make it an even dozen. They'll look really nice set in with the beds you planted this morning."

Looking satisfied, Leigh Ann turned to Dee Dee. "Can you spare two dozen?"

Two things her oldest sister didn't want for—time and

money. When she wasn't volunteering, she often entertained herself with expensive projects. Take her recent kitchen remodel, for example.

Over the spring months, Leigh Ann had spent hours pouring over appliance selections, tile choices, deciding which was better—granite or silestone countertops.

With that finished, she started planning an upstairs bathroom redo. Once again, her dining room table was stacked with decorating magazines.

Now, it seemed, she'd turned to landscaping.

Karyn leaned over a pot filled with a miniature rose bush and sniffed. Disappointed there was no aroma, she moved to a pot of brightly colored chili peppers, the kind you put in your kitchen window. It was then that her phone vibrated in her back pocket. She pulled it out and brought it to her ear. "Hello?"

"Karyn? It's Crusty."

Her heart immediately sank. "Yeah?"

"You need to come pick her up."

WITH NO WAY TO shed Leigh Ann, Karyn had little choice but to let her sister accompany her downtown.

"I'm afraid I don't understand. Why did Crusty call you and not me?"

Karyn gripped the steering wheel a bit tighter. "Maybe K comes before L in his phone directory—I don't know. Quit reading something into nothing."

Her sister's lips drew into a tight line. "You don't have to get snippy."

Karyn sighed and tilted her head, considered how to defuse the matter. "Look, I'm sorry. I didn't mean to take what I'm feeling out on you." She flipped on her blinker and turned onto

Main, knowing it was easier to end this quibble now before the exchange took on a more complicated dimension.

She adored Leigh Ann, but she could be stubborn and a little idealistic, and a firm believer that anything could be fixed with a bit of grit and some hard work. There was little point in trying to convince her of the one thing she didn't want to see—the fact that not everything worked that way.

Still looking a bit offended, her sister lifted her chin. "Apology accepted."

Minutes later, they were parked in front of the establishment their younger sister often called her own private oyster bar—a place that covered over the irritants in her life.

In reality, Crusty's was where local blue collars hung out, the ones who would never be caught inside the more distinctive Cornerstone or the Sawtooth Club—or heaven forbid, one of the trendy breweries that dotted the county.

Originally opened as a casino in the forties, the bar had been passed through many owners. Crusty, or Byron Gentry as his driver's license would reveal, purchased the establishment after losing his wife and two boys in a car fire in the seventies. He lived in an apartment on the second floor and dispensed not only alcoholic beverages to his patrons, but a lot of non-muddled wisdom.

When Dean died, Crusty had quietly stood at the back of the church during the funeral, hands folded, tears streaming down his face.

"I suppose there's no talking you into staying in the car?" Karyn asked her sister, hopeful. One look gave her the answer. "Okay, but try not to—"

"To what?"

She bit the inside of her cheek to keep from plainly stating what was on her mind. "Just—well, now might not be the time to light into her."

Inside Crusty's, the interior was dark and smelled of a

strange mix of stale cigarette smoke and Pine-sol cleaner. Karyn stood for a few seconds, letting her eyes adjust to the dim light.

The stools lining the bar were filled with guys. Neon beer signs lined the sparce walls. On the far side, a game of pool was underway. Snippets of talk about the upcoming BSU Bronco football game filtered through the latest Band Perry song, loudly accompanied by their little sister who sat on the floor leaning against the base of the billiard rack singing at the top of her lungs.

Crusty came from around the bar, wiping his hands on a towel. "Hey, girls. I cut her off over an hour ago, but she wouldn't let anyone drive her home, and well—"

Karyn patted his boney shoulder. "You did the right thing."

Leigh Ann scowled at the scene their sister was making. "Yes, thanks for calling us."

Crusty flipped the towel onto his shoulder. "I considered calling Edwin, but I thought—"

Karyn quickly shook her head. "No, better that you called us instead of dad."

Leigh Ann skirted around them both and made a beeline for Joie.

Joie pushed herself up from the floor, wobbled slightly. "Oh look, it's Nancy Reagan." She hiccoughed and wiggled her finger. "Just say no."

Leigh Ann took her arm and steadied her. "Come on, let's go—"

Their younger sister slowly smiled. She thrust an open palm toward Leigh Ann. "Here's my halo. Needs a bit of shining —but you look like you're up for the job."

"Oh, stop it," Leigh Ann scolded. "Do you have any idea—"

Karyn wedged herself between them. "Enough you two. Not here." She folded Joie's limp arm around her shoulder and grasped her sister's waist. "Let's just get you home."

From up at the bar, Terrance Cameron pulled the pipe from

his mouth. "You cannot escape the responsibility of tomorrow by evading duty today." When they looked at him in confusion, he added, "A famous Abraham Lincoln quote."

Leigh Ann leaned close to Karyn and whispered. "One of the main reasons we wouldn't allow Colby to consider Berkeley."

With more than a little effort, they got their little sister outside and into the car. Karyn quickly climbed in and started the engine. Before pulling out, she snuck a quick peek in the rear view mirror.

Sitting next to Joie in the backseat, Leigh Ann reached and pulled their little sister's head down onto her shoulder. Karyn waited for resistance. Surprisingly, there was none.

"Leigh Ann?" she heard Joie say.

"Yeah?"

Her little sister rubbed her nose with the back of her hand. "Not one of my shining moments."

Leigh Ann tenderly kissed the top of Joie's hair. "And you have so many to choose from."

12

J on Sebring smiled at Karyn from across his desk. "All media inquiries you might receive should be directed to my office." He stood. "I think that about wraps up this part of your orientation. Tomorrow we'll go over what the accountants need for payroll and then you're ready to be on your own." He circled the desk and motioned her down the hallway leading to the lobby.

Karyn followed him. "Right. That sounds good," she said, with far more conviction than she felt inside. There was way more to this job than she'd expected. The responsibility was definitely going to push her limits.

"We got a lot done today," Jon said as they neared the registration counter. "I can tell you're going to fit in just fine."

Despite feeling overwhelmed, she wanted desperately to appear like she had it all together. "Thank you, Jon. I'm really going to enjoy working here."

They bid each other goodbye and Karyn headed for the lobby.

Over the past days, she'd been introduced to the employees and associates of the Sun Valley Lodge. She'd planned the new menu with Amelio DelCorte, the head chef, booked reservations with the desk manager, reviewed snow removal contract renewals presented by their grounds manager, and approved a purchase order for linens for the housekeeping department.

No doubt she was going to be extremely busy with her new responsibilities. Busy was good.

She'd said as much to her father the other night. In a rare occurrence, both of her sisters had begged off their family dinner leaving her precious time alone with her dad.

"I'm so proud of you, sweetheart," he said as they stood washing the dinner dishes together. "Landing that job was no small thing."

"Thanks, Daddy. No doubt I'll be busy. But I'm really excited about what's ahead." Her throat tightened. "You know, it's been a while since I could say that."

Her father reached across the counter for a mug and dipped it into the soapy water. "We don't get to pick our circumstances, but each of us can decide whether or not to be happy."

She nodded, knowing he too had been forced to say goodbye to his life partner too soon. With three little girls to raise, he didn't have time to wallow in the loss he no doubt experienced.

She toweled off a spoon and returned it to the utensil drawer. "So, I probably need to tell you about Joie."

He reached for the dirty sauce pan. "I already heard."

Karyn raised her eyebrows. "That was quick. Who was the Katie Couric this time?" She loved the Dilworth sisters, but if either of them was the culprit, news of her younger sister's indiscretion would no doubt be all over town by now.

"Joie told me."

"Ah—" She watched him scrub the sudsy pot.

"You sound surprised."

"Not surprised really, only—" She paused. "Okay, yeah. I'm surprised she told you."

He handed off the pot and pulled the stopper in the sink, letting the water drain. "Your sister makes her share of mistakes, but she always owns up to them."

She nodded. "True."

"She'll find her way." He'd offered the often repeated phrase with confidence. "Same as all of us."

Karyn continued through the lobby, realizing her father was spot on. Joie would find her way—and they'd all be right beside her until she no longer teetered.

For now though, she had repair guys showing up. An auger bearing was grinding on the Zamboni and she couldn't take a chance of it going completely out before the Fourth of July ice show next month.

She was almost through the doors leading to the rink when she noticed Grayson step from the elevator. She slowed, unable to look away, especially when he hung back and let the elderly man and woman, who were holding hands, pass by in front of him without showing any sign of annoyance.

Something warm and pleasant set up camp inside, put an immediate smile on her face.

She waved and decided to head over his way.

GRAYSON CHANDLER FOLLOWED AN OLDER couple out of the elevator. The white-haired man gently threaded his fingers with his wife's and they shuffled through the lobby holding hands.

He smiled and checked his watch. If he wanted to make his appointment with the realtor, he'd need to get a move on. Even so, he waited patiently for the couple to make their way forward.

"Grayson?"

He looked up, surprised to find Karyn Macadam heading

his way. She wore a pretty sweater that matched the color of the sky and a wide smile. "I wondered when we'd run into each other again."

He moved to join her, appreciating how she wasn't one of those girls who had to try to look pretty. "So, I take it you're officially on the job now?"

She nodded. "It's official."

"Everything you hoped it would be?"

"Even more. There will no doubt be challenges, but I really think this job is a perfect fit."

Something in the way she looked at him made his heart idle a little too fast.

"Good. That's great." It felt a bit awkward to stand there staring like a pimply-faced eighth grader. He shuffled a bit. "Well, I was just heading out—" He pointed toward the front entrance.

"Oh goodness!" She held up her hands. "Yes, don't let me make you late."

"No, it's—you didn't." An idea formed. "Hey, what time are you done here? I'm supposed to meet a realtor and go look at some places. Shopping for houses isn't exactly my forte. In fact, I can tackle just about anything, unless the task is remotely domestic. I once rented an apartment and never noticed there was no stove. For months, I had to cook on a hotplate." He was rambling. There was an awkward pause before he took a deep breath and forged ahead. "Look, I certainly don't know the area like you do. The truth is I could really use a friendly bit of help in evaluating where to buy. Real estate is a big investment. Especially here in Sun Valley."

She looked uncertain. He'd gone too far, he could tell.

A concierge passed by wheeling a cart loaded with bags. A family with three small children followed closely behind. The youngest tugged at the woman's shirt. "An ice-skating rink! Can we go?"

Grayson felt himself sliding on thin ice.

With an embarrassed grin, he anchored his gaze on Karyn and offered her an out. "I'm sorry. I didn't stop to consider you might not have time—"

"No—I'd like to go! But, I still have a few things I need to wrap up here." Karyn examined her watch. "I could meet you at the realtor's office. Say, in a half hour?" Their eyes met. "Would that work okay?"

He gave her an enthusiastic nod. "Sure, that'd be just fine." He handed her the realtor's business card. "Here's the address."

"Oh, you're using Tessa McCreary. She's a great realtor."

"That's good to hear. So, I'll see you in a bit." He turned for the door, then glanced back, grinning. "Hey, Karyn?"

"Yes?"

"Uh—thanks."

Her lips pulled into a tiny smile. "No problem.

KARYN ENTERED Tessa McCreary's office wondering why she was even there. A guy, still a stranger in many ways, had up and asked her along to go look at potential real estate and she'd said yes? And, with little to no hesitation?

It's the neighborly thing to do.

The reception area was empty. Voices echoed from somewhere down the hall.

"Karyn? We're in here," a familiar female voice rang out. "Come on back."

She followed a wall lined with framed sales awards and made her way to an office with windows overlooking Baldy. "Hey, Tessa."

Grayson jumped up from his seat. He extended his hand, which seemed like a formal thing to do, given he'd invited her. As a friend.

He must've thought so too because he immediately dropped his hand and smiled. His face flushed, he pointed to the chair next to his. "Have a seat?"

Tessa leaned over her desk. "So, Grayson tells me you've agreed to join us on the great house hunt."

She nodded. "Yes, I hope that's okay."

"More than okay. Glad to have you along." She turned to her client. "I helped Karyn find her house a couple of years ago." If Tess thought it odd that Dean's widow was helping Grayson Chandler find a place to live, she didn't let on.

Karyn sat and nestled her purse in her lap. "By the way, thanks for the generous check you gave at the memorial event. Your support is so appreciated."

Tess waved her off. "No problem. Glad to donate to such a great cause."

The realtor pulled a piece of paper out of the file on her desk. "Grayson, I've narrowed the selections down to three listings I'd like to show you today."

The first was a condominium in Elkhorn, which Grayson quickly nixed. "I'm not the kind to live stacked so closely with the neighbors," he said. "I think a place where I can drink coffee outdoors without putting a shirt on might be a better option."

An image formed in Karyn's head of his bare chest. She quickly chased the notion from her mind, but not before remembering the easy way Dean strode from their bathroom in the mornings wearing only his drawstring pajama bottoms.

"I have what might be perfect for you. A place up Warm Springs that backs up to a creek lined with willows and aspens." She gave him a wide smile. "You won't feel the least crowded."

He nodded his approval. "Sounds good."

They left the office and climbed in her car, she and Tessa up front and Grayson in the back seat. A short drive later and they were parked in front of the potential property.

Even at first blush, the log structure was stunning. Spacious, but not too big.

Grayson seemed pleased. "Yeah, this is what I was hoping for." He turned to Karyn. "What do you think?"

"I love the timber elements. The river rock. Great curb appeal."

"Curb appeal?"

She exchanged an amused glance with Tessa and motioned for him to follow her up the sidewalk. "C'mon, let's take a look."

The home consisted of two levels, the bottom floor a large open area with vaulted ceilings and massive windows overlooking a stand of quaking aspens lining a brook.

Overhead was a loft. The railing of rough-hewn posts called to mind the early frontier days of this part of Idaho, when the Sun Valley area was a thriving silver mining town. Besides timber, and stunning river stone, portions of the interior had the traditional look of square-cut logs and chinking—sturdy and dependable, like the house could protect the inhabitants from even the harshest winter.

She sighed. "I think this house is perfect for you."

His eyes twinkled. "Oh? And why is that exactly?"

Karyn moved to the fireplace and ran her finger along the mantle. She could almost see the flicker of flames casting their warmth, imagine sitting in front of the crackling fire nestled on a flannel throw with a glass of wine.

She turned and their eyes met. "The house has a homey feel, and the craftsmanship is remarkable," she answered in part, skirting his question.

Tessa didn't waste the opportunity to make her own sales pitch. "I agree with Karyn. This house displays rugged strength, yet is completely warm and inviting. No frills. Just raw, dramatic elegance." To make her point, she led them to the open guest bath door. "Look at that mirror frame made of elk horns."

Grayson's face broke into a wide smile as he stepped to the counter and saw the basin made of stone. "Okay, I agree. All this is pretty cool."

Tessa gave a satisfied nod. "Let me take you upstairs. The master has an unsurpassed view of the backside of Baldy that is stunning, most especially at night."

Minutes later, they stood in the center of the main bedroom admiring the light-filled space.

Karyn could barely form words for the ambiance created by the windows. "Wow! It's almost like sleeping outdoors."

"You think so?"

His teasing tone didn't stop her from going on. "You'd have to put the bed right over there, facing the fireplace." She pointed. "A flat-screened television would be perfect in that spot right above the mantle. That way you can watch the news while drinking your morning coffee in bed."

She whirled and parked her hands on her hips. "You need to buy this house."

He laughed and held up open palms. "Point made. You like the house."

She laughed too. "Yeah, well—" She looked around the room, appreciating all the details. "I do." She nodded. "I really do."

Tessa stood in the doorway, clipboard in hand. "Sounds like my job may have just gotten a lot easier."

Grayson rubbed at his chin. "Is the house on city water and sewer?"

"I have more details if you'd like. Follow me." She turned and headed in the direction of the stairs.

Before trailing after her, Grayson looked back at Karyn. "You coming?"

13

"Wait, you're telling me Karyn went house shopping with Grayson Chandler?" Leigh Ann pulled her red sweater a little tighter across her bare shoulders as she followed Joie across the church parking lot.

"Yup." Joie lifted a compact mirror from her pocket and applied lip gloss as she walked. "Dad heard it from Ben at Atkinson's Market. Ben learned the news from the Dilworth sisters who had lunch with Tessa McCreary, Grayson's real estate agent.

"I just talked with Karyn on the phone last night. She said nothing." Leigh Ann followed the winding sidewalk leading to the front doors. "I don't understand why she didn't tell me."

"Oh, I don't know, Life Expert Barbie. Let me guess."

Leigh Ann gave her younger sister a sharp look before quickly pasting a smile as they neared the entrance to Grace Chapel. "Morning, Father John."

The rector handed each of them a bulletin. "Morning Leigh Ann. Joie. Glad to see you girls this delightful summer morning."

Leigh Ann nodded at the man who was also her dad's closest friend. "It is gorgeous. Summer never lasts long enough for me."

He smiled. "Ah, yes—but winter will return before we know it. I can't wait to get back on the mountain myself."

Inside, she and Joie made their way to their regular pew— middle section, third from the front, directly behind Andre and Dee Dee Hamilton and to the right of where Nash Billingsley always sat. Grace Chapel parishioners were nothing if not creatures of habit.

Leigh Ann slid in next to her dad and Karyn. Barely settled in her seat, she leaned over to Karyn and whispered, "Why didn't you tell me?"

"She's upset that Karyn didn't tell her she's seeing Grayson Chandler," Joie explained, dispelling their father's puzzled look.

Their middle sister huffed. "What are you talking about? I am most certainly not *seeing* Grayson Chandler. He's new to the area and he simply asked me to weigh in on a house he's considering purchasing. Despite what you might want to think, that's not exactly a romantic rendezvous."

Leigh Ann slipped her arms from her sweater and folded it over her lap. "Well, half the town is talking about it."

"Yeah? Well half the town needs to get a life."

Joie reached for a hymnal from the rack in front of her as Mrs. Miller positioned herself at the organ and began playing. "Sounds like Grayson Chandler wants to take wire cutters to that fence you've had up."

Karyn rolled her eyes before turning to their father for help. He sat silently with a wide grin on his face.

"Oh, now don't you start too." She looked around at her family. "Are you all intent on making a mountain out of a mole hill just to torture me?"

They nodded in unison.

"Well, job well done." Karyn whipped a hymnal from the rack and flipped the pages to *Blessed Assurance* before securing it across her lap. "The fact that I've become friends with Grayson Chandler isn't even remotely connected to anything romantic. Sorry to disappoint, but this isn't a Hallmark movie, folks."

Her dad's eyes sparkled with amusement. "I hear that Chandler guy bakes a mean apple pie." He winked at Leigh Ann.

Karyn slapped at his arm. "Oh, please. All of you. Stop already."

Leigh Ann grinned and lifted a hymnal from in front of her. "Speaking of pies, I saw Elda Vaughn in Atkinson's Market yesterday, her shopping cart heaped with baking supplies. She had a mega bag of chocolate chips. Perhaps she's diverting tactics and her next ploy will be a plate of hot cookies."

Joie quietly laughed as Father John stepped to the podium. "On top of petitioning for world peace, we need to pray we don't end up with a Bo Peep in the family."

Their father cocked his head in her direction. "A what?"

She patted his arm. "Nothing, Dad. Just bow your head."

HALFWAY THROUGH FATHER John's sermon, Joie picked at her nails, a habit she knew drove Leigh Ann crazy.

Only yesterday, her older sister caught her pulling at a ragged edge on her thumb and had chastised her. "Why do you do that and mess up your pretty hands? People are going to take one look at your nail beds and think you're a prisoner who recently dug out of Guantanimo."

She'd rolled her eyes. "Speaking of Guantanimo, I believe sister torture was banned under the Hague Convention."

A disapproving look fixed upon Leigh Ann's face. "You might not care what others think of you, but you should.

Despite how diligent you are in denying the fact, your reputation matters."

"Are we still talking about my fingernails?"

Leigh Ann shook her head. "Doesn't that chip on your shoulder ever get heavy? Seriously, Joie. At some point in your life you are going to have to grow up and—" She'd stopped mid-sentence, likely realizing the repeated warnings never did any good.

Truth was, that wasn't entirely so.

Her older sister's disapproval was nothing compared to the conga line playing in her head constantly reminding her of the ways she'd screwed up. Most recently that little stunt she pulled at Crusty's. Her sisters were never going to let her live that down— especially Leigh Ann.

Joie closed her eyes and tried to focus on Father John's message.

"We would all be wise to embrace the following truth." The rector gently smiled out over his congregation. "We are beloved by our Creator and each of us has great purpose. Any dead fish can go with the flow. We are called to climb out of the boat and grip our destiny in order to fulfill what we alone were created to accomplish here on earth."

Father John seemed to look directly at her.

"And in order to do that, some of us need to forgive. Maybe even ourselves."

She drew a deep breath and looked at the floor. "Easy for you to say," she thought.

Despite her steadfast public bravado, she'd marred more than her fingernails, and no one sitting in the pews of this chapel, let alone her family, knew the half of it.

Light filtered through the artistic spate of windows located behind the altar, a commanding view of Mt. Baldy anchoring the background.

She appreciated what Father John had to say. Unfortunately, standing tall and moving into her destiny wasn't all that easy.

She glanced sideways at her dad and sisters.

Not when she'd had to make her choices.

KARYN SHOULD BE LISTENING to Father John's sermon, but her mind kept wandering. People in town were talking, and she didn't like being the subject of their chatter.

Sure, her family and friends loved her and wanted her happy again. She wanted that too. The dangerous side effects of receiving such generosity of spirit were the pesky symptoms of expectation—her every move and motive examined like she was a specimen on a tiny glass slide.

Her world had definitely tilted after losing Dean. That didn't mean she was incapable of maneuvering her own life without people weighing in, no matter how well intentioned.

She was making every effort to right herself and stand straight again. Life moves on—even after tragedy. Sometimes you had no choice but to say goodbye to the one you loved, stare down that long road ahead of you and take the first step forward.

Karyn glanced across the aisle to where Dean's parents sat. Without honing in her gaze, she knew Aggie's eyes would fill with tears at the first strains of *Amazing Grace* . . . still.

Her heart filled with sadness at the notion. Yet, did that mean she couldn't break from following suit? Wasn't it healthy to want to walk away from the pain and feel good again?

Her hand slid into the pocket of her jacket and she quietly lifted her cell phone out and stared at the text message on the face.

"Thanks again for helping me the other day. I really enjoyed

your enthusiasm for the new house. Would love to see you again. Dinner sometime?"

She swallowed.

After having read the text multiple times, each letter of that message was now imprinted on her brain. Before responding, she needed to consider all the angles.

Was she really ready to start dating?

No doubt each of her sisters would want to offer counsel on every detail, smother her with concern and advice. Not to mention how having dinner with Grayson Chandler would only serve to create more fodder for discussion in the supermarket aisles.

What about Bert and Aggie? She knew Dean's parents wanted her happy, but they might be hurt to know she'd allowed someone new a place in her heart so soon—even if the relationship was limited to friendship more than anything else.

There would be no turning back after taking such a huge step. Yet, hadn't she vowed to start living again?

Her thumbs slowly moved to the keyboard.

Leigh Ann leaned over. "Who's that?" she mouthed.

Karyn glanced up at her nosy sister. "No one," she whispered and pocketed her phone.

Father John stood at the podium, his familiar voice clear and strong. "Any dead fish can go with the flow. We are called to climb out of the boat and get on with our destiny—"

A slight line of sweat formed at her hairline. She nibbled at her bottom lip and stared at the morning light streaming through the windows at the front of the church.

She might be a young widow, but she was no dead fish.

Before she could change her mind, she grabbed her phone and quickly tapped out a response.

"Sure, that would be nice."

Her finger wavered slightly as it hovered over the face of the phone. She took a deep breath, held it and pressed send.

GRAYSON CHANDLER STRODE across the asphalt of the Friedman Memorial and headed for the hanger where he kept his Cessna 206, the way he habitually did on so many beautiful mornings like this.

Being a backcountry pilot suited him—the quiet, simple routine, the work of packing and loading supplies for delivery, doing a flight check, and ultimately taking to the wide-open sky.

While his ex had discounted the value of his career choice, had even pushed him to consider a more conventional option that might carry more prestige, he'd never once regretted his decision and the lifestyle his avocation provided.

Today, instead of cargo, he'd be transporting an author and his publishing team to Roosevelt Lake for a photo shoot. The little known spot located in a remote mountainous area near Yellow Pine had been the seat of mining back in the early 1900s when a mud slide blocked Monumental Creek and flooded the entire area, leaving the town of Roosevelt under water. Remnants of the historic buildings could still be seen below the surface.

Normally, he left before dawn on such a trip, but he'd received a text from the head publicist that the group had stayed out a little too late on Saturday night and they were late rising from bed. She hoped that didn't cause him too much trouble.

"No trouble," he'd written back. He was here to serve the needs of his customers. He scrolled up to the even more important message he'd sent over a day ago.

Karyn had a great time looking at houses, and while it was a bit unnerving to venture out and send the message in the first place, he'd hoped she'd be happy to see it and would agree to move the relationship forward a tiny step.

But she hadn't responded, leaving him feeling unsettled, and yes, disappointed. Maybe he'd misread the situation, jumped ahead. Might even have made a fool of himself.

He shook his head.

Wouldn't be the first time.

He was getting ready to pocket his phone when it dinged. A message appeared.

"Sure, I'd love dinner. That would be nice."

Grayson's face broke into a wide grin.

A good day had instantly turned a whole lot better.

14

L eigh Ann reached into her grocery cart and grabbed the Oreos. "Like you need those," she scolded before placing the package back on the shelf. No one would say she was fat. But neither did she enjoy the fine-boned structure both of her sisters took for granted.

She pushed her cart down the aisle and away from the temptation with determination, instead heading for the pasta aisle. Another food item that went straight to her hips, but Mark loved anything with basil and garlic. Tonight, she'd surprise him with her special lasagna recipe using the canned tomatoes in her pantry, and would serve a loaf of crusty garlic bread he loved.

A night filled with all his favorites would provide a perfect springboard for her idea for his upcoming birthday and the trip she'd arranged to Seattle.

Normally, she'd prepare her lasagna noodles from scratch using her fancy pasta maker, a Christmas gift from Mark. Okay, admittedly she'd ordered it out of the Williams Sonoma catalog and put his name on it. Today, she was running late and she'd have to make do with the packaged variety.

On the way to the other side of the store, she passed the wine aisle and stopped to consider the selections when she overheard Mark's name.

"Are you sure it was Mark Blackburn?" While muted by the music piped from the overhead speakers, the familiar voice on the other side of the aisle clearly belonged to Trudy Dilworth.

"Well, no. I didn't personally see it," responded her sister, Ruby. "But Maxine over at the Moose Café was in the Opera House the other day and said she saw Mark with her in his car. They were driving south of town towards Hailey."

Leigh Ann frowned. Without regard for hidden store cameras, she crouched to listen.

Trudy's bracelets bangled on her wrists as her hand no doubt went to her mouth. "And you're sure it was her?"

Ruby lowered her voice, making it even more difficult to hear. Leigh Ann leaned closer to some bottles of chardonnay, the effort to no avail. She couldn't catch what Ruby said.

Trudy cleared her throat. "That's just awful. Oh, poor Leigh Ann! Do you think she knows?"

Leigh Ann pressed her forearm into her stomach to settle the rolling motion. Her mouth went dry and she couldn't breathe.

What was Mark doing with some gal in his car? And who was it?

As quickly as the questions formed, so did a reality check.

Despite what the Dilworth sisters had conjured in their minds, Mark came into contact with a lot of real estate investors, and it would not be out of the question that many of them were women. He might even have occasion to drive someone to look at a piece of property.

Tension melted from Leigh Ann's shoulders. How silly to let the Dilworth sisters' chatter get her all flustered.

Still, she bit at her lip.

Leigh Ann took a deep breath and lifted from the floor,

tightly gripping the cart until her knees felt steady. She looked up just as the Dilworth sisters rounded the aisle. Their eyes locked.

Immediately, Leigh Ann planted a bright smile. "Trudy! Ruby! How are you?" She prayed the two women wouldn't realize she'd been eavesdropping. It would require her to confront the situation and she simply couldn't. Not until she had more to go on.

Trudy's eyes lit up. "Leigh Ann! It's so good to see you. You were just the subject of our conversation. Wasn't she, Ruby?"

Leigh Ann held her breath, and immediately went into self-preservation mode, mentally calculating the nearest exit just in case she needed to fake a sudden stomach ailment and make a quick departure.

Ruby exchanged a nervous glance with her sister. "Yes, we're most thankful for those many jars of yummy home-canned tomatoes you shared with us. As God is our witness, we'll never be hungry again." She gave Leigh Ann a broad smile.

Trudy nodded, a bit too enthusiastically. "Oh, yes. We've both had a hankering for tomato basil soup and dropped in to get ingredients."

Momentary relief washed over Leigh Ann as she realized they had no intention of sharing what they thought they knew —at least to her face. She quickly regrouped. "What a coincidence! I'm using the tomatoes in my dinner as well. The beefsteak variety was especially good this year." She chattered on about how she and Mark had gone to Boise and stopped at the u-pick farm in Hagerman on the way back. "In fact, I'm making his favorite—lasagna with Bolognese sauce. It's our date night." She added a sweet smile to the conversation, for good measure. "I suggested we skip it this week since I had a big tourism council meeting tomorrow and I knew he had some important meetings looming as well, but he insisted."

She knew she was rambling. She couldn't help it.

"No matter how our calendars fill, Mark never wants to skip our date night. Even after all these years of marriage." She looked at the Dilworth sisters, knowing she could easily be awarded an Oscar for this performance. "He brags it's those little things that keep our marriage fresh."

On the overhead speaker, someone called out that an additional checker was needed up front.

She stubbornly lifted her chin. "On that note, ladies—I'd best scurry home. I need to get started on that dinner. Oh, and I need to pick up the new nightgown I ordered from Panache. It's the prettiest shade of aqua, accented with cream-colored French lace. Not that I'll wear it long." She winked. "If you know what I mean."

The Dilworth sisters exchanged confused glances. From the looks on their faces, she'd successfully supplanted the notion her marriage was in any kind of trouble.

"Oh, honey—why yes!" Trudy swept her caftan-draped arm dramatically toward the front of the store, relief evident on her pudgy face. "You need to get home and take care of your man!"

After bidding each other farewell, Leigh Ann threw some pasta in her basket and hurried for the butcher counter where two other women were in line. The first appeared to be in her late forties or early fifties, was exquisitely dressed with well-preserved facial features. Likely a part-timer or perhaps a tourist. The woman tapped a beautifully manicured nail at the glass. "What is that?"

Marley, the butcher, smiled cordially. "A ribeye roast, ma'am."

The botox queen struggled to lift her perfectly shaped eyebrows. "What is a ribeye roast exactly?"

Marley looked confused. "Ma'am?"

"I mean, how exactly do you cook . . . a ribeye roast?"

Leigh Ann moved into the line forming. Marley noticed her and waved. She waved back.

"Could you excuse me?" he asked the woman standing at the counter. "I'll only be a moment."

He quickly made his way to the end of the refrigerated case where a white butcher-paper wrapped package waited, all tied up and ready. He retrieved the bundle and handed it across the counter to her. "Here you go, Leigh Ann. Ground chuck and Italian sausage blended just like you ordered."

She thanked him, ignoring the glare of the woman standing at the counter. "Sorry," she expressed to the rest of the people in line before heading for the check-out counter.

At home, Leigh Ann quickly unloaded her groceries and put them away, then called Karyn and reported her grocery store encounter with the Dilworth sisters. "Can you believe those two? Those gals latch onto a rumor like hungry dogs on a bone."

"Ah, don't be too hard on them," Karyn responded. "Granted, they're nosy. But they don't mean harm. I'm sure they were primarily worried for you. Mark wouldn't do that. So, don't let their talk get to you."

Leigh Ann reminded her sister that she too had complained about being on the receiving end of their generous concern on occasion, that earlier that morning she'd been the one to lament the attention her relationship with Grayson Chandler was getting around town.

"I guess the trick is to keep the skeletons in our closets well organized," Karyn offered, trying to diffuse the situation with a bit of humor.

Leigh Ann huffed. "Well, I took action and dispelled any notion that my husband is out trouncing around with some bimbo."

"You did? How?"

Leigh Ann pulled a large pot out of her cupboard and positioned it in the sink under the tap and turned on the water. "I told them a tiny white exaggeration—that Mark insists on a date night to keep our marriage fresh. I made sure they understood that is why I'm cooking his favorite lasagna dinner tonight, and that I bought a special nighty for the occasion. For good measure, I made sure they also saw me buy an over-the-top dessert. The thing looks like some Pinterest fantasy."

"And that worked?"

"The effort seemed to do the trick. The Dilworth sisters bought that my marriage is not on the rocks. And they'll spread the word soon enough."

"Very clever of you."

"Take lessons, my sister. Well, I'd better go. I've got sauce to make."

She bid Karyn goodbye and turned off the water, then moved the pot to the burner.

The date night notion wasn't exactly a bad idea. The truth was, it wouldn't hurt to put in a little extra effort. Spice things up a bit.

Especially given that her husband had occasion to be driving around with clients of the female persuasion. She was pretty sure there was nothing to be concerned about. But it never hurt to add a little frosting to the marriage cupcake. Remind Mark the only sugar he needed was right here at home.

LEIGH ANN STOOD in front of the full-length mirror, her arms folded across her stomach. The show-stopping aqua gown, with its sheer off-the-shoulder straps, fitted bodice and plunging neckline were meant to be alluring, yet she suddenly felt like the insecure nineteen-year-old who had given herself for the first time to a young kid with big-fortune dreams.

"You have to be where the money lives," he'd told her on their wedding night, which explained why later he'd passed on the choice to remain in Seattle or move to Los Angeles, instead settling for her hometown area. "There's a reason investment bankers from all over call Sun Valley a summer camp for billionaires."

He'd hugged her tight. "We're going to have a great life, baby."

And they had. Their quick romance morphed into resolute companionship, allowing Mark to foster a lucrative real estate investment firm and for her to remain close to family after graduation. Together, they'd raised a son and built a life many envied.

Still, the years had been a little kinder to Mark. Thanks to regular exercise sessions, he still had the muscular build of a thirty-year-old. Only the gray at his temples betrayed his real age.

Leigh Ann leaned toward the mirror, taking into account the extra pounds she'd put on over the years, a reflection that her priorities had been arranging play dates, helping with homework and chauffeuring their active son to all his events. She didn't mind. In fact, she'd been sad when it all ended and Colby didn't need her anymore—at least not like that.

She wasn't bad looking by any means. A few heads still turned when she entered a room. Those who knew her would say she was also bright, socially adept and cultured—traits her husband placed high on his list of desirable character attributes.

Leigh Ann stared at her reflection and timidly dropped her hands. She might as well quit dwelling on her body image. The extra twenty pounds couldn't be erased in the next five minutes, especially after eating that big pasta dinner earlier, so why let her mind park on the matter?

She spritzed cologne across her décolleté, took a deep breath and reached for the doorknob.

Suddenly, the voice of Trudy Dilworth pushed its way into her mind.

Poor Leigh Ann. Do you think she knows?

She determinedly shoved the crazy words from her head. She knew Mark. He was a lot of things, but the man she'd spent her life with was not an adulterer. He'd never hurt her like that.

With her hand resting on the doorknob, she forced a deep breath.

Yes, she could be stubborn, a little idealistic, and a firm believer that anything could be fixed with a few carefully offered recommendations. But the truth was, Mark was one person she'd rarely been able to recalibrate. He simply nodded in agreement, brushed off her helpful suggestions, and then did what he intended anyway. It made her half crazy sometimes.

Often she wondered what had enticed him to marry her in the first place. Yet, in the dark recesses of her mind, she clearly remembered the reason. And, he was away at school.

She opened the door slowly and entered their bedroom, taking special care to hold in her stomach as she walked across the plush carpet.

The candle she'd lit earlier gave off a nice glow. Very romantic.

Mark was already in bed, his face tucked behind the Wall Street Journal under light cast by a bedside lamp she'd bought him on the trip to India they'd taken three years ago.

Cool night air drifting from the window he'd opened earlier caused her skin to tighten—or maybe it was anticipation. A tiny smile pulled at her lips. "Mark?"

"Yeah?" He peeked from around his paper, then went for a glass of water at his side table and took a drink.

She swept her long dark hair to one side, letting it cascade over her bare shoulder as she moved to her side of the bed. She lifted the covers and slipped in beside him. "Honey, why don't you turn off the lamp?"

"I will in a minute." He straightened his paper and returned to reading.

Not to be deterred, she let her hand glide across the expensive linen until she reached his upper thigh. Her nails lightly scraped across his bare skin, travelling slowly upward until they hit against the hem of his sleeping shorts. She hesitated for a brief moment, then let her fingers drift further north. "Mark?" she repeated.

She felt, more than heard, his breath catch and smiled knowing she still had that effect on him. "Sweetheart, why don't you put the paper down and turn out the light?"

The paper crumpled as he dropped the pages to his lap. She smiled and leaned in.

"Leigh Ann, I appreciate the gesture, but I have an early morning meeting and—well, I think it's best if we take a rain check."

The impact of his words hit her. Before she could process the moment in her mind, her hand recoiled, as if burnt.

A rain check?

She felt like she might implode. Rarely had she been the one to instigate any bedroom activity, yet he'd elected to pass?

"Sorry, Leigh Ann. I'm just really tired." He offered up an apologetic smile before folding the paper and tossing it to the floor. He then reached and turned off the lamp. He punched the pillow and turned over, pulling the duvet up around his chest. "G'night."

With blistered emotion, she blew out the candle and slid deeper inside the bed, the darkness a welcome cover for the humiliation that heated her face—and the single tear that made its way down her cheek to the pillow.

Her teeth bit at the tender flesh of her cheek as she tried to clear her racing mind, and the image that insisted on forming —that of her husband in a car with another woman.

15

"I think something's wrong."

"Wow, big surprise. Here's what's wrong." Joie yanked the latigo strap from the tall blonde's manicured hand. "The saddle's loose because you forgot the saddle blanket."

Chelsea Rae popped her wrist against her forehead. "Crap! You're right."

Joie gathered all the patience she could muster, plucked the saddle from the horse's back, and waited for this new hire, one of Clint Ladner's choices, to lift the saddle blanket into place.

"A little higher," Joie instructed.

"What?"

"Move it up. You have it too far down on the horse's back."

The girl wearing blue jeans distressed to the tune of several hundred dollars huffed. "What's with the attitude? Do you think you can quit being such a witch?"

Joie held her breath for several seconds. Self-control had never been one of her strong suits and right now she wanted to beat this girl with a stupid stick. And what was with the two names anyway? Couldn't she just go by Chelsea, for goodness sakes?

From outside the stables, she spotted Clint crossing the yard and heading their direction.

She slowly exhaled and buried her head against the horse's front shank and unhooked the breastplate from the saddle. She wanted to tell the girl she'd quit being a witch when she quit being dumb as a broom. Instead, she re-threaded the cinch through the buckle, and said nothing.

"Oh, Clint. Hi!"

Joie looked up just in time to catch Chelsea Rae push her ample chest forward and give their boss a flirtatious smile. Disgusted, she yanked the rawhide gloves from her hands and tucked them under one arm before nodding in his direction. "Hey."

After giving Chelsea Rae an appreciative glance, he focused on Joie. "Turns out I need your help picking up a horse I bought."

"Right now? But I'm scheduled to take a group of ladies from some book club in Texas—the Pulpwood Queens, I think they call themselves—on a trail ride. We're supposed to leave in a half hour."

"Saw that on the schedule. Patty's going to cover." He turned and told her to follow him.

She trailed him through the jumping arena and out the gate into the parking lot, stopping behind a pickup truck with a horse trailer hitched behind. She didn't have any choice, she told herself, thinking back to the bar. It's part of the job.

Ever since Clint Ladner's hire had been announced, she'd done her level best to avoid him whenever possible. She argued with herself continuously that the day in Crusty's didn't matter. So what if her first impression hadn't been stellar?

Truth was, if she wanted to resurrect a better reputation, it would take a very long time to rewind that clock and start over.

Every time Clint looked at her, something inside her squirmed. He had a way of making her feel like he could see into the very depths of her soul with one glance, like he knew all her secrets.

No one knew all her secrets. She'd seen to that.

"Get in." Without waiting for her to answer, he headed to the driver's side and climbed in.

That was another thing. She didn't take to anyone barking orders at her. She didn't jump for any one. Not even Clint Ladner.

He honked the horn impatiently.

"I'm coming!" She stomped to the passenger side and threw open the door. "Gads, what's the big hurry?"

As soon as she climbed in, he shoved the gearshift into drive and they took off. "You ever load a skittish horse?" he asked.

She stared straight ahead. "Yep."

"Well, the BLM was holding a herd of wild horses they'd collected from the Saylor Creek herd management area in one of their selective removal campaigns. One got injured and won't easily be adopted. I offered to rehabilitate him."

Joie glanced across the seat at him in surprise, then forced her gaze back to the road ahead. "So, a rescue horse."

"Yep," he answered, mimicking the tone of her earlier response. "In the process of vaccinating him several weeks back, he kicked and gashed his leg pretty badly. The wound got infected and the BLM believes he might end up lame. They're holding him on a ranch in Stanley."

Miles passed in silence as they made the drive north on State Highway 75, stopping at the overlook at Galena Summit so he could check the hitch.

While Joie took in the stunning panoramic view over the Sawtooth valley below, Clint dug into a cooler in the back of the pickup. "Want something to drink?" He held up a Dr Pepper. "I know you're used to something a bit stronger, but 'fraid this is all I've got."

"Do you know how much sugar you're putting into your body when you drink one of those? What will all your admirers think when you get all flabby?"

He grunted and popped the tab. "I'm not into caring much about what others think."

She sidled around him and thrust her hand into the cubes of ice and pulled out a can. "Yeah, I could see that this morning."

Clint frowned. "What are you talking about?"

"Ha, what am I talking about? I'm referring to your new hire. Chelsea Rae, isn't it?" She held up one open-palmed hand. "Maybe she deserves some slack—it's a lot of work holding up all that hair. Where's she from anyway—Texas? No Idaho mama would hang a ditzy name like that on her kid." She popped the tab, tipped the cold can up and chugged the ice cold drink like a pro.

"That was a favor."

She tossed her empty can in the back of his truck. "A favor?"

"Sometimes a manager has to bend to politics." Clint jumped up inside the back of his truck and picked up her empty, tossing both of their empty cans back in the cooler. "We'd better get going," he said, closing the lid, and the subject.

They made it the rest of the way to Stanley in a little over an hour, again riding in silence. Normally, it took less time to drive the distance, but the horse trailer slowed them considerably.

At the junction to Highway 21, she finally spoke up. "How far to where we need to pick up the horse?"

"Less than ten miles," he answered.

She gazed out the window at the grassy banks of a stream, at criss-crossed pole fences winding through grassy meadows and the jagged mountains beyond.

In some ways, the craggy vista reminded her of the guy

sitting inches away. He was most certainly a fine specimen, a man she could easily find herself physically drawn to. He had a careless look, his jawline angular and rugged, even strong. But there was something in his eyes that told her Clint Ladner was not someone easily traversed, that he was studded with icy snow-capped spires extending too high to successfully climb.

Clint slowed the pickup and eased from the paved highway onto a rutted, potholed road that meandered through heavy sagebrush that scraped against the door of the truck. He looked across at her and apologized when he hit a particularly deep furrow.

She braced herself by holding onto the dash. "You ever take in a rescue horse before?"

"A couple," he answered. Slowing, he maneuvered around the biggest of the dips, until they came to a wide-open space with nothing more than an empty corral and a small shed-like barn. A BLM vehicle was stationed nearby.

They parked and got out. As two BLM officials headed their way, Clint grabbed a lead rope from behind his pickup seat.

"Hey, there!" one of the light brown-uniformed guys extended his hand. "Glad you made it."

Clint shut his pickup door and shook hands with both of the officers. "So, where is he?"

The tallest officer pulled his cap from his hand and swiped his forearm across his brow. "Sure is hot for this early in the summer." He nodded in the direction of the barn. "Horse is in there."

The other officer stepped forward. "Here's the paperwork." He handed the envelope to Joie. She noticed the ground surrounding his side of the government vehicle was littered with discarded Tootsie Roll wrappers.

Holding her tongue, she took the paperwork and tucked it inside the truck before following the three men to the barn that was in need of much repair.

At the door, the officers both hesitated. The one who had handed her the paperwork cleared his throat. "Well, that's really all we need. Guess you can handle it from here."

Joie wanted to ask if he was kidding. Didn't they intend to help? A wounded horse was predictably hard to manage. It could very well take all of them to load the horse safely. She opened her mouth to say as much when Clint's hand went to her arm. "Thanks, guys. We've got it."

"Okay then, we'll be going."

She and Clint waited a few minutes for the men to get in their truck. As they were driving away, Joie turned. "What was all that? Don't you think those guys should have helped?"

"It ain't help when it's not freely given." Clint had already turned and his hand pulled the rusty handle on the door. The broken wooden panel creaked open. The entire structure looked like the rotted boards might collapse at any time.

Joie glanced back at the truck making its way in the distance, leaving a plume of dust trailing behind. There were many great governmental employees, but a few lazy ones like those often gave the entire organization a bad reputation.

Inside, the barn was dusty and dark. At the last stall, Clint held up his arm, blocking her from going any farther. She paused behind him. The black stallion nearly got lost in the shadows except for his bared, yellowed teeth and the whites of his eyes. His ears lay flat back and he snorted, blowing snot and air.

"Whoa, boy." Clint slowly opened the stall door and took a cautious step forward. The young horse reared and lunged lopsided, striking out with his front hooves.

Her eyes widened. "I thought he was crippled."

Clint sidestepped easily and snapped the lead rope onto the horse's halter as the horse's hoof banged into the wooden panel.

It took nearly twenty minutes to get the terrified animal out of the dank, smelly stall packed with old hay caked with manure and urine.

In the sunlight, both she and Clint got a good look at the horse's injury—a gash that had nearly severed a tendon on his rear right leg. The wound was definitely infected, the surrounding flesh dark purple, puffy, and oozing with what looked like weeks-old pus.

Clint let out an expletive.

Joie felt the start of tears and dashed them away before her new boss could see. She never got used to wounded horses, especially injuries resulting from neglect of this magnitude.

She thought of the government officials, how quick they'd been to exit the scene. Anger burned behind her sternum with such intensity, she wanted to hit something. Or someone—but the men she ached to pound on were already gone.

Clint stroked the horse's velvety muzzle, but the young stallion yanked back from his touch, his eyes rolling wildly. "Best to get him loaded and out of here," he barked in her direction. "I think I noticed a loading chute in the back. Might be safer to use that to get him loaded."

"I'll go get the trailer," she told him. Seeing the doubt in his eyes, she immediately turned defensive. "What? You don't think I can back a trailer?"

With only one try, she positioned the trailer at the chute with impressive precision. She climbed from the truck with great satisfaction and opened the back gate. "Your turn, cowboy."

Clint nodded tightly. He slowly coaxed the horse forward, cueing him with a kissing sound. "Atta, boy. That's it." He gave the horse a gentle tap on the hind quarter with his open palm, urging the skittish animal toward the pile of hay placed at the front of the trailer as incentive.

The process took time, and several tries, but with Clint's carefully executed effort and softly-spoken assurances, they got the job done. "Atta, boy. That's it." He fastened the safety bar and then the back gate.

He swiped his face with his bare forearm, then moved to the ice chest in the back of his truck for a cold soda. He retrieved one for himself, and tossed her one. "Well, that should do it."

Joie couldn't help but admire the way he'd handled the horse, with extraordinary patience and never showing anger. Animals sensed whom they could trust, and the young stallion responded accordingly.

On the way back to Sun Valley, she turned to Clint. "How can people be so cruel?"

He beat his thumb against the steering wheel, clearly sharing her upset. "He's in good hands now. With some strong antibiotics and a little care, the horse will be good as new physically."

She stared at the tattoo running up his arm, the bear claws appearing especially fierce as they extended across his bulging bicep. "What about mentally?"

"That's where you come in."

"Me?"

"Yeah, I've watched you. You're good." He shifted gears. The truck and trailer shuddered and groaned before gathering speed again as he made his way to the main highway. "And you're going to work with me to get this one back on the upside."

She couldn't help but smile at that.

"I think it'll do you both some good," he added, ruining it.

She whipped around to face him. "What do you mean?"

He slowly brushed his fingers across his stubbled chin. "Pain can change an animal, make it reckless."

Suddenly, Joie didn't think they were talking about the horse anymore. "Are you implying something here? Because if you've got something to say, I invite you to just spit it."

Clint gave her a sideways look. She could see the gleam of

his perfectly straight teeth as a stealthy smile nipped at the corners of his mouth. "I just have one question," he said simply.

She challenged him with a frosty look. "Yeah? What's that?"

He looked back at her, still brandishing that half smile. "What's a badass trial lawyer doing playing cowgirl?"

16

K aryn tried to convince herself that her good mood was simply a byproduct of the comment Jon Sebring made at the lodge earlier that afternoon. "You're doing a fabulous job," he'd told her, inciting an immediate smile.

It was true. She'd been performing far over what she'd even expected from herself. Still, it was nice to have her boss acknowledge her effort and his praise had gone a long way toward elevating her disposition.

Even so, she had to admit the real reason she was happy and bouncy and okay, giddy, could only be attributed to what lay ahead—an evening with Grayson Chandler.

Admittedly, she was slightly nauseated at the same time.

She stepped out of her shoes as she entered her bedroom. She'd have to shower and redo her makeup, curl her hair and get dressed—and she needed to make it out the door by seven in order to be on time. She hated being late.

They'd agreed to meet at the restaurant. So much better than the awkward greeting at the front door, not knowing whether or not to invite him in and for how long. Goodness, was she really going on a first date again?

She set her phone on the docking station by her bed and selected a playlist. While easy jazz filled the bedroom, she walked to the kitchen and poured herself a glass of wine, then returned to the bathroom.

After her shower, she dried her hair, then twisted the long strands into wavy spirals and stared at her reflection in the mirror. While she definitely wanted to look cute, she didn't want to look like she'd tried too hard.

Satisfied with her appearance, she headed for her closet. Her wardrobe would take a little more thought.

She pulled a sleeveless black dress from the closet and held it up.

No, too formal. And too . . . black.

Her hands ruffled through the hanging items, considering options. Casual slacks and a cute top might be good.

The red sweater was tight and accentuated far too much. She wasn't some lonely widow looking for action. The blue polka dot top was cute, but a bit too juvenile for this occasion.

Twenty minutes later, her bed was piled with apparel she'd tried on and discarded. Nothing seemed right.

That is, until she landed on a little sweater set from her bureau drawer. She'd nearly forgotten about the tangerine-colored cashmere tank and cardigan she'd never yet worn.

She'd ordered it after thrusting her iPad in front of Dean's face. "Honey, look at this."

Dean reluctantly pulled his attention away from the basketball game on television. "Look at what?"

"This. Do you like it?"

Dean had great taste in clothes and she often sought his opinion before making any addition to her wardrobe.

He shook his head. "Wrong color. Green washes you out."

"It comes in other colors."

Her husband pulled the electronic device closer and rang his finger over the screen, scrolling through colors until he landed on an image he liked. "Here, this one. This orange shade."

Her hands pulled the garment from the drawer, letting the tissue drift to the thick carpet. Despite the memory connected with Dean, the brightly-toned sweater set would be perfect for the evening ahead.

After dressing, she stood in front of the full-length mirror in her bathroom for a final look. The outfit she'd chosen skimmed her curves nicely. Not too fancy, wasn't super sexy, and Dean had been spot on. The tangerine sweater set made her look happy and really set off her dark brown hair and green eyes.

She looked really good.

Even so, her satisfying appearance did nothing to quell the nervous emotions now roiling in her stomach.

Despite the time showing on the clock and the need to get moving in order not to be late, she sank to the bed and stared at Dean's photograph on the bedside table.

"Well, here goes," she told him out loud, feeling her throat constrict. She swallowed, not knowing how to articulate her teeming thoughts beyond those few spare words. She stared at her wedding band, twisting it much as Dean had done the many times he'd held her hand while they watched television.

Karyn stood and went to the tiny wooden box positioned on her dresser. Her fingers slowly drifted over the crossed skis and his engraved name. She turned to her jewelry box and opened the tiny top drawer. Dean's wedding band lay there, gold, barely worn and inscribed with a single word: *Always*

The same was inscribed in hers.

Her fingers lifted his ring and she held it for several seconds before she gently placed it back in the jewelry box. Her heart immediately grew heavy.

Karyn took a deep breath.

With renewed resolve, she returned to the bed and grabbed a tube of rose-scented hand cream from the bedside table drawer and squirted a dollop into her palm and began working a bit around her third finger. She twisted the band back and forth, then took hold of the ring and pulled. It caught momentarily on her knuckle and then finally slid free, revealing a permanent line of smooth white skin.

This moment was the first time since Dean had placed the ring on her finger that she'd not worn that symbol of his love. She felt naked without it.

Trembling inside, she stood and laid her ring in the jewelry box beside Dean's, noticing as she did so that her hand was also shaking.

Karyn stood there for several long seconds. Finally, she forced herself to close the little drawer and turn away.

THE HISTORIC RAM RESTAURANT was located in the heart of what was known as the Sun Valley village, a centrally located area with walkable access to resort pools, golf courses, shopping, dining and many special events.

The Ram was one of Karyn's favorite places to dine. Despite its notoriety, the Ram was the kind of place that served extraordinary food while still maintaining a relaxing and unpretentious atmosphere.

With her clutch tucked under her arm, she made her way into the restaurant and glanced around. Grayson was already there, standing just inside the entrance. He smiled when he saw her—a warm, welcoming smile that made her all tingly inside.

"Hi, Grayson. I hope I'm not late."

As she moved toward him, she saw his gaze drop to take in what she was wearing. The appreciation evident on his face both eased and sent her nerves dangling from the ceiling.

"Oh, no. You're not at all late. I showed up early." He grinned. "A bad habit of mine."

He took her elbow, a little tentative, like he wasn't exactly certain if the gesture was too forward.

She quickly reassured him with a smile.

"You look—uh, you look really nice."

"Thank you," she said, likewise admiring his chinos and crisply pressed button-down shirt.

"I thought you might like to sit outside. The evening's fairly warm and they have gas heaters."

She nodded, wishing she didn't feel so nervous. "I love dining al fresco."

As if on cue, a maître d showed up and escorted them to an outdoor courtyard dotted with linen-draped tables, sheltered by umbrellas with tiny lights. Flower boxes filled with colorful blooms topped the wrought iron railing. Beyond, an expansive green lawn led to a large pond with paths leading around the border, all landscaped with tall pines and bedding areas brimming with more brightly-colored flowers.

They were seated at a table a bit away from other diners.

"Are you sure it won't be too cold out here for you?" Grayson asked.

She shook her head. "No, this is perfect."

A musician played a soft melody on a piano located closer to the entrance. She waved in his direction and he nodded back at her.

"Someone you know?"

She tilted her head and let out a little laugh. "I know most of the locals. That's Larry Harshbarger. He plays for a lot of area weddings and events. A really nice guy."

"It must be great living in the community you grew up in."

She smiled, starting to feel a bit more at ease. "Well, yes.

Sometimes that's true. Of course, we have a regular influx of tourists. Those of us living in Sun Valley get the best of both worlds, I suppose, where we get to enjoy our small community and the world comes to us."

A waiter appeared at their table and handed them large green menus embossed in gold lettering.

"Anything you'd recommend?" Grayson asked as he opened his.

She offered a big smile. "All of it."

Grayson ended up ordering the braised lamb shanks with parmesan polenta and roasted baby carrots. She selected the seared wild King Salmon in ginger plum crème sauce.

"Could you also bring us a bottle of the Regusci cabernet?" Grayson added as they handed back their menus.

"Certainly, sir. Fine selection." The white-gloved waiter retreated from their table.

She looked across at Grayson. "A wine connoisseur?"

"Hardly." He placed the large linen napkin across his lap. "My wife—'er ex-wife's—family lives in Napa Valley, California. I picked up a couple of pointers." He paused. "I'm sorry, I never meant to start off our conversation with—"

"What? That you've been married before?" She shrugged. "Goodness, we both have histories. We're not exactly teenagers."

He really smiled then, a broad smile laced with laughter. "Yeah? Then why did I feel like a pimply-faced-fifteen-year-old while I was getting ready tonight? I don't date much," he admitted.

"Then we're well matched." Their eyes met across the table. "This is my first since—well, since the accident."

That information wasn't likely a surprise to him, not after seeing her come undone at the Hemingway Memorial that day.

"I'm honored to be the first." He paused, looked at her seriously. "I really mean that."

He fingered his butter knife. "I hate to admit this, but early after the divorce I kind of swore off ever doing any of this ever again."

She found his admission charming. "Yeah, that's my story too. But we'll get through this," she assured him.

He leaned back. A grin sprouted at the corners of his mouth. "I think the problem is that you look so pretty tonight."

She raised her eyebrows. "Oh, is that so?"

"Yes, true story," he said, giving her a warm smile that left her feeling a bit untethered. "I'm really glad you agreed to spend the evening together."

"I'm glad too."

There was a time she could never have imagined this day. Sure, she knew a time would come when she'd be compelled to take this brave new step, or face a lifetime filled with loneliness, but she'd dreaded the aspect of the actual doing. Heavens, her Facebook status still said *married*.

It's as if one day she'd sent her favorite well-worn jeans off to the cleaners only to learn the washing machine had malfunctioned and ripped them up, forcing her to shop for another pair. That, or stay in her house to avoid walking around naked.

And, you couldn't buy just any pair. The new brand had to be sized perfectly and suited to fit your body type.

He reached across and lightly touched her arm. "You look like you just drifted a million miles away. You okay?"

She quickly nodded. "Oh, yes. I'm fine. I was just thinking about how nice it is when you find someone who fits," she blurted, immediately embarrassed by her unfiltered admission.

Thankfully, the wine steward appeared and uncorked their wine. Grayson took the obligatory sip and nodded his approval. Their waiter then placed the salad course—pears and arugula lightly dressed with a huckleberry vinaigrette.

Karyn went for her fork, determined to change the subject.

"I'm curious. Of all the places you could have landed, why Sun Valley?"

"Well, after the divorce I knew I wanted to leave everything familiar behind." He stabbed a piece of lettuce. "Too many memories."

"I bet you loved Alaska."

"I did. Winters were harsh though. The long hours of darkness were as tedious as one might suspect. The landscape was magnificent though. Thankfully, this area has its own stunning beauty."

She nodded in agreement. "It sure does. I pity people who live back East. They think they've seen mountains until they get a good look at the Sawtooths." She shook her head and scooped a bite of salad. "I never take living here for granted. Despite the surrounding beauty, the entire area has such a ripe history."

She explained how Averell Harriman, the chairman of the Union Pacific Railroad and a lifelong skier, had determined America needed a resort like the ones he'd once visited in the Swiss Alps.

"Harriman launched an extended national search for the perfect location," she told him. "He finally purchased the nearly four-thousand-acre Brass Ranch bordering the tiny mountain town of Ketchum, Idaho and commenced construction. Seven months later, he dubbed his new resort Sun Valley and people from across America packed up their ski equipment and rushed to ride state-of-the-art chair lifts up Baldy Mountain." She paused. "I'm sorry. I must sound like a tourist guide."

"No, not at all." Grayson slid his empty salad plate aside and reached for a second piece of bread. "I find all this extremely interesting. Please, go on."

"Well, celebrities soon flocked to the area—Gary Cooper, Clark Gable and Errol Flynn. Lucille Ball, Marilyn Monroe and later, the Kennedys. In fact, Marilyn Monroe ate at this very restaurant back in 1956 when she was here filming *Bus Stop*. I believe there's a framed photo on the wall inside."

She paused as the waiter approached their table with their entrees. "Can I get either of you anything else?" he asked after he'd placed their food. He looked in Grayson's direction. "More bread, sir?"

Grayson sheepishly glanced at the empty basket and shook his head no. Once the waiter retreated and they were alone, he scooped and sampled a bite of his lamb shanks. "I think these are the best I've ever tasted," he said appreciatively. "Hands down."

Karyn tasted her salmon. "If you like lamb, wait until you attend your first Trailing of the Sheep Festival."

"I heard a bit about that. Sounds like a great time."

"The festival is held every fall. My sister, Leigh Ann, chairs the committee. Lots of fun, and unbelievable food. You've got to go."

Grayson beamed. "I'd really like that."

As they talked over dinner, she learned he liked to cook, and rarely followed a recipe. She really didn't like to cook, but when she did she rarely veered from the ingredient list. They both loved to eat. And read. He was a James Patterson fan, which made her giggle.

"What? You're a book snob?" he teased her.

"Not necessarily. I just figured you'd gravitate more to—" She paused and considered his apparent affinity for the outdoors. "—well, more towards someone like Larry McMurtry."

"You got me there. I loved Lonesome Dove."

As their discussion turned to growing up in Sun Valley, she recounted a funny story about Rory Sparks, the sheriff in town and her former classmate. "The final week of our senior year in high school, we arrived on Monday morning to find a half dozen cows on the school roof. To this day, no one knows exactly how Rory got those cows up there, only that he finally confessed to the prank at our class reunion last year."

Grayson's eyes widened. "You're kidding! How'd they get them down?"

"A hoist borrowed from over at the county building. Followed by several shovels."

"Shovels?"

She nodded and grinned. "For what was left behind."

They both laughed.

Somehow, each of them finally relaxed and their discussion now came easily. She studied his face as he spoke, taking in the way his mouth moved and enjoying how he looked at her while he was talking, like she was the single most important person in the entire restaurant.

When the dessert menu was delivered to their table, she reviewed the selections carefully and ordered crème brulee, her favorite.

She gave Grayson a rueful smile. "Dessert calories don't count."

He laughed. "In that event, I'll have the same."

The waiter offered them coffee and her date ordered them both a cappuccino.

"I've really had a nice time tonight, Grayson. But, I feel like I did most of the talking. In fact, I believed I rambled on a bit. I learned very little about you."

"In that case, maybe you'd agree to a little walk around the village before I take you home?"

"That'd be wonderful," she told him.

They ate their crème brulee while listening to Larry Harshbarger play show tunes on the piano.

"Do you like movies?" he asked.

"I love movies," she told him. "But not many of the current releases. They seem far too violent. Nothing like the great epics from years past."

"And your favorite?"

"I can't say I have one favorite, but—" She paused, weighing whether he might scoff at her choice like Dean had. Men rarely understood a woman's heart when it came to great stories. "Well, very near the top of the list is *The Titanic*. I loved how Rose shed the need to please everyone and became her own person—stepped into a life she wanted to live leaving the one that had been designed for her to inhabit behind."

She waited for a mocking comment. None came.

He only smiled and said, "Yeah, that's a really good one."

Karyn returned his smile and scooped a final creamy bite into her mouth, savoring the slightly caramel flavor of the egg custard. "What's yours?"

"Mine?"

He thought a minute. "You'll laugh."

"No I won't," she assured him.

He hesitated. "Superman."

She couldn't help but raise her eyebrows in confusion. "The guy with the cape?"

"See? There you go."

She giggled and covered her mouth with her hand. "I'm sorry. But, that one really doesn't fit."

He quickly clarified. "Maybe, but every boy grows up hoping to be a hero."

When they'd finished, Grayson paid the bill and they wandered out the door and into the star-filled night.

"Which way?" he asked.

"Let's circle the pond and then browse the shops on the boardwalk."

He nodded and they headed past the European-styled Sun Valley Inn, with its chalet gabled roofline, shuttered windows and overflowing flower boxes all beautifully illuminated with uplighting. "When I was little, I used to think this was the same house where Snow White ran into the dwarfs."

"Quite the imagination." He chuckled and reached for her hand, weaving his fingers in her own. She focused on the feel of his calloused skin against her own, fighting the flash idea she was betraying her dead husband.

"Oh, yes," she continued, pushing the intrusion from her mind. "Me and my sisters used to pretend a lot. Often, we'd play like our nighties were glamorous gowns, march up and accept our Prell shampoo bottles and take turns giving magnificent Oscar speeches."

This time Grayson tossed his head back with laughter. "Love that. I once took the cardboard box our new Sears range came in, drew elaborate instruments with my crayons and spent hours flying the countryside."

She tilted her head in his direction. "Do you have siblings?"

"Nope, only child."

She immediately felt sorry for him, and told him so. "I don't know what I'd do without my sisters. And my dad, of course."

They walked in silence for several seconds. "What happened to your mother?" he finally asked.

They passed a stand of quaking aspen trees, the limbs thick with tiny green leaves barely visible in the dark.

"She died when I was ten. Cancer.."

"You've had to deal with a lot of loss." He gently squeezed her hand.

She appreciated his comment, one she'd heard often from others in various forms. "What about you?" she asked, diverting the conversation. "Did you grow up in Alaska?"

He shook his head. "No. A little town in the middle of Washington State—Toppenish. Located on the Yakima Indian nation."

"Yeah?"

"Not much to do there, except hunting, fishing and sports. My mom and dad owned a tackle shop. They both passed away years back. Dad a heart attack and mom cancer."

"So, you've known loss as well."

He nodded. "And extreme happiness."

She liked that about him. He didn't pretend life wasn't hard, but instead of getting mired in the unfairness and hurt, he'd determined to embrace the good things and be happy.

They neared the Opera House. The lights on either side of the entry reflected brightly on the sidewalk.

She took a deep breath. "Tell me about her," she ventured.

The question may have crossed the bounds of proper manners. Especially on a first date. But she had this overwhelming curiosity. All he had to do was look up Dean on the internet and he could find out all he wanted to know. On the other hand, she was a bit handicapped.

His voice grew thoughtful. "What do you want to know?"

She shrugged, wishing now that she'd restrained herself. Obviously, she'd made him uncomfortable. "I'm sorry. I didn't mean to pry. I just—"

"No, that's okay," he assured her. "I'm an open book. Well, maybe not with everyone—but if you want to know, I'll tell you."

He led her to nearby bench facing the pond. They sat.

"Are you getting chilly?" he asked. Without waiting for a response, he placed his arm around her shoulder to ward off the cool night air.

"Hmm—where do I start? I guess at the beginning." He stared out over the pond water. In the light from the posts lining the sidewalks, she could see him thinking about what he wanted to say.

"I met Robin at a Seahawks post-game party. She was gregarious, funny—one of those individuals who shine in the spotlight. Like everyone else, I was drawn to the way she made a person feel like you'd been her friend for years—even if you'd just met. Guys were constantly hitting on her."

Karyn nodded. She knew the type. Everyone had flocked to Dean as well.

"It was nearing the end of the evening. I don't drink a bunch, so I figured I was going to be the designated driver and chauffeur all my buddies safely home. That is, until Robin made her way over and introduced herself. We hadn't talked ten minutes and she asked if I'd give her a ride. Apparently, her girlfriends had already headed back and left her."

The corners of his lips drew into a slight smile. "I was terribly flattered. Any of those guys at the party would have fallen all over themselves to be alone with her, and she'd picked me to escort her safely back to her hotel."

His thumb lightly rubbed against her shoulder.

"We married six months later. I don't even remember who asked who. All I know is, before much time had passed, we'd set a date and she was shopping for a dress and I was trying to scrape enough funds together for a ring that she wouldn't be embarrassed to wear." Grayson chuckled. "I wasn't exactly rolling in dough back then."

Karyn sensed a shift in his demeanor. His voice held an intensity that was honest and raw and irresistible at the same time. She urged him to continue.

"Anyway, fast forward through the next few years. We moved to Seattle and she landed a job as a stockbroker and did really well. Her earnings allowed us to buy my plane and together we made the decision to move to Alaska when she was offered the opportunity to open an office in Anchorage. Alaska was the perfect place for a backcountry pilot and Robin believed there was a lot of money to be made advising people in the oil industry. She was right, of course. On both counts."

Karyn watched a duck glide silently across the pond water and nestle in a stand of reeds. "Sounds like things were pretty good."

He nodded. "They were. Until they weren't."

He paused briefly. Took a deep breath. "She stopped coming home for dinner. Traveled more. She quit calling and checking in." She could feel him tense. "And then she fell in love with someone else."

Karyn's chest caved with empathy. "I'm—I'm so sorry."

Grayson sighed. "Yeah, not a great ending. I'm generous but there are some things I never share. I left her to her oil exec, gave her the house and all our belongings. I took the plane, moved here and I've never looked back." He gave her hand a little squeeze. "That's it. Now you know my story."

Karyn eyed him, realizing for the first time there might be a loss more painful than her own situation. She simply couldn't imagine that kind of betrayal and how a person could not be filled with bitterness after something like that. "Grayson—" She muttered his name with a tone that was warm and caring. "Thank you for telling me."

"Your turn. What about you?"

"Me?" She took a deep breath and considered what to say. "Well, before Dean died, I'd generally considered myself a cheerful person. I opened my eyes each morning and felt excited to be alive, know what I mean?"

He nodded.

"And then the call came—the one that shattered my world."

The night air suddenly sent a chill across her skin. Grayson seemed to sense her need for warmth and lent her his by pulling her closer. He rubbed her arm.

"I raced to St. Moritz, wanting to see him. I knew he'd have a long haul ahead, that his racing career had ended. But I would be there for him. I'd help him adjust." She paused. "But when the doctors finally came out to report his condition, one look in their eyes told me he was already gone."

Now it was his turn to express his sorrow over the pain she'd endured.

She drew a much-needed breath. "In the days following the

accident there were spans of time—minutes, hours and even days when blinking and breathing and speaking all took so much effort that I thought I might as well give up. I was in a dark hole of sadness and anger and confusion." She paused, realizing this was the first time she'd admit what was to follow. "I didn't think I was going to make it."

"But, you did."

"Yes," she agreed. "My sisters never left my side. They literally held my hand and never let as much as a finger untie from our grip. My dad too.

She bit at her lip as emotion clogged her throat. "When my world was torture, they gave me hope, a breath of fresh air, and a tiny scrap of faith that the dark tornado that threatened to eat me whole might begin to change—and get better."

"We have a lot in common," he said. "Most especially that life can shift under your feet."

She reached for his hand and gave it a squeeze. "Yes, life shifts. But we're still standing."

There was something about that moment—a kind of shared vulnerability that established an affinity between them. She was not the only one who had taken a leap of faith and decided the darkness wouldn't win.

She stood and lifted him to his feet. "C'mon, let's go." Together they walked the short distance around the pond to the boardwalk lined with shops. Some were darkened, but a couple of storefronts remained open.

"Hey, do you think there's a place where we could get some ice cream?"

Her hands went to her very full stomach. "You're kidding right? I couldn't possibly eat another bite."

He grinned. "Okay, I 'fess up. I guess I simply wanted to prolong the evening just a little."

"Well, we'll just have to agree to do this again—soon."

In the parking lot, Grayson walked Karyn to her car and

waited while she dug her keys from her purse. When she'd successfully unlocked the driver's side door, she turned to face him. "Thank you again for inviting me out tonight. I really had a great time." She paused and grinned. "And that's the truth."

"Yeah, same for me." He moved closer, stopping a breath away. His approach launched a nervous ripple through her. *Was he going to kiss her?*

She almost wanted him to. At the same time, it felt too fast.

He must've thought so too. He simply rested his broad hand on her shoulder and squeezed. "I had a great evening. I closed on the house earlier this week. Once I get moved in, perhaps you'd allow me to grill you a steak?"

She nodded enthusiastically. "I'd like that."

This was the awkward part, but she meant what she said. She really hoped they could spend more time together. She liked Grayson, the easy way they seemed to connect. He was warm and charming. At no time in the evening had she felt the need to adjust herself to fit his expectations. Or even impress him really.

"What about tomorrow?" she blurted before she could censor herself. "What I mean is, you must still have boxes everywhere. So, we can grill at my house." She cleared her throat. "I mean, if you want to."

He was grinning from ear-to-ear. "Sure, that would be great."

"Excellent!" Her heart wouldn't seem to stay still. "Let's plan on seven."

Karyn climbed in her car and bid Grayson goodnight as he closed the door, then started the engine, waved her fingers and backed out.

She couldn't help it. Unexpected happiness bubbled up from inside and overflowed in the form of a wide smile—a smile she carried with her as she drove away, knowing he was watching.

17

Joie curled up on her sofa wearing her robe with a towel wrapped around her head. It'd been a long day. Normally, she'd have stopped in to check on her father, especially since the lights were still on over at his house. Tonight, she'd arrived home from the trip to Stanley and had simply gone straight to her own place, too tired and far too upset to do anything but climb into a hot shower.

Despite her exhaustion, twice she'd had to talk herself out of driving in to Crusty's. Throwing back a few and a game of pool with the guys certainly sounded good—and a fairly effective distraction—until morning dawned with her head pounding, a blunt reminder that no shot of tequila could erase Clint Ladner and the issues he'd created.

The day had started out a bit rocky, yet she'd soon let her guard down believing Clint might have a redeeming streak after all. Especially after seeing the way he handled that horse.

Sadly, she had a history of misreading men.

While she had no way of knowing exactly how much he knew, her current boss had snooped where he didn't belong. The knight in shining armor turned out to be a jerk in tin foil.

She'd shot him a look after he lobbed that bomb into their conversation. "You talk too much. Has anyone ever told you that?"

"Has anyone ever said you have trouble answering questions?"

"How did you find out?" she'd demanded, pissed.

"Didn't know the fact you're an attorney was some big secret. I mean, it's on the internet for anyone who cares to look."

Rage whirled inside her chest like a bad storm. "Used to be an attorney," she corrected. "I'm not currently licensed." She squared her shoulders. "And my personal life is none of your business, if that's okay with you."

He looked taken aback, if not at what she'd said, then at least at the tone in her voice. She'd confused him. That was obvious.

No matter. At least she'd shut down the conversation before the dangerous subject had a chance to jump the fence and run away with her.

Joie had no illusions about who she was and what she deserved. She'd known long ago she would spend the rest of her life trying to overcome what she'd almost allowed to happen. She'd taken the hit—done the right thing. That did not translate into opening the matter up for public consumption.

Especially with him.

There was a time she'd been proud of graduating at the top tier in her law school. Recruiters had come knocking and she had her choice of law firms and quickly climbed to junior partner at a prestigious litigation firm headquartered in Denver with satellite offices throughout the Rocky Mountain corridor, including Boise. She'd been brilliant and downright bold—yet in a blink she'd nearly morphed into the woman everyone scorned. And, she'd never even seen it coming.

Joie's phone buzzed causing her to startle. She reached and shuffled several stacks of papers on the coffee table before her hand finally landed on the smooth surface of her iPhone and she freed it from the pile.

Her sister.

She glanced at the clock and noted the late hour.

"Karyn? What's up?" She rubbed at her aching temple, wishing she hadn't skipped dinner. "Is everything all right?"

"Oh, yes. Everything's fine. I was just driving home from my date and wanted to talk."

Her sister's words infiltrated Joie's strained thoughts. "Did you say *date*?"

"Mmm-hmm. I did."

The elation in her sister's voice was hard not to catch. Joie set her own distress aside. "Well, well—who's the lucky guy? Or can I guess?"

"Okay, yes—you got your Hallmark movie. I spent the evening with Grayson Chandler."

"The back country pilot you adamantly denied you had any interest in?"

"Yes, that one," she admitted. "He moved here from Alaska and recently bought a house up Warm Springs."

"Uh-huh. The place you helped him pick out." Joie grinned as she tucked her feet up under the hem of her bathrobe.

"Look, are you going to cooperate here? Or do I have to hang up and call Leigh Ann?"

"You mean the woman who doesn't think twice about walking in on you when you're in the tub in order to go about the business of prying?"

"Yes, that one," her sister retorted with a mocking tone.

Joie couldn't help but laugh out loud. "Okay, okay—spill. What's he like? What did you guys do? Did he kiss you?"

"Whoa—slow down! No, we did not kiss," Karyn quickly

clarified. "We went to dinner at the Ram. Admittedly, it was a little hard. I mean, this was the first time since—"

"And now the first is behind you," Joie finished, intercepting her sister's trip down Dark Memory Lane. "Just think, from here on out this whole thing will be a breeze."

"Yeah? Well, breezes can mess up your hair." Karyn answered back. There was a long pause before she added, "Joie, you don't have to worry about me anymore. Dean will always hold a very special place in my heart. I'll love him until the day I die. But I agree with you. I can't keep living like I'm the one who died. No matter how hard, I know it is time to move on."

"Preach it, sister. Takes a lot of string, but tying up life's loose ends is a good thing. I'm proud of you, Karyn." She slipped from the sofa and slowly paced the floor. "So, tell me about him."

"Grayson?"

Joie rolled her eyes. "No—Peter Pan." She wandered into the kitchen and pulled the refrigerator door open. "Spill. I want to hear everything."

"We had dinner at the Ram, like I said. After that, we walked—and chatted. Grayson is so easy to talk to. I mean, Dean was a blast to be around and he made life fun, but he often teased me out of every conversation that grew deeper than a puddle."

Joie reached for a lone container of deli potato salad and set it on the counter. "Mmm-hmm. Go on." With her free hand, she lifted the lid. She bent and sniffed, then quickly tossed the whole thing in the garbage.

If only all the rotten things in her life were as easily disposed of.

"I couldn't believe how quickly we moved to deeply emotional topics. He wanted to know what it was like for me after Dean died. It was amazing to share that heartbreak without him flinching. But then, he understands. He's divorced.

Grayson admitted he had a crush on his wife, and it ended up nearly crushing *him*."

Joie took a sharp breath. "That's awful."

"I know. I have little understanding for extra-marital betrayal. Why can't people learn to park in their own garages?"

"I know, but it can happen," Joie ventured. "Just because someone steps over the line and allows themselves to get caught up in the heat of a situation doesn't mean the person is bad. It only means they made a mistake. A bad mistake. And sometimes that person wishes they could take it back—but they can't. Even if they stop in time."

"I'm not sure what you're talking about, but I don't think that was the situation here. I didn't get the impression his ex-wife's transgression was a one-time oops. More like a *"I like him better"* thing."

Joie closed the refrigerator door with her foot. "Regardless, I'm glad you had a good time. When do you see him again?"

She could swear her sister giggled. "Tomorrow night. He's busy packing, so I offered to have him over for dinner."

"Good move!" A pleased grin lifted the corners of Joie's mouth. "I hope you have a tingle-your-toes fling."

"Well, that's a lot of pressure to take on. But the new me is all about taking risks and grabbing as much joy as possible while I'm still on this earth."

"First a new job and now this."

"Yup," Karyn said. "The world is going to be my oyster this year."

"And your oyster is Grayson Chandler?"

"Who knows? Anything's possible, I suppose. All I know is that I'm happy for the first time in a long while. And that feels good."

"Well, I'm waving sparklers and celebrating with you."

Joie hated to bring it up, but curiosity got the better of her.

"What about Bert and Aggie? Do they know you're seeing someone?"

There was momentary silence on the other end of the conversation. "Dean's parents will understand. I'm not even forty. I'm sure they don't expect me to remain a widow forever."

Joie wasn't so sure. "We're talking about Agnes Macadam, right?"

Her sister brushed aside her concerns, and immediately turned defensive. "No doubt it'll be hard. It's difficult for me too. None of us elected this. It would be too simple to say I will always love Dean. But, that's the truth. Like I already said, he'll forever remain in my heart and nothing will change what he means to me. No matter what."

"No, I get that. I'm just saying—"

"It'll be fine," her sister assured. "You'll see."

"You're probably right. Besides, hot sex will make up for a mother-in-law pout any day."

"Joie!"

"What? I'm just saying."

They bid each other goodnight and Joie clicked off, relieved to hear Karyn was picking up the pieces of her splintered life and starting over.

She pocketed her phone and leaned with her back against the counter. Across the room hung a series of framed photographs of her, Leigh Ann and Karyn when they were young.

One in particular caught her eye.

It was summer and they were running across their dad's lawn in swimsuits, laughing like nothing could ever prick their happy bubble.

Minutes after their dad clicked that image with his camera, she grew tired of playing in the sprinklers with her sisters and snuck off to the horse barn where she discovered baby kittens nestled in the straw bales.

With great care, she'd bent and gently lifted two of the tiny black and white balls of fur and cuddled them against her swimsuit. Suddenly, a loud hissing sound caught her attention. She turned to find an angry mama followed by the worst odor she'd ever smelled.

She always meant well, even back then, but her best intentions often led to skunky consequences—it was hard to lose that reputation, even when the incident happened a long time ago.

The world might be Karyn's oyster, but after today's exchange with Clint Ladner, Joie knew her own life could easily turn to stink again.

If the full story came out, Leigh Ann and Karyn wouldn't only view her as their irresponsible little sister. They'd learn the truth.

She might as well hang a scarlet skunk around her neck.

18

Karyn looked into Grayson Chandler's eyes, remarkably blue like summer lupines, his trimmed beard stubble punctuated with deep dimples. He smelled like the laundry aisle in the grocery store mixed with the deep scent of leather.

He took her face in his hands. She closed her eyes and waited with expectation, the desire for what was to come nearly unbearable.

One might expect a widow would miss sex, but it was this—the kiss that she most longed for these past months. The brilliance of a rust-tinged sunset, the velvety brush of rose petals, the power of a salty sea wave—all wrapped into that single moment when lips joined and her stomach tightened at the feel of his breath.

The pleasure of the simple act washed over her until the moment he gently pulled back and whispered her name.

Karyn startled at the unexpected familiar voice. Pulled back. Suddenly, her dead husband's face smiled back at her.

Dean?

A cold sweat broke across her brow. Her breath stopped and

a door slammed inside her. The familiar sound of her heart closing shut. Tight.

She bolted upright in bed and clawed herself fully awake, her insides quivering with emotion. "A dream—it was only a dream," she reassured herself out loud as she pushed drenched hair from her face.

Still feeling shaky, she tossed the down comforter off her legs and stared at the alarm clock on the bedside table. It was almost nine a.m. Hours later than she normally woke, even on her day off.

For several seconds, she sat in silence, trying to collect herself.

It'd been months since she'd had these vivid and disturbing dreams. Why now?

Instinctively, the answer came. Her evening with Chandler had stirred up her emotions, made her vulnerable to all the old feelings.

While moving on and forming a new relationship gave her great hope, she had to admit the thought of starting over also terrified her. The familiar was—well, familiar.

If anyone asked, Karyn could easily recite so much about Dean—how he preferred only white toothpaste, not striped or for goodness sakes, or any brand that was red. He loved grilled steaks, but wouldn't dare pour steak sauce over the top, only garlic salt sprinkled liberally. He never wore sandals because he considered his toes too hairy.

Nothing caused him to grouse more than when he attended a party and the host served red wine chilled. Or white wine at room temperature. He preferred button-down shirts to polos, used Aqua Net hairspray to keep his unruly cowlick in place, and he hated lima beans.

She knew his every touch, what each moan and sigh communicated, what signaled he was in the mood. Or the rare occasion when he wasn't.

Dean had known her just as intimately. How reluctant she felt around people she considered inauthentic. How disjointed she sometimes felt in his circle of wealthy friends. He anchored every situation by simply placing his hand at the small of her back.

He believed she was beautiful, she could see it in his eyes. And when he made love to her, his body took her to places she could never imagine going with anyone else.

How could another man ever know her like that?

New was exciting, but scary. Kind of like jumping off a cliff without knowing where you'd land.

Dean was scored on her heart, but he'd been gone nearly as many days as they'd been married.

She closed her eyes to keep tears from forming, imagined his hand on her back and heard him gently remind her he was no longer her husband, and that meant she needed to move on.

Certainly, there was no predicting where this budding relationship with Grayson Chandler might lead. But something told her she had no choice but to jump.

With renewed resolve, she pulled herself from the bed and headed for the shower, and over the next minutes let her angst wash down the drain along with the soapy water.

She stayed there until the water started to turn cold, then she stepped out of the shower and onto her bathroom rug feeling clean—and a lot more settled. Her hand grabbed for a towel when she heard what she thought was someone knocking on the door.

She quickly wrapped the towel around her wet hair and donned some jeans and a sweatshirt. The knock became more insistent.

She raced for the living room. For goodness sakes, why the knocking? She had a doorbell. "Coming," she hollered. "I'm coming."

She heard a key in the lock and a click. The unexpected

sound caused her to jump back. Suddenly, fear moved in and she wished she'd put on her bra under the sweatshirt.

"Aggie, perhaps you shouldn't—"

"Nonsense Bert, there must be something wrong. Her car is in the garage and she's not answering the door."

Karyn's hand tightened on the towel. "Aggie?"

Her mother-in-law startled and jumped back, her hand clutching her chest. "For goodness sakes, Karyn. You scared me."

Bert scrutinized the situation with amusement. "I think the feeling is mutual, Aggie."

His wife waved off his comment. "Bert, honey—be a gem and retrieve the breakfast rolls from the car. Would you?"

Her former father-in-law gave his wife a resigned look and turned for the door. "Whatever you wish, dear." For her benefit, he added, "Sorry, Karyn. We didn't mean to barge in on you."

Aggie gave him a pointed look before moving inside the living room. "We're most certainly not barging in, Bert. We're leaving for Morocco this afternoon and only wanted to say goodbye."

"Morocco?" Karyn watched as Bert headed for their car.

"Yes. Remember? We're taking a trip with Arthur and Trixie Banducci. They've never been and we agreed to show them around a bit."

Nothing good would come from telling Aggie she didn't recall, so instead she simply nodded. "Do you want some tea?"

Aggie slid her Lugano sunglasses from her face and nested the expensive shades on the top of her stylish cropped blonde hair. "Do you have any of that Dragon Tears loose leaf I brought you back from China?"

Karyn nodded and went for the teakettle.

Agnes Macadam, by anyone's account, would be considered a brand snob, something she and Dean used to laugh about in private.

"Would you like me to rub your feet with this Louis Vuitton Cadillac Coach lotion?" he'd mock after spending an evening with his mother at dinner.

"Only if you first carry me to the bed on your Carradan Mambas skiis."

"Ha, what are you saying?"

She smiled coyly. "Only that you have your own penchant for high-end brands."

"Take it back. I am not my mother!" He pulled her into his arms and squeezed until she burst out laughing.

In between heaving breaths, she'd managed to squeak out a response. "Okay, Little Pauper Boy—I give! You are nothing like your mother."

Bert returned with the rolls. "Karyn, dear. What are you smiling about?"

"What? Oh, nothing." She turned back to the stove and removed the steaming kettle with a hot pad.

She was in the middle of pouring Aggie's tea when Dean's mother looked up from the counter with a startled expression. "Karyn—where's your wedding ring?"

On impulse, she pulled her left hand behind her back, which caused her to slop hot water onto the counter with her other hand.

"Honey, where's your ring?" she repeated.

"Uh, I'm soaking it in some cleaner." Yes, the hasty response was a lie, but she was caught off guard. She most certainly wasn't prepared to disclose her evening with Grayson and the real reason she didn't have Dean's ring on her finger.

"You're soaking it? Honey, the diamond on that band was my mother's. It's very expensive and should only be cleaned by an experienced jeweler."

Karyn blinked several times. "I—I didn't think a little ammonia would hurt." She took in the look on Aggie's face. "But, yes. Of course, you're right."

Dean's mother waved her hand. "Go—get that ring back on your hand and I'll call my jeweler." She looked at her husband for support.

Bert nodded. "I'm afraid I have to agree with Aggie. Fine gems require special care."

LESS THAN AN HOUR LATER, Karyn stood on Leigh Ann's doorstep, angry that she'd allowed her in-laws to bully her into putting Dean's ring back on. It'd been hard enough to take the step of removing it in the first place.

If there was anyone who would be willing to commiserate with the situation, she could count on Leigh Ann.

She rang the doorbell. When no one answered, she glanced at her wristwatch. Her sister was normally an early riser and should be up by now.

She rang again.

No answer.

Rarely would Leigh Ann buy a banana without calling and telling her, so it would be odd if she had an early morning meeting without her knowing.

She pulled out her phone and texted.

At your front door. Where R U?

For several seconds, she stared at the face of her phone waiting for a reply. Nothing.

Karyn frowned and called her dad. She quizzed him to see if he knew where Leigh Ann was. He didn't.

Neither did Joie.

Now, she was beginning to worry. Going AWOL was entirely out of Leigh Ann's character. Even if she'd headed out of town on a sudden trip with Mark, she'd have responded to the text.

Karyn wandered across the portico-covered driveway and headed for the garage, stood on her tippy-toes and peeked inside the windows. Even though the garage was fairly dark inside, she could make out Leigh Ann's car.

Now she was really concerned.

She made her way to the side of the house. The open plantation shutters provided an opportunity to glimpse into her sister's kitchen. The overhead light was on and dishes were stacked on the counter.

Leigh Ann never left dirty dishes.

She wandered farther around the house hoping the gate wouldn't be locked. No such luck. Then she remembered seeing Leigh Ann hide a key back when Colby was still living at home. "In case he loses his and needs to get in the house and we're not here," she'd explained.

Karyn closed her eyes and concentrated, trying to recall where her sister had placed the key. Somewhere out front, she knew that much. Suddenly, she remembered.

Karyn scrambled for the front of the house and stood on the step, again on tippy-toes. With her fingers extended, she felt along the base of the light sconce mounted on the left side of her sister's front door. Relief flooded as the tip of her forefinger brushed across the key taped there.

Even though she knew her nails would likely break in the process, she dug at the adhesive, lifted the key and slid it into the keyhole.

"Leigh Ann?" she called out, pushing the door open. "Are you in here?"

No answer.

Her sister's favorite jazz music played from somewhere at the back of the house. Her bedroom maybe?

Karyn closed the front door and headed that way, pausing to look around the house and into open doors as she moved down the hallway.

"Leigh Ann?" she called out again, padding across a floor made of wood imported from Brazil.

Then she saw her.

"Leigh Ann! Honey, what's the matter?" She rushed to where her sister was sitting on the bedroom floor carpet, her face all blotched from crying. "Are you sick?"

Her sister miserably shook her head. She looked wrecked.

Karyn crumpled down beside her. "Colby? Mark? Are they—"

"They're fine," her sister managed to say through chest heaves, the kind that come after a hard cry. She held up a cell phone. "Mark especially."

Karyn scowled. "What do you mean?"

"It's Mark's. He's having an affair."

19

The startled look on Karyn's face was not exactly a surprise. Leigh Ann barely grasped the harsh reality of the phone message herself at first. Now, after several hours, the shock had soaked in and there was simply no denying the verity of that text.

Her younger sister tried to argue. "Are you sure you're not reading something into this? I mean, it's hard to comprehend that Mark would do something like that."

Karyn read the message again as Leigh Ann recited the words from memory. "*I got your message. I agree, it's time to take things to the next level. Let's meet in Boise this weekend where being seen together won't raise any suspicion.*"

Leigh Ann shook her head in miserable disgust and shared what she'd overhead at Atkinson's Market. "True, while the full story is not yet known, the implications about all this can hardly be misinterpreted. If my husband hasn't already done the dirty deed, he's about to."

Karyn looked dumbfounded. She handed back the phone. "What are you going to do?"

When she didn't answer, Karyn reached out her arms for a

hug. Leigh Ann pulled back and held up her hand. "No—I can't."

Karyn nodded. "Okay—I know you're good at being the strong one, but I'm here. For whatever you need."

Leigh Ann knew her resolve was often misunderstood. People, even her family, dubbed her tough as nails attitude as bravado. In reality, she was as fragile as anyone. Maybe more.

She'd learned early on that some situations warranted her full attention, without constantly bending to her feelings. What purpose did falling apart serve when your world was already cracking into a million pieces?

She'd had her pity party. Now, she needed a plan.

"Look, I love you," she told Karyn. "But what I need right now is time alone. I need to think."

Her sister looked at her like she was crazy. "What do you mean? I'm not leaving you alone right now. I can put off going in to the office."

Despite temptation, Leigh Ann stood firm. "No, like I said, I need time to think—to figure out how to react. This situation has far-reaching implications. Financial implications. Social implications. And I have Colby to consider."

Karyn went wide-eyed. "If Mark goes to Boise this weekend, you've got to kick him out!" As soon as she blurted that statement, she recanted. "I—I'm sorry." She ran her hand through her long dark hair. "It's just that, well—"

"I need time to think," Leigh Ann repeated, rubbing at her forehead. Suddenly, she dropped her hand. She didn't want everyone knowing. Not yet—and hopefully not ever. "You must promise to keep this confidential. Not Dad. Not Joie. No one."

"Oh, Leigh Ann. Do you really think that's wise? Secrets never benefit anyone."

It didn't matter what Karyn said. She couldn't bear for anyone else to know her husband's attention had drifted to another woman. "Not open for discussion. I want to get my feet on the ground before everyone starts running at me." She grasped Karyn's hands. "Promise me."

Her sister slowly nodded "Oh, all right," she said, reluctantly. "But I think a cataract of misplaced concern has clouded your vision on this thing."

"Thanks, but this is for me to work out—with Mark." This time she gave in and they embraced. The comfort she found in her sister's arms led Leigh Ann to have to fight to keep her emotions at bay.

More than anything, she needed to know this white-knuckle fear was unfounded, needed to be assured her life had not just shifted beneath her feet, that she had no real reason to be this scared and unsteady. She needed to be held. Really held —by someone who could protect her from the oncoming storm.

Mark was the one she'd normally turn to. As it turned out, another woman had butted in and usurped her wind shelter.

She walked Karyn to the door. On the steps, her sister turned suddenly. "Who is it?"

"What do you mean?"

"I mean—who's the woman who sent the text to Mark? You never said."

A weight pushed against Leigh Ann's chest as she considered again what she'd overhead in the store—what the Dilworth sisters chattered about. A silly rumor now steeped in truth. "I don't know her name. But I can promise I intend to find out."

After Karyn left, Leigh Ann took advantage of the time before Mark was due home and went on a little reconnaissance mission in her husband's office only to find his desk drawers locked and his computer passwords changed.

Frustrated, she tried to regroup.

She needed to talk to Colby. It would be tricky not to let on, but he might know something that she'd find helpful. Information was power.

Often Colby failed to pick up when she phoned. At times, she'd have to make multiple tries and leave a scad of messages before he'd call her back. She should remind him who bought his phone and paid his bill. Luckily, today he answered on the second ring.

"Hi, Mom. What's up?"

"Nothing in particular. Just wanted to hear your voice and check in."

There was a slight pause on the other end of the phone. "We talked two days ago, Mom. Not much has changed."

Her son had registered for summer school and remained in Seattle against her wishes. "It'll look good on my record if I apply myself and finish my undergrad a bit early," he'd explained. Never mind Colby was only a sophomore and wouldn't be applying for engineering school for at least two years.

"How'd you do on your physics exam, sweetheart?"

"Oh, I did okay. The test covered material the professor never mentioned in class and I have yet to find in the textbook any reference to tachyons.

"Tachyons?"

"Yeah, something having to do with particles that are faster than light."

She should warn him not to fall into a pattern of excuses. Then again, she couldn't risk him tuning her out. Prodding him to be a better student wasn't why she'd called.

"Son, have you talked to your father lately?" she ventured, hoping to ease into a conversation that would mine any information her son might have that would shed light on her precarious situation.

"Not lately. Why?"

She couldn't help herself. She threw caution aside and got defensive. "Why? Can't a mom just ask her son a simple question? I'm simply wondering if you've checked in with your dad. That's not exactly prying—just being interested. You're my son and I want to know about you—about school—about you and your dad and if you've talked lately. That's not out of reason."

Goodness, she sounded like a blathering idiot.

"Mom, you're being weird."

She paused, took a deep breath. "Sorry, you're right." She laughed his comment off. "I—I'm distracted. The housekeeper is over an hour late this morning and she just pulled up. I'm probably going to have to let her go. She's just not punctual. That's how everything starts. First they're late, then their work gets shabby. Really, it's so hard to find domestic help here in Sun Valley. Too much competition for the good ones."

"Mom!" Colby interrupted. "Look, I need to go. Class starts in a few." His tone was impatient, leaving her no choice really but to end the conversation.

"Oh—sure. I understand honey. I'll call tonight. We can talk then."

She clicked off her phone and slid it into her pocket.

Well, that was a waste of effort.

Colby and his dad were fairly tight. Even if her son knew something was up, he wasn't likely to share the news with her. Besides, Mark would never be so careless as to allow his son to know he was about to break his wedding vows. Not directly, anyhow.

Her heart skipped a beat.

If he hadn't already.

She took a deep, painful breath.

What she needed was a course of action. She couldn't very well just sit back and allow things to proceed in the wrong direction without intervention. Not when Mark's choices had the power to bomb her world to smithereens.

This was war!

She'd watched enough Dr. Phil to know her plight wasn't all that unusual. Long-term marriages could grow stale. She'd been foolish enough to believe her own relationship was immune.

Well, her head was no longer buried in the foxhole.

She wasn't one to give in and allow another woman to steal her husband—her life. It was time for a good old-fashioned fight!

No way would her future include shared holidays. Colby and her someday grandbabies would never gather around some bimbo's Christmas tree and drink eggnog from another woman's punchbowl while she sat home miserable, wondering how she'd let all this happen.

The voracity of her growing anger surprised her as she moved to the iPad on the kitchen counter. There had to be blogs about all this. There were blogs about everything.

She'd do the research necessary and devise a plan to hold onto her marriage.

And God help the woman who failed to keep her mitts off her man!

20

Karyn shuffled the stack of invoices and put them in her desk drawer, then turned her attention to the computer.

Most days flew by, in part because she loved her job. She didn't even mind working these occasional Saturday afternoons. But today, the clock hands couldn't move fast enough. A thousand demands were building up in her personal life, and the stress of juggling this new life was not as easy as she'd expected it to be.

In less than a few hours, Grayson would show up at her front door, hungry and expecting a meal worth eating.

What had she been thinking? At best, she could boil an egg or perhaps grill a tuna sandwich. Even after following a recipe to the letter, her meatloaf turned out dense as wood, her puddings runny, her homemade mac and cheese burnt on the bottom.

There were other factors pulling at her attention, mainly her former in-laws. Aggie had called no less than a dozen times seeking her opinion about packing for her trip to Morroco.

That woman would take the foam right off her latte if she let her.

Typically, when life pulled at her from all directions, she'd run to Leigh Ann for help. She'd planned to do just that, but never expected to find Leigh Ann in the state she was in this morning. Rarely did her older sister give in to fear, yet there were pieces of Leigh Ann's heart scattered all over that room. What she suspected of Mark was causing her world to split at the seams. Karyn was worried about her.

Could it really be true that Mark was seeing someone on the side?

Her brother-in-law was a lot of things—at times arrogant and often too ambitious for her liking. Still, there'd never been any doubt that he loved Leigh Ann, never seemed disconcerted by her sister's quirks.

Rarely did they argue or get cross with one another. At least not in front of her.

Still, that text message certainly raised some questions. Especially coupled with what the Dilworth sisters claim to have seen.

Oh, she hoped none of her sister's suspicions were true.

Karyn closed out of the accounting program on her computer. She reached for her purse and forced her mind to her shopping list, determined to think about something she could do something about—like tonight's meal.

Perhaps she should make eggplant parmigiana. Goodness knows, she had plenty of home-canned tomatoes. Then again, why risk a sauce catastrophe when she could sneak and use a bottle of premade sauce?

Overhead, the intercom crackled. "Karyn, I'm afraid we need you down here. Pronto! A pipe burst and the kitchen is flooding."

Alarm shot through her. She grabbed the phone receiver from her desk and pressed it against her ear. "I thought we had the problem fixed?"

"Apparently not," Amelio reported. "And we're in the middle of plating the reception dinner for the Idaho Bar Association."

"What?" She mentally paced as she tried to think through what all that meant.

"The kitchen is flooding," he repeated, this time with even greater urgency. "Come quick!"

Rattled, she promised she'd be right there. All she'd need is a bunch of attorneys waiving their convention contract in her face and calculating damages.

In a haze, she set the phone back in the cradle, dropped her purse and sprinted down the short hall. The lobby was filled with guests checking in for the convention, many of them with heads tucked down at their phones while they waited their turn in line.

"Excuse me. Pardon me," she called out, as she maneuvered through the crowd.

Melissa Jaccard hollered after her as she passed the front desk. "Hey, they're having an issue in the kitchen."

Karyn nodded. "Yes, I'm heading there now." She'd taken several steps before the fact Melissa was now sporting a huge streak of purple hair sunk in—a clear violation of dress code she'd have to address later. Hopefully, before Jon spotted the situation.

Amelio met her at the entrance to the kitchen. He spread his white-sleeved arms wide and gestured frantically. "Come quick. We've got a mess." He pulled her through the double metal doors.

Her head chef had not been exaggerating.

Ankle-deep water covered the floor and spilled out into the carpeted hallway. Karyn glanced around at the stunned kitchen staff and their silent plea for guidance. Instinct kicked in and she turned to Amelio. "Has anyone called the plumber who was here earlier?" When he shook his head to the contrary, her hand moved to her pocket. She realized she'd left her phone behind in her office and barked, "Hurry, make that call!" They needed to get this water stopped—now!

She tossed off her shoes. "Got any sacks of flour? Sugar?"

Amelio's staff nodded.

"Let's line that hall and create a barrier so the water doesn't flood further."

They all worked to do as she instructed.

With hands on her hips, she turned to Amelio who was hanging up from his phone call. "The plumber is on his way."

"Good. You stay here and wait for him. I need to go warn our dinner guests that their meal will be delayed this evening." She'd have to offer a substantial discount to the group. Perhaps some free wine would soften their reaction as well.

Grayson pulled into Karyn's driveway ten minutes early. Perhaps he should have circled her neighborhood another time, but someone might notice and report the fact back to her. Small communities were great, but there was a downside.

Yes, okay—he'd been anxious to see her again. Had even stopped unpacking so he could shower and get ready far earlier than necessary, which sounded like a girl thing to do.

After Robin, he'd sworn off women. But that was before he met Karyn.

He barely knew up from down whenever she was within twenty feet of him. In the weeks following that chance meeting at the Hemingway Memorial, no matter what he had going on, thoughts of her crowded his mind and shoved aside the minutiae in life. And everything seemed like minutiae compared to her.

It was out of character for him to allow a woman to consume his thoughts like this.

His inexplicable obsession only got worse after taking her to dinner last night. He'd tossed and turned all night in a fitful sleep, first dreaming about that smile of hers and then about drawing her into an embrace. Just as he was about to kiss her, her former husband's face appeared on the scene and she faded away.

It didn't take a psychologist to unravel the meaning of what his subconscious was saying. And it didn't take a genius to understand she might not be ready to move into another relationship after losing her husband.

Still, no matter how he argued with himself, how sternly he told his emotions to settle down, it was as if she'd moved in and taken over his mind. He was falling and there was nothing to grab onto to slow this thing down.

Grayson climbed the steps to her front door and rang the doorbell, nervously clutching a mason jar filled with red roses from his new yard.

He waited, imagining Karyn in those cute jeans he'd seen her wear—the ones that were just tight enough to show off the contours of her figure. Maybe a pretty white top made of some kind of silky stuff. Her long dark hair fastened up and gold hoop earrings dangling from her ears.

He liked a gal who didn't try too hard, yet always looked so classy. That was Karyn Macadam—pure class. Not the haughty kind, but the perfect mixture of swank and warm grace.

And, oh—when she smiled. Her whole face lit up. His stomach tightened with anticipation.

A bird squawked from the branches of a nearby tree. He shifted his feet, took a deep breath and rang the doorbell again.

No answer.

When she didn't come to the door, he juggled the jar to one arm and pulled his phone from his pocket. Maybe she'd sent a message that she needed to run out to the store for some ingredient she'd missed.

Nothing.

He rubbed at his chin. Confused, he pushed the doorbell one more time, just for good measure.

Aw—to heck with that.

He rapped on the door. Then, a second time, much harder.

Disheartened, he finally turned and slowly made his way back to his car.

There must a good reason she'd stood him up. Karyn wasn't the kind of person who would be callous enough to just brush him off.

Unless maybe like Robin, she'd had second thoughts after all.

21

L eigh Ann wrestled the bed sheets trying to find a comfortable position. Lying on her back, she stared into the dark in the direction of the ceiling. Beside her, Mark snored like a congested grizzly bear in heat.

Wonder if his new lady friend would find his nose trumpeting sexy?

She turned over and punched the pillow, then plopped her head back down.

As usual, her husband had arrived home late. By the time he'd snuck in the bedroom door and quietly undressed, believing she was asleep, she'd had plenty of time to get hold of herself and devise her plan.

After Karyn left, she'd spent hours on the internet. According to all the relationship blogs, she wasn't the only woman in America in danger of losing her marriage.

What she'd learned was both reaffirming, and terrifying.

While cooking that man's meals *and* raising his son, in addition to fulfilling all her civic responsibilities, she'd fallen behind on trends and what was hot.

Well, those days were over!

She turned and punched the pillow yet again, then settled in and clasped her eyelids tightly shut. For now, she'd focus on getting much needed sleep.

Tomorrow—project makeover.

IT WAS LATE when Karyn had finally threaded her way past linen-draped tables, juggling several plated salads. Despite complimentary liquor flowing liberally during the water fiasco, she knew the room full of hungry attorneys might start growling if not fed soon. So, she'd donned a server's apron in order to help out.

"Conservative or liberal, doesn't matter. Just so long as tort reform stays off the table." The woman who was speaking wiggled her glass in the air at Karyn. "Could you be a dear and get me another?"

Another guest, a formidably stark man with an even more imposing nose, spoke up from cross the table. "Ma'am, do you have any thousand island?"

She nodded and set the plates. "I'll get some right out to your table, sir." She retrieved the glass from the woman's hand. "You're drinking?"

"Bourbon. Straight up, with a lemon twist. And could you make that Bushmill's single malt?" The tedious woman turned back to her tablemates. "The single malt has far greater depth than standard Irish blends." The others at the table nodded approvingly, especially the wives.

There was a time when she had tried to be friends with these types, and fought to fit in. She'd have been satisfied to bump into these stylish female varieties in Giacobbi Square and have them admire something she was wearing. Maybe invite her to join them for lunch.

Suffering tragedy had changed her perspective—freed her

from listening to them whine about their husbands, the high cost of private schools, or complain about how hard it was to find a good housekeeper while they cackled over martinis.

These days, she was totally satisfied having a long and meaningful conversation with someone who didn't care about how much a watch cost. Someone like Grayson Chandler.

Grayson!

Her chest tightened and prickles raced up her spine.

She'd forgotten their date!

She passed off the woman's empty glass to another server and waved down Amelio. "Look, I need to go. You got this?"

He nodded. "Do what you need to do. We can manage now."

She raced through the now nearly empty lobby and to her office, grabbed her bag from her desk and dug out her cell phone to check for messages.

None.

With anxiety crawling up her throat, she sunk into her office chair and swept her thumb through her contact list until his name appeared.

She dialed, silently vowing to make it up to him.

Ring . . . ring . . . ring.

No answer.

Karyn was about to hang up, determined to drive to his place and tape a note of apology to his door if necessary, when he finally picked up.

"Hello."

A rush of relief filled her lungs. "Grayson? Goodness, I am *so* sorry. We had a flood. In the kitchen. A mess, really."

"This is Grayson Chandler. Sorry I missed your call. Please leave a message."

Karyn's heart dropped several notches. She impatiently waited for the beep. "Grayson, I am so sorry! I was really looking forward to seeing you. But, you won't believe what happened tonight at the lodge. We had a flood in the kitchen—

Beep.

Her insides filled with frustration. She quickly redialed, waited again for the opportunity to leave a message. "Look, it's a long story. Call me so I can explain?"

She hung up.

Well, that was that. What more could she say?

She sighed and grabbed her bag. Of course, she'd done what had been necessary this evening, but that was of little consolation right now.

She couldn't imagine how he felt when he showed up at her house and she wasn't there. Worse, she'd not even thought about him, not even remembered their date and the need to give him a heads up that she'd been held up at work.

What kind of person does that?

On the way out to her car, she shook her head and told herself to be reasonable. Grayson wasn't the type to hold a grudge. When given the chance, she'd explain more fully and he'd forgive the snafu.

She climbed into her car and tossed her purse in the passenger seat. Yes, she'd just recount the impossible situation she'd faced tonight and he'd understand.

Then again, perhaps he may consider her the biggest flake ever. He'd tell her he was busy and wouldn't be able to see her over the next few days. The days could stretch to weeks, possibly months.

She'd be stuck in the chair at home, looking out at the golf course knowing she'd been given an opportunity for male companionship with someone she really enjoyed, yet she'd blown it by failing to show the common courtesy of a text explaining what had happened and why she couldn't meet him for their date.

Feeling a little sick inside, Karyn turned on the engine and pulled from the parking lot.

Then again, she often gravitated to the worst-case scenario.

Her sisters would agree. "Life isn't a television drama," Leigh Ann would remind her. "Yeah, lighten up," Joie would add.

Her father would join in and chastise her for beating herself up like this. He'd tell her (like he often had) "Don't camp out on your mistakes. The good Lord made you perfectly you. And that's a good thing."

She believed that. She did.

That meant she needed to reign in these wild thoughts. Grayson would completely understand. The magnitude of this slip-up was all in her head.

She'd almost convinced herself the mistake was no big deal —until she pulled up in front of her house and spotted what was on the doorstep.

A mason jar filled with wilted roses.

22

L eigh Ann casually flung her new Kate Spade purse—
bright green and very spendy—over her shoulder and
pushed the hair salon door open. Inside, she pulled
her new Tory Burch cat eye sunglasses from her face and
looked around.

Ever since the trendy shop opened, Mark had pushed her to
make an appointment at Vertu, instead of with her standard
stylist. "We can afford the extravagance," he told her. " Why go
to the same gal you've known since high school?"

Her husband believed appearance mattered, that a person's
public persona was something to be carefully cultivated. So
much so, that he only wore custom suits and spent a great deal
on manicures and facials. Even had his own hair tinted a darker
shade of brown.

"But, graying temples are sexy," she'd argued.

He laughed a little, brushing off her opinion. "When you're
competing in business, you can't afford to look dated."

A gal with short spiky blonde hair looked up from the
counter. She flashed a brilliant smile. "Hi, can I help you?"

Leigh Ann nodded. "I called this morning for an appointment." She slid her sunglasses into her purse. "Leigh Ann Blackburn."

"Oh, yes. We've got you down with Shania. Come on back."

At barely thirty-eight, she wasn't about to be pulled from the shelf because she'd grown stale. If Mark now longed for a freshly-baked croissant, this Wonder Bread was ready to cook up a few changes.

The stylist's station was at the rear of the shop, past an indoor water fountain and walls lined with glass shelving filled with designer hair products. "Have a seat," she was told. "I'll alert Shania that you're here."

Leigh Ann thanked her.

While waiting, she couldn't help but stare across the way at how a young hairdresser with wild bright orange hair and purple tips expertly wielded a hairdryer and a brush nearly the size of the rolling pin in Leigh Ann's kitchen drawer. The client's hair looked like someone had chopped it off with a butcher knife from that same drawer.

She panicked.

Perhaps she should've slowed down, maybe gotten a referral before she moved forward with her plan. Sure, she wanted a change, but nothing so drastic she looked silly.

"Leigh Ann?" A young woman approached with her hand extended. "Hi, I'm Shania."

Turns out, her reservations were unfounded.

Her stylist had the classic good looks of Carolyn Bessette Kennedy, with long straight blonde hair and blue eyes. Leigh Ann had encountered the celebrity and her husband, John Jr. when they'd visited Sun Valley for a brief ski weekend in the months before their tragic plane crash. Leigh Ann remembered wondering how anyone could look so good wearing so little makeup.

"So, what are we doing for you today?" Shania asked.

She took a deep breath. Surely someone who looked like that would not make a mess of her hair. "I'm hoping for something different. Very fresh and updated."

The girl smiled. "I know just the thing. How are you with a color change?"

Leigh Ann exited Vertu's almost three hours later looking very different from how she'd walked in. While the image looking back at her in the rear view mirror of her car was shocking—she liked what she saw.

She hoped Mark would as well.

She plucked her sunglasses from her bag and planted them on her face. Now, it was time for the next step in her carefully designed plot.

In order to be discreet, she drove south to Hailey, a community about thirty minutes south of Ketchum. As far as she could tell from her internet research, a guy named Thor Magnum, who worked out of his converted garage, came highly recommended. The state board showed no complaints or violations of the health code.

Still, she rang Mr. Magnum's doorbell feeling extremely nervous. Only after she'd punched the button twice with no answer did she notice the sign instructing customers to enter from a door located at the side of the house.

The gravel walkway played havoc on the heels of her chocolate suede booties, a gift from her husband last year. She'd been both delighted and horrified when she opened the package. Valentinos often ran in the high three-digits—more than what she personally allotted for her entire year's wardrobe. She liked stylish clothes, but wasn't used to wearing anything that cost what she called *stupid money*.

A small placard on the door at the side of the house simply read *"Enter."* She turned the doorknob and pushed.

Inside, the space was not at all how she'd imagined a tattoo parlor might look. Instead of red walls and dim lighting, the area was brightly lit and had an almost clinical feel. To her great relief!

A stocky man with a shaved head and a black goatee, appeared from a back room. He wore ratty cowboy boots, gray and crisscrossed with deep scratches that scarred the leather. Faded jeans, a belt with a John Deere buckle, a plaid shirt tucked in neatly over his flat stomach and rolled up at the sleeves.

"Hi, you must be Leigh Ann."

She shifted a bit, trying to quash the tingles at her ankles, a sure sign her nerves were on the rise. She'd felt the same the day she got her ears pierced and that was nearly twenty years ago.

"Yes, that's me. I'm Leigh Ann. I called earlier about a tattoo?"

"Sure, do you know what you want?" He wiped his hands on a towel and tossed it on a nearby counter.

She shook her head, losing a bit of her nerve. "Not really. Something . . . I don't know, small."

"Well, come on over here." He pointed to a table. "Take a few minutes and browse in these books. Maybe you'll find an image you like."

She nodded. "Yes, that would be great. Thank you."

Leigh Ann smiled for the first time since she'd stepped inside the door. The walls above the table were pasted with images of dangerous looking men with racy women on their arms, all sporting tattoos.

Secretly, she'd always wondered what it would be like to be one of those women, the ones with internal engines that idled a bit too fast. Those types didn't wait at the stoplight, playing their expected roles perfectly. And certainly, not one of them ever got shoved aside for a shiny, sleeker model.

She flipped the front cover open on the thick three-ring binder. A large skull with snakes crawling out the eye sockets stared back at her.

She shuddered and quickly turned the page.

The next sample was a naked woman with very large assets.

Yeah, right.

Then, an anchor with a long winding rope, tattered at the end.

Not her style.

She flipped several pages forward. A rose.

Better, but overused.

Thor returned to the room. "So, how are you doing? Finding anything you like?"

Rethinking how bold she had the nerve to actually go, she shook her head. "I'm afraid not." She looked up at him, noting for the first time he had a tiny gold ring in his nose. "I—I'm often in settings where some of these might not be appropriate," she tried to explain.

"I know who you are."

He looked at her with appreciation, a look she hadn't seen in Mark's eyes for some time.

Flattered, she lifted her chin. "What would you suggest, Mr. Magnum?"

He gave her a slow grin. "The name's Thor." He leaned over her shoulder and flipped the book to a page near the back.

She couldn't help it. Her heart raced a bit. Especially when she noticed his muscular forearm, deeply tanned and thickly dusted with black hair. And the way he smelled—like rich leather soaked in the finest brandy.

Leigh Ann swallowed.

He pointed to an image. "What do you think of this?"

She leaned forward to get a better look. "A seal?"

He nodded. "Wedell seals swim under the ice to avoid predators—orcas and such. That is unless their pod is threatened, then look out." He threw her a second look that made her insides teeter. "What do you think?"

"I—I think it's just right," she stammered.

Thor Magnum was decidedly handsome—all angles and lines and broad shoulders. Mark wasn't the only one who could appreciate a member of the opposite sex.

She squared her shoulders. "A seal it is!"

A slow smile broke on his face. "Next decision. Where?"

"Huh?"

"Where do you want the tat placed?"

If she were bold, she'd have the image inked on the top of her breast. Of course, that was wholly inappropriate, given the way this Thor guy continued to stare at her.

In fact, a week ago she'd likely have made some excuse and left already. But that was last week.

Noticing her hesitation, his finger reached and brushed the skin at the front of her right shoulder. "How about here?"

There was that smile again.

Leigh Ann felt as if she was suspended somehow. Dangling had never been her thing. She swallowed a second time, no longer caring that the tattoo might show more than she'd planned. "How long will this take?" She glanced at her watch. "I have an important meeting—"

"Not long," he assured her.

All she could manage was a deep breath and a nod. "Okay, let's get this done."

For the next hour and a half, Leigh Ann leaned back in a reclining chair with her eyes squeezed shut, listening to the high trill of the tattoo gun and trying to block the sensation of the needles.

Every so often, Thor would stop and dab a cloth against her skin and ask, "You doing okay?"

Without opening her eyes, she forced the words, "Doing fine. Thank you."

She wasn't, of course. The process felt a lot like a cat scratching a bad sunburn. More than once, she had to talk herself out of calling an end to the procedure, but the idea of a seal on her shoulder looking like an orca had bit off half of its face kept her quiet.

"I'd like to add a little something. Trust me?" His voice was low and husky.

She drew a deep breath. "I do—trust you." For the next several minutes, she savored the feel of his fingers against her bare skin—the way he pressed and dabbed—daring to imagine things no married woman should conjure in her mind.

No doubt her body had been starved far too long. If her plan worked, that situation would soon be remedied. A storm was brewing and Mark wouldn't even see his little tornado coming. And neither would that lady friend of his.

Finally, the buzzing stopped. "All done," Thor reported.

Leigh Ann dared to open her eyelids. "It's over?"

He nodded. "Yup, all complete." His hands reached for hers and he lifted her from her reclining position. He handed her a mirror. "Take a look."

She maneuvered the reflection so she could survey the results. Staring back at her was the face of a tiny seal pup, eyes dark and wide. Not your typical sexy tattoo, but she had to admit she liked how the tiny animal appeared both vulnerable and secure at the same time. "Perfect," she said, noticing for the first time Thor had added the word *strong* in a tiny artistic font right beneath the seal's face.

She grinned up at him.

"Glad you like it." He grabbed some bandaging. "You can remove this in about three hours. After that, just follow these instructions." He gave her a sheet of paper. "Call me if you have any questions." His hands took hold of hers and he helped her to her feet.

She paid him with cash and headed for the door, anxious to

arrive home before Mark. With her hand on the doorknob, she turned back. "Thank you, Thor."

His sultry brown eyes stared back at her. "Anytime, Leigh Ann."

23

Joie jogged on the treadmill keeping rhythm to the tune blasting through the ear buds plugged in her ears. Adele's *Rolling in the Deep* was one of her favorite songs, which made running in a gym more palatable, especially at this early morning hour.

She'd much prefer exercising outdoors, but a cold front had moved in with dark storm clouds, forcing her inside. Even though several months of summer remained, snow would appear on the peaks of the Sawtooths before she knew it. That would make ski enthusiasts happy, including her. But the stables would take a hit with business not picking up again until the following spring.

That would mean a hit to her income as well, which could be a problem.

She felt a tap on her shoulder. She yanked the ear buds out and turned. "Leigh Ann? What are you doing here?"

Dressed head-to-toe in neon pink and green spandex, her sister looked as out of place as a Kardashian wandering the aisles of Walmart. She turned off the treadmill. "Nice outfit."

Leigh Ann's eyes inspected the room. "You think so?

Because it seems I have overdressed compared to everyone else."

"Let's just say you'll fit in perfectly with the ten o'clock crowd." Seeing her sister's confused frown, she quickly moved on. "I didn't know you came here."

Leigh Ann nodded with enthusiasm. "Mark bought me a membership last year for Christmas. I've just never had time to use it until now." She looked around. "Where do I start?"

Joie groaned inside. What had she done to deserve this? All she wanted was to run her ten miles in peace. Even so, she gave her older sister a weak smile. "Did your gift include a trainer? If you've never been here before, you might want someone to set up a regimen for you."

Leigh Ann adjusted her color-coordinated gym bag on her shoulder. "Well, if Mark didn't think to include a trainer, I can pay for one." Confusion crossed her face. "Where do you find a trainer?"

Joie pointed toward the back. "There's always at least one on the premises. Check with the girl at the counter."

Her sister thanked her and headed that way. Joie returned the ear buds to her ear and hit replay on the song, determined to finish and get out of here. She loved Leigh Ann, but getting chummy this early in the morning was out of the question.

Her relationship with Leigh Ann was . . . well, complicated.

For one thing, Leigh Ann never gave her credit for anything, passing over the fact she'd passed the bar first try to focus on the fact she too often hung out in one.

Of course, if Leigh Ann knew the whole story, and the reason she'd moved back home, she'd be even more disappointed. Worse, she'd be hurt.

Joie slowed her pace and surveyed the gym looking for her sister. Leigh Ann was still at the counter, digging through her wallet.

Relenting, Joie turned off the machine. She stepped down and headed that way.

"I don't understand," Leigh Ann said, her voice filled with agitation. She lifted another card and handed it off to the woman behind the counter. "Try this one."

Joie swiped a towel across the back of her neck. "What's up? Did you get lined up with a trainer?"

"My gift package didn't include one, so I went to pay the extra fee and my credit card won't authorize the charge." She shrugged. "It worked this morning, so I don't know what the problem might be. Thankfully, I have a card for Mark's business account."

"I have some cash if you need." Joie wouldn't risk lending her much-needed funds to just anyone. Leigh Ann was good for it.

"Won't be necessary. I'll call the bank if I have to. It's got to be a glitch of some sort."

The clerk looked up from the point-of-sale machine. Her face broke into a broad smile. "Looks like the second card went through fine." She handed it back to Leigh Ann. "I'm so sorry for the trouble, Mrs. Blackburn." Her face turned apologetic. "It's possible the trouble may have been at our end."

Leigh Ann's disposition brightened. "No worries. Now, about that trainer—"

Joie liked to believe she was fit, but the woman who stepped up to the counter looked like some sort of gymnasium goddess.

"Hi, I'm Arina." She held out her chiseled hand, which was connected to a long arm with well-defined muscles. Her shoulders bulged like those of a body builder. Her skin was darkly tanned and glistened with some sort of oil that smelled lightly of coconut.

While Joie was impressed with the fact this gal had so little body fat, the entire look was a bit repulsive.

Leigh Ann, on the other hand, was clearly enamored. "It's

nice to meet you, Arina." She took the trainer's hand in her own. "Such a pretty name."

"Thanks. I was conceived when my parents were on a trip to the Ryukyu Islands in western Japan. I'm named after a hot spring near the city of Kobe." She pulled her long black hair into a ponytail at the back of her neck. "So, which one of you am I working with today?"

Joie quickly shook her head. "Not me. I've got to head out. We've got a group of elk hunters coming in tomorrow from Portland and I have to inventory and get the riding gear ready."

She noticed Arina taking in her sister's outfit and couldn't help but grin. "Leigh Ann, you're in good hands." She leaned and brushed her sister's cheek with a kiss, then headed for the door.

Outside, dark clouds rolled in off the surrounding mountaintops. A clap of lightning boomed overhead sending her running for her car to avoid the inevitable downpour she suspected was only minutes away.

"Joie?"

Her heart stopped. She turned in the direction of the familiar male voice. Someone she'd hoped never to see again.

"Andrew. What are you doing here?"

Leigh Ann watched Joie leave, before turning to her new trainer with a mixture of excitement and dread. "So, where do we begin?"

Arina took her arm and led her on a quick tour. She was introduced to machines that looked more like torture equipment—the Pec Dec, the Squat Rack, the Kettle Bells, and the Stability Ball.

Arina parked her hands on her hips. "A very important thing to mention is that utilizing proper form when using these workout machines cannot be stressed enough." She gave Leigh Ann an encouraging smile. "Let's get started, shall we?"

An hour later, she'd finished her first circuit wondering if Mark was indeed worth the way she felt—which in one word was *pooped!*

She simply couldn't imagine—what was it Arina said?—building up to a routine that would maximize her effort to tone and contour her body. She'd barely survived the starter regime.

Even so, all she had to do was look around at all the hard-body competition—women who were younger, prettier, and definitely more fit—to determine she had no choice but to stay the course if she wanted to attain her goal. No matter how exhausting, her marriage was at stake!

"You did very well today, Mrs. Blackburn."

Leigh Ann lifted her forearm and swiped back the hair sticking to her sweaty forehead. "Please, call me Leigh Ann," she said, still somewhat winded. She really wished she could just collapse on the leather sofa in the entry area and sleep for seventeen hundred hours or so. Instead, she forced herself to stand straight and smile. "So, when do we do this again?"

"I have an open slot tomorrow?"

Inside, Leigh Ann groaned. "Great. I'll take it."

Wearing a satisfied look, Arina pulled the band from her hair and shook out her shiny black tresses. "I don't know what your time allows, but I often suggest my first-timers get a massage to keep their muscles from tightening up."

Now, that was the best thing she'd heard out of this gal's mouth all morning. "That sounds lovely."

Arina walked her to the counter. "Can we get Leigh Ann in with Liz?" While the girl studied her computer monitor, her trainer turned and lowered her voice. "She's the best."

Leigh Ann was too beat to do anything but give her a weak smile.

The girl at the counter looked up. "You're in luck. We can fit you in."

In less than fifteen minutes, Leigh Ann was undressed and lying on a massage table, draped in a large white cloth, waiting for the masseuse. She was trying hard not to doze off when her ears perked at a familiar voice outside the curtained door.

"Ruby, dear. Have you ever seen Zenergy this packed?"

"Well, you know what they say, Sister? The only thing that separates us from the animals is our ability to exercise."

"Well, I for one am completely comfortable with the ample body the good Lord gave me."

That made Leigh Ann smile. No doubt Trudy Dilworth had been mightily blessed in that regard. Of course, she should talk. Without this self-imposed intervention, who knew what her own future might hold relating to the scales. She'd never been one to follow the latest exercise craze, or diet fad. Never felt like she had to. She was married and secure in the fact her husband loved her, cellulite and all.

Until now.

"And I'll tell you another thing, Ruby. If ever my art studio goes belly up, I could pay the rent by turning that space into anything health related."

"Maybe you could be proprietor of a waxing studio. I see a new one opened near Spruce and Sun Valley Road. It's called LunchBox. I hear they have a three-week waiting list to get in."

"LunchBox? What kind of name is that?"

Leigh Ann's ears perked up. She could almost see Ruby shrug when she said, "Does it matter? All I'm saying is you can tell if someone is a good witch or a bad witch by their broom—know what I'm saying?"

Trudy let out a loud chuckle. "I feel sorry for this new generation of women. All we had to worry about as girls was shaving our legs and armpits."

"Oh, I know," Ruby commiserated. "But not anymore. Not if you're in the current dating scene."

"How do you know that?"

"Magazines, Sister. I read magazines."

Their voices faded as they moved on down the hall, leaving Leigh Ann to contemplate what she'd overheard.

It wasn't long and she'd added yet another tier to her plan.

24

Karyn shut off her car engine and carefully slipped her wedding ring from her finger. She tucked it securely inside a pocket in her purse before stepping out onto the pavement of the Friedman Memorial Airport parking lot. Overhead, the skies were growing ominously dark, not exactly a hopeful sign except that it might mean the weather had grounded Grayson and she'd find him in the hangar.

When Grayson hadn't called, Karyn knew she had a choice —dwell on the situation, or do something.

In a snap decision, she'd elected to try to make up for her poor manners, even if it meant skipping church. Nothing said *I'm sorry* better than baked goods fresh out of Nash Billingsley's oven.

She reached for the plate of freshly made oatmeal raisin cookies from the passenger side of her car and raced to the entrance hoping to beat the rain. It'd taken nearly an hour to perfect these curls.

Outside the gate window, a twin prop aircraft taxied in from the runway.

"Hey, Dale," she said, greeting the airport manager as he crossed the small terminal.

His eyes lit up. "Karyn, what brings you out to the airport? Heading off somewhere?"

She shook her head and held up the plate of cookies. "No, just bringing a peace offering to a friend." In answer to the quizzical look that crossed his face, she simply inserted, "It's a long story." Her gaze cut to a couple walking past, broad smiles on their faces and hands tightly woven. "Uh, Grayson Chandler. Do you know what hangar he flies out of?"

Dale nodded in the direction of a door leading out to a small tarmac to the north. "Second to the end."

"Thanks." She smiled her appreciation and headed in that direction.

Minutes later, she stood at the open entrance to a small metal building. The wind was wreaking havoc on a red windsock hanging nearly straight out from a long pole. The bluster was also doing a number on her hair.

Suddenly, she found herself having second thoughts. Maybe he wouldn't appreciate her just showing up like this. What if he hadn't called because he was mad?

Taking a deep breath, she peeked through the crack in the door. Inside, Grayson was crouched over a toolbox at the wheelbase of a small white plane.

She forced a smile and stepped into view. "That doesn't look good."

He looked up. "Karyn? What are you doing here?" He stood and wiped his hands on a rag before moving to meet her.

She held out the plate of cookies. "A token of my sincere apology."

He grinned and lifted the plastic wrap. "Now, how did you know I had to skip lunch?"

Relief flooded her gut. She smiled at him. "Nothing chases hunger better than a warm cookie."

He filled his mouth and rolled his eyes with pleasure. "Mmnn—" he muttered through the crumbs. "Darn, you're absolutely right. Nothing much better" He shot another grin her way, causing dimples to peek through a jawline covered in stubble.

"Glad you like them." She mentally kicked herself yet again. "Grayson, I'm so sorry about last night." She explained what had happened, how the kitchen had flooded. "It was awful. We had an entire convention room filled with people waiting to eat. I can't even begin to describe the pressure we were all under. Still, I hate that I didn't call and alert you."

There was a bit of devil in his eye as he grabbed another cookie. "So, I think there's a rule that for every date you skip, you have to commit to two more—maybe three. I'd have to check the rule book to be sure."

She laughed. "Guilty as charged and more than willing to submit to the maximum punishment."

His face eased into a wide grin. "Okay, then. So, I have lunch packed in the cooler. Would you care to join me for a picnic of sorts? And before you answer, let me remind you that proper restitution requires you to say yes."

"I'd love that." She tucked a strand of wayward hair behind her ear, grateful he'd forgiven her so easily.

He grabbed two large plastic buckets, turned them upside down and placed them on either side of a large white Yeti cooler. "Hope you don't require a table cloth," he said looking around the hangar. "I didn't expect a guest, but maybe there's something here we could—"

"It'll be fine," she assured him.

He opened the lid on the cooler and pulled out several containers. "Do you like quinoa?"

She nodded enthusiastically. "One of my favorites."

Despite the chilled air, a tiny trickle of sweat coasted down her back. Goodness, the man standing before her was as amazingly handsome as he was sweet. Hard to believe she'd left him standing on her doorstep with a mason jar of roses in hand.

"Do you always eat like this?" she asked, taking the spoon he offered.

"Like what?"

"A backcountry pilot who makes himself gourmet lunches is a bit off the expected grid. I mean, Dean would never have—" She stopped mid-sentence, horrified she'd slipped and mentioned her former husband. "Oh, Grayson. I'm sorry."

His expression went soft. "Karyn, Dean was a big part of your life. I don't expect you to never mention him." He dug in the cooler and handed her a can of soda. "Perhaps it's time we put some cards on the table, okay?"

She nodded, not even fully understanding what she was agreeing to. "Yeah, okay."

"We're not exactly kids hooking up. Both of us were once married. Like it or not, a piece of us remains tethered to our history. I don't believe you can ever give your heart to someone and then act like that person never existed. Know what I mean?"

She dried the top of the can with a corner of her shirt. "But—"

"Look—I really like you, Karyn. Let's agree right here at the start to be absolutely authentic with each other. No poker faces allowed." He smiled and offered her a napkin.

Boy, he had a way of cutting right to the chase of things.

"That may take a little practice on my part," she ventured. "But I'd like to try." The thought of being free to express herself without first evaluating the impact of her every word sounded refreshing. "And just so you know—I like you too."

Over the next hour, they ate lunch and enjoyed each other's company while sitting on buckets perched on a cement floor, amidst a slight smell of oil and airplane fuel. He asked more about the flood at the lodge and if she expected any further problem, offering to come take a look if necessary.

She assured him all was now well. The plumber guaranteed they'd experience no further problems.

He grabbed another cookie and told her about how he'd been scheduled to fly a group of researchers from the University of Utah to the base of Mount Regan to count big horn sheep and study their mating rituals. "Weather doesn't always cooperate. We had to reschedule."

She looked at him full on. "Mating rituals?"

He grinned. "Apparently, in many parts of the country, highways are keeping the sheep from moving freely into other areas. Soon, the animals get inbred and numbers start dying off. The Sawtooth National Resource Area in one of the few pristine areas remaining that duplicates the natural habitat these animals flourished in years ago, and still."

"I know it must be hard work on many levels, but you must pinch yourself and wonder how you maneuvered into making a living doing something you love."

He laughed. "Ha, well—most days that would be true. There is the occasional big city group of aging men who simply want to get away and act like frat boys in the wild." His blue eyes twinkled. "I want to fly hung-over bald men home and listen to them fill their sick bags, said no one ever."

She cringed. "Yuck, I guess every job has its down side."

Suddenly, Grayson stood. He pointed outside the hangar door. "Hey, looks like a break in the weather. Would you like to go for a ride?"

"Who, me? Now?"

He looked around the hangar in an exaggerated manner. "I don't see anyone else."

Karyn took a deep breath. "I—I don't know. I've flown commercial, but not sure I—"

"Oh, c'mon," he urged, grabbing her hand and pulling her

up. "It'll be fun. Just a short loop around the valley. You'll love it."

"But, what if another storm rolls in? The weather can be unpredictable around here."

By now, Grayson was outside the hangar. He looked up and inspected the sky. "Nah, we're good. But I'll check with the tower just to be sure the Doppler doesn't show another front coming in."

Twenty minutes later, she was seated next to him, seatbelt tightly fastened and an aviation headset in place that included a little microphone so she and Grayson could communicate during the noisy flight.

"Ready?" he asked.

She wasn't, but nodded anyway and watched wide-eyed as Grayson pressed several switches on the cockpit dashboard filled with knobs and gauges. This set off a series of whirring sounds. He leaned to the partially open side window and hollered, "Clear." Next, his hand reached for the ignition and he started the engine.

She smiled across at him over the loud sound that followed. Her stomach fluttered with excitement—and nerves.

The propellers cranked into motion. He grinned over at her briefly as they taxied out to the runway. He adjusted his microphone. *"KSUN Tower, Cessna One-Niner-One on thirteen thirty-one. Request taxi."*

A voice interrupted the slight crackling sound. *"Cessna One-Niner-One standby."* Grayson pulled a clipboard from a slot to his left and made a few notes. A few seconds later, the voice came on again. "Cessna One-Niner-One, go ahead."

Grayson stored the clipboard back. *"Cessna One-Niner-One ready for departure."*

"Ready?" he asked her.

Karyn nodded enthusiastically and leaned back in the

leather seat, watching as he pushed the throttle forward and they hurtled their way down the long paved airstrip.

She felt the plane lift. Seconds later, they were airborne and the ground receded below. They climbed steadily through a slight haze of cumulus clouds and into a sky so penetratingly blue, the vivid sight nearly hurt her eyes.

Grayson banked to the left and the tiny town of Hailey came into instant view. On the northern horizon, she could make out Ketchum and Sun Valley bordered by majestic mountains, including Baldy with its ribbons of ski runs breaking through vast spreads of pines.

"What do you think?" he asked through the sound system.

"Oh, it's stunning. Absolutely beautiful. I can see why you adore flying."

"Mark Twain once said, '*The air up in the clouds is very pure and fine, bracing and delicious. And why shouldn't it be? It is the same the angels breathe.*'"

Karyn sighed, loving that he was quoting one of her favorite novelists. "My sentiments exactly."

They flew north toward a misty blue horizon, reaching Galena Summit before circling wide and making their way across the Pioneer Mountain range. He pointed out Goat Lake with its sparkling blue water and Johnstone and Hyndman peaks, both topped with craggy rock croppings poking out from glacial snow.

She couldn't help but hold her breath, the beauty of the moment too much to completely take in. As was the man sitting next to her.

She did something bold then—something she never would have imagined herself doing a month ago. She reached across and folded her hand over his and squeezed. Despite his aviators, she could see his face brighten.

He grinned and quietly squeezed back.

25

The man's voice turned Joie's blood to ice. "Andrew, what are you doing here?" she asked in a choked voice.

He reached for her, and she yanked her arm back. "Don't touch me!"

"Joie, wait."

She quickly glanced around to see who might be watching. "I told you it was over." And she had, over a year ago.

"Joie, please. Just listen. I'm in town for the bar convention—"

Her eyes narrowed. "And let me guess—you didn't bring your wife?"

"That's not fair."

"Funny, I believe that was my line." She turned and stomped toward her car, determined to escape this scene at any cost. She'd nearly reached her jeep when she felt his hand on her shoulder.

"Joie, please."

She whirled to face him, her eyes drilling his own with her anger. "What part of *not interested* do you not understand?"

Despite the enmity she felt toward this man, her breath caught. *God, did he have to still make her entire being buzz just by standing there?*

It'd been many months since she'd last seen Andrew Merrill, and he looked the same. Same jet black hair that refused to stay in place, a lock escaping his precision haircut and falling carelessly over one of his coffee-brown eyes. His clean-shaven face held a shadow and in place of his typical tailored suit and crisp white button down with a striped tie— his law firm uniform—he now stood there in designer jeans and a plaid shirt. Black hair peeked from under his rolled sleeves. Hair she'd run her fingers lightly across more than once.

Andrew saw her staring and his face drew into a slow smile, one that left Joie unsettled.

"Look, all I want is to be left alone," she told him.

"I miss you," he said, daring to take a step closer. She could smell his signature cologne, a woody aroma that drew her mind back to memories she vowed to forget. Despite her pledge to do the right thing and move on with her life, she now found every cell in her body viscerally responding to the closing space between them.

"Please stop," she begged, her eyes now filling with unexpected tears. She angrily wiped them away. "I can't do this."

"I only want to talk." His eyes pleaded with her own, asking for something she wasn't going to give.

"I can't." She forced herself to turn away. She opened the door on the jeep and climbed inside, finding it impossible to breathe normally.

"I'm at the Sun Valley Lodge—room 23."

She slammed the car door closed.

"Room 23—," he repeated, pressing a hand against the closed window.

Joie started the engine. Her foot slammed the gas pedal to

the floor, gunning the engine and she roared off, leaving the man who had nearly destroyed her standing on the sidewalk.

Karyn stood at her father's sink, scrubbing potatoes for dinner, when the door opened and Leigh Ann entered, her arms loaded with sacks filled with groceries.

"What's all that?" Karyn asked. She shut the water off and wiped the counter with a dishtowel.

"The farmer's market," her sister reported. "I couldn't stand to pass up all this fresh produce."

"So, you bought out the entire market?"

"Don't be silly," she said. "Besides, you'll be glad when you get a taste of this pepper jelly from a new vendor in Stanley. She mixes red peppers with choke cherries."

Karyn scowled. "Why are you walking funny?"

"Don't ask."

Karyn folded the towel and placed it by the sink. "What do you mean?"

A slow smile sprouted on her sister's face as she slid the sacks onto the counter. "Let's just say my broom went in for repair."

Karyn reached for a grocery bag and began emptying the contents. "Goodness sakes! And, what did you do to your hair?" She leaned closer to get a better look.

Her sister fingered the sides. "Just a few highlights. Do you like it?"

"Like it? You're nearly blonde!" She reached to touch her sister's hair.

Leigh Ann beamed and pulled her shirt collar aside, proudly exposing her shoulder.

Karyn scowled and moved closer to get a better look. "Oh, my goodness! And what is this?"

Leigh Ann gave a defensive shrug. "Just a little tattoo."

"A tattoo? Are you kidding me?" Karyn inspected the inked outline of a tiny seal with large puppy-dog eyes. The surrounding skin was bright red. "A seal? I think a few nuts have left the Planters can."

"It's a Wedell seal," her sister patiently explained. "A cute, yet ferocious little female predator who will stop at nothing to protect her own."

Understanding dawned. "Oh, I see what this is all about— the hair, the tat." Karyn's gaze dropped lower. "And everything."

"Yeah? So what?" The look in her sister's eyes grew challenging. "I've been married since I was as old as Colby. Over all those years, Mark not-so-subtly suggested I lose a little weight. He criticized the fact I spent all that time filling my days with volunteer work." She used air quotes. "Accused me of neglecting all that stupid exercise equipment he gave me for Christmas. Oh sure, he noticed other women on occasion, but never did I dream he might leave me." Her eyes filled with tears. "Well, I'm not going to let that happen."

The vehement tone in her sister's voice took Karyn aback. "So your plan is to make yourself over? To mold into what you think Mark wants and expects?" She reached for her sister's arm. "Oh, Leigh Ann. Surely, you see how—"

Her sister yanked her arm back. "You wouldn't understand."

Karyn wanted to argue, but the door opened and their dad strode in, unaware of what he'd interrupted. He looked between them and frowned. "Something up?" he asked, taking his jacket off.

"Karyn and I were just talking. Hey, any reason Joie hasn't shown up yet?" Her sister quickly skipped over what had promised to become a rare point of contention between them. "I told her we'd be having dinner tonight."

Their dad joined them in the kitchen. "I'm sure she'll be

here eventually." He brushed both the tops of their heads with a kiss.

He leaned back and looked over Leigh Ann's new appearance. "Say, that's a bit different." His weathered face broke into a broad smile. "I like it. Very pretty."

"Thanks, Daddy," Leigh Ann squeezed his arm, all the while staring down Karyn in an unspoken challenge not to add anything to his remark. "I hope you're both hungry."

JOIE PULLED into the stables lot, parked her jeep and climbed out. She headed for the horse barn with renewed purpose. Ever since she was little, she'd found solace in animals every time life's challenges reared their ugly head.

Tonight was no different.

With her stomach tied in knots, she made her way to the tack room and grabbed a halter. All she wanted to do was to take Fresca out—ride off some of the angst tangling in her gut.

Why now?

She saddled the gelding and led him into the ring. Why after nearly a year had Andrew just shown up like that? Especially after she'd made her wishes entirely clear when she'd left.

She mounted the horse and pressed her heels into his sides, urging him into a slow lope. She circled the ring, wrestling the idea of Andrew in her mind.

No matter how tempted she'd been to reach and brush the hair from Andrew's face, the way she once had, she'd done the right thing in standing firm and leaving no room for misunderstanding. Their relationship was over the minute she learned he was married. She'd left the firm and moved back. And, it was still over.

She made a clicking sound against her cheek and Fresca

broke into a gallop. Joie let her body move to the rocking motion created by the horse's lanky strides. With every movement she felt the tension ease from her own muscles.

Joie rode the horse hard, round and round the enclosed area. His hooves made almost no sound beating against the thick, soft dirt. Soon, the gelding would be ready for the barrels. She'd be able to line up some sponsors and compete again. Perhaps by next summer.

Or maybe she'd split for a while and go to Perris Valley and participate in the planned formation skydivers hoped would beat the world record. California weather was great, even in the winter. She could try to fit in some surfing at Laguna. Or abalone diving in Mendocino.

Nothing was keeping her in Sun Valley—well, except her family. And of course, her lack of money. There was always that.

Both she and Fresca were in sync—in mind and body—as she slowed the horse to a trot and then a slow walk. After circling twice more, she dismounted and led the gelding out of the arena and back down the wide aisle lined with gated enclosures to a cement pad where she tethered him and grabbed a hose and brush.

"Hey."

She turned toward the familiar voice. Clint Ladner headed in her direction.

"Hey," she answered back, wishing he'd just go away. She'd finally settled herself down and only wanted to be left alone.

"Did that guy find you?" he asked.

Her heart instantly filled with dread. "What guy?"

"Said his name was Andrew. Told me that you used to work together and he needed to find you." His eyes carefully watched her. "I said he'd likely find you downtown. You hook up?"

Her lips drew into a taut line. "Guess not," she fibbed, sweeping the brush across Fresca's flank. "Besides, any friend of mine has my phone number and can reach me if they want to."

Clint rubbed at his jawline. "That's funny. He left the impression you were close." He stared at her with casual knowing. "Maybe even more than friends."

JOIE RACED UP THE STAIRS, taking two at a time, then hurried down the thick, carpeted hallway until she stood in front of Room 23. She banged on the thick wooden door with her fist, waited for several seconds, then banged again.

From inside, a voice called out, "Coming. I'm coming."

The door flung open and Andrew gazed out at her, not bothering to hide his surprise—or his pleasure at seeing her.

"Joie," he breathed. "You came."

She pushed her way past him. "Yes, I came. What did you expect?"

"You're mad," he stated, no matter how stupid that made him sound.

Joie whirled. "Mad? Why would I be mad?" She jabbed his chest with a finger. "You went to law school, passed the bar exam—so I know you understand the English language. What part of *stay out of my life* don't you get?"

For good measure, she hauled off and slapped him.

Hard.

Andrew grabbed her wrist. At the same time, he kicked the door closed.

Only then did it sink in she was alone with him, in a hotel room. The idea flustered her, and she didn't fluster easily.

As if speaking to a toddler throwing a tantrum, his voice lowered and he calmly suggested she come in and let him pour her a drink.

"I'm not going to have a drink with you. I simply want to

drill it through your thick head that you are not to show up at my work, you are not allowed to meander Sun Valley looking for me, and we most certainly have nothing to talk about. We're over. Go back to your wife."

"That's done. The decree was signed two months ago."

The news shocked her, but failed to dissolve her stance. She shook her head. "Doesn't matter. You lied to me. You lied to her."

He reached for her and she stubbornly pulled her hands out of his. "What? Did you think all you had to do was waltz back into my life and we'd start over? At square one?"

He shook his head vehemently. "No, that's not at all what entered my mind. I simply wanted to talk. I think about you all the time—the way it was between us." He gazed over at her, looking miserable. "I miss you."

She stared back at the man she'd chased from her dreams night-after-night. Ebony hair—like that of a black stallion's mane. Squared shoulders that lent a certain gravity to his countenance. And those cognac eyes that nearly seared the depths of her soul every time he looked at her.

Like now.

She closed her eyes and drew a deep breath before facing off with him. "So, you want to create a crisis out of your nostalgia?"

Andrew reached for her again, his eyes filled with emotion. "Please don't be angry."

This time her resolve wavered slightly. She allowed his hand to linger.

Even all these months later, she had yet to adjust to being without him. Even so, she would never completely forgive herself for not having seen what was right in front of her flipping face. But wasn't that the way things were sometimes? Passion often makes you blind and you only notice what you want to see.

She stepped from him and swallowed. "Please, Andrew. If I ever meant anything to you at all—let me be. Go home and don't contact me again."

Despite her determination, tears formed. She made the mistake of hesitating before moving for the door.

"You miss me too, I can see it."

This was not the way she wanted this conversation to go. Andrew, somehow, taking control.

"I missed you," he quietly repeated.

He reached and lightly brushed away the moisture collecting at the corner of her eye. That's all it took. She couldn't . . . didn't seem *able* to move. Even as he folded her into his arms.

Her emotions suddenly broke and she now wept openly, something rarely allowed. A deep ache rushed through her gut as she took in the smell of him, felt the strength of his arms.

She made a final weak attempt to turn away. He jerked her back. "Joie, I know you love me."

She struggled to clear her mind, to pull free but he only held her tighter. Suddenly, his lips were everywhere—her throat, her earlobes, her cheek. She could feel the heat coming in waves as she melted against him. Finally, he lifted her chin and pressed his lips to her own.

God help her. She kissed him back.

26

L eigh Ann uncorked a bottle of Mark's favorite wine and pulled two stemmed glasses from the cupboard. While the wine aerated, she retrieved her purse from the living room and plucked a blue envelope from the interior, the one containing the airline tickets to Seattle.

According to the clock on the wall her husband should be home anytime. It had cost a chunk of change to move up her surprise birthday plans to coincide with his planned trip to Boise, but she'd have spent any amount to keep him from a weekend in another woman's arms. All she needed was time—an opportunity to recalibrate his intentions.

He'd fallen in love with her once, and she could rekindle those feelings again. She had to, or face losing everything that was important to her. Her marriage and family, her financial security and even her status in this town. People may not all like Mark, but they respected him, admired his business acumen. His development projects and investment opportunities had padded a lot of pockets in the Sun Valley area, even if indirectly.

She carefully leaned the blue envelope on the counter, and waited.

And waited.

Nearly two hours passed before his headlights finally appeared through the front windows and she heard the front door open.

Tamping down her frustration, she pasted a smile on her face and went to greet him. "There you are," she said, handing him a glass of wine. "I was worried."

Mark scowled. "I told you I'd be late."

"Yes, but not this late." She internally scolded herself, remembered to keep the evening upbeat. "Doesn't matter. Come on in and get relaxed. Tell me about your day."

He made it into the living room before he stopped and cocked his head. "What did you do to your hair?"

She smiled, glad he noticed. "Thought I'd just change it up a bit. Do you like it?"

He hesitated. "A little lighter than I'm used to, but sure. Looks fine." He threw his computer bag on the sofa and sampled the wine, then placed his glass on the table. His hands went to his collar.

"Here, let me." Leigh Ann reached and unfastened his necktie and placed it neatly aside.

"For goodness sakes, what's that?" he stepped closer and pulled the neckline of her blouse a bit lower for inspection. "You got a tattoo?"

She grinned. "I did. Something inside me felt a little adventurous. It's a Wedell seal."

"A what?"

"A Wedell seal," she repeated. She started to explain the significance but let it go when she noticed he wasn't paying attention.

"I have a surprise for you," she told him.

Mark sunk to the sofa, slipped off his shoes and lifted his

stocking feet onto her Steinberg coffee table. Any other night, she'd have harped at him not to treat a piece of furniture worth several thousand dollars so casually, and would have asked him to please remove his feet.

Instead, she went to the kitchen and retrieved the wine bottle and the envelope. She sat next to Mark, who leaned against the cushions. "Honey, you've been working extremely hard. All these terribly late nights. Anyway, I wanted to do something really special for your birthday." She handed him the envelope.

His eyebrows lifted. "What's this?"

"Open it," she urged.

He did as instructed and extracted the electronic tickets, inspecting them with a puzzled look. "Seattle?"

Leigh Ann let a wide smile sprout on her face. "Yes, Seattle. I booked a room in a little boutique hotel minutes from the wharf and thought you might like to spend the weekend with a tattooed blonde who's crazy about you." She knew she was gushing, but her nerves were starting to buzz like a circus of tiny mosquitos. "You deserve some time off, babe. Just think . . . a little coastal therapy, including a night at that little oyster bar we visited a few years back. Remember?" She reached and refilled his wine glass. "Maybe I'll even let you get lucky again, Mister."

"This weekend?" He rubbed at his forehead. "It's just not possible."

She expected a bit of opposition, so she launched a second round in her argument. "I considered our schedules carefully, and this was really the only open window. As you know, I have the Wine and Arts Festival on the horizon and I saw on your calendar—"

"You checked my calendar?"

She lifted her chin. "Yes, I checked the calendar open on your desk and you had nothing noted until the following

Wednesday." She clasped her hands signaling the decision was made. "So, it's a done deal. The tickets are booked, the hotel is waiting."

Mark shook his head. "Leigh Ann, I'm sorry. It's impossible for me to get away this coming weekend. Not everything is noted on my calendar. I have to make a trip to Boise."

"But, can't that wait? Maybe until early next week?" she protested, her stomach twisting with worried disappointment. "We really need this trip."

"I'm sorry, Leigh Ann. It's just not possible."

She parked her wine glass on her expensive table, anger muscling in on her disappointment. No matter her earlier plan, unchecked irritation raised its ugly head. "What meeting could possibly be so important that you can't reschedule by only a few days in order to celebrate your birthday? Or, maybe I could go with you. We could at least salvage the situation and go to dinner at the Cottonwood Grille."

He shook his head. "That won't work this time."

His response made her burn inside. "No, of course not. That wouldn't be very convenient given your important plans."

He looked at her like she was a petulant child. "Look, I'm too tired to argue."

She wasn't a child. She was his wife!

She stood, rage building. "I'm tired too, Mark. Tired of getting shoved aside and being expected to live life solo. You leave early, come home late. When you do drag in, you're too exhausted to have a decent conversation, too drained to eat the meals I slave over, because you're distracted with—with your little text messages."

His eyes narrowed. "What's that supposed to mean?"

"It means, I know," she blurted, unable to hold back. "I know all about your get-away trip to Boise. Your secret's out."

He bolted up. "Now you're just being ridiculous."

"Am I?" She was yelling, but couldn't help it. "I'm not yet

forty. Gals older than me are regularly having clear-your-sinus-out, pay-off-the-credit-cards-with-cash-left-over, whole-body sex on a regular basis. Me? I can't even get my husband to look my way, let alone touch me." She whirled on him. "I mean, I dyed my hair blonde, got a tattoo and had a date with hot wax —and I'm not talking candles, baby. So, is giving me a little time and attention just too much to ask after all these years?"

"You've gone crazy, Leigh Ann. Life isn't some damn romance novel," he shouted back. "You're not married to a bare-chested hunk of a hero who doesn't have to make a living. And a good one, at that. A financial status you've become quite accustomed to, I might add."

She literally growled and turned, bumping the table and sending wine toppling. Deep red spilled onto her white shag-style carpet. The rug that she'd special ordered from Pottery Barn and waited ten weeks for.

The sight was too much. Leigh Ann went over the edge.

She glared and air-jabbed her finger in his direction. "You listen to me, Mark Blackburn. If you go to Boise with that woman—"

"What woman?"

"The woman who sent you the text, the one you've been feeding the gossip mill with by riding around town with your car top down. If after all these years, you plan to leave me, then you can just push that Christmas treadmill up your backside until your tonsils are jogging."

Her insides shattered into a million tiny pieces as she ran from the room.

Footsteps thundered right behind her. Mark caught her wrist and turned her to face him. "You think I'm having an affair?"

"Oh, please." Her lip quivered. "Now you're going to treat me like I'm stupid?"

Mark's face turned to stone. "You've got everything wrong, Leigh Ann."

Her fingers drifted to the tender place on her shoulder in an attempt to draw strength from the inked image. "Sadly, not everything. Or, have you not been listening?" She turned then and raced down the hall and into the bedroom, locking the door behind her.

aryn climbed the steps leading into Bistro on Fourth, bent and stroked Chelsea's head. "Morning, girl. Enjoying the sun?" She glanced at the sky as she grabbed for the doorknob. Deep powder winters drew the crowds to Sun Valley, but like many, she loved summertime the most.

Inside, she headed for the counter where Nash Billingsley was taking orders. "Hey there, Karyn. Whatcha in for today?"

Without needing to look at the menu mounted on the wall behind him, she rattled off her standard. "Large coffee to go—splash of sugarfree caramel and skim."

"Coming right up," Nash reported.

Karyn glanced around. Dee Dee Hamilton and her husband Andre sat at a table near the window. She waved. A short distance from them Sheriff Sparks stood talking with elderly Mrs. Carter.

Nash slid her coffee across the glass-topped counter and she handed him a twenty. He opened the cash register to make change. "Looks like the 'ole gal got herself busted again," he said in a lowered voice.

Karyn nodded. "I saw her driving last week too."

He handed over several bills and some coins. "Her son is about ready to pull his hair out. She's nearly blind, you know. It's a wonder she hasn't hurt herself, or someone else."

Lucy sashayed out of the kitchen with a tray of apple scones. "Her son needs to toss her in a nursing home." She slid the tray into the display case. "Problem solved."

Nash and Karyn exchanged glances. Nash waited until they were alone again, then leaned over the counter. "She's a pretty good worker, but I'd hate for her to be the oarsman if my boat was sinking. Know what I mean?"

Karyn nodded. "Boy, you're not exaggerating."

"Well, some things need no embellishment."

She laughed out loud, then turned to find Grayson walking in the door. Her insides went all tingly as if she were some schoolgirl who'd spotted the star football player heading her way a week before prom.

His face lit up. "Hey, I thought that might be your SUV parked outside."

"So, you thought you'd pull over and casually see for yourself?" she teased.

Nash walked out from behind the cash register, wiping his hands on a towel. "Back again already?" He winked at Karyn. "He was in here less than a half hour ago."

Grayson sheepishly threw his head back and laughed. "Can I get a side of bacon to go with that egg on my face?"

Nash seemed tickled with himself. "We don't serve bacon, but I have some apple scones fresh out of the oven."

"Well, there you go." Grayson turned to Karyn with a smile. "Do you have time to sit and have a quick bite?"

She hesitated, glanced at her watch. "I have a meeting at eight. But a girl's got to eat. Right?"

Grayson's hand rested lightly on her waist as he steered her to a table near a window overlooking the street. Lucy delivered two plates with hot scones and a carafe of coffee. "Nash says these are on the house." The girl made a point of brushing her hip against Grayson's arm, a move that irked Karyn.

Even so, she responded the same way she always had—with a sweet smile and words of gratitude, but not before boldly tucking her hand into the crook of his elbow.

Lucy gave her an icy stare. "Well, enjoy your breakfast."

She innocently picked her scone from the plate. "So, I thought of a way I can pay my debt to society."

He lifted his eyebrows and gave her a curious look. "Yeah? How's that?"

"Another date." She placed her scone back on the plate. "Attend the Wine and Art Festival with me this weekend. Leigh Ann's in charge and it's always a fun time."

"Done." He smiled across the table. "Now eat your scone."

28

If Joie were keeping count—and who was keeping count? —this wasn't shaping up to be the best day of her life.

Harsh sunlight heaped through the large hotel window and mixed with her guilt as she slipped from the satiny sheets. She bent and gathered her strewn clothes. The last thing she needed was to have her sister catch her here at the lodge this early in the morning and have to explain.

She quickly pulled on her jeans and top—the same slightly dusty ones she'd worn at the stable the day before—and crammed her bra into her bag. After a quick look around the room, she hurried for the door.

Before she could make her escape, the water shut off and Andrew stepped from the shower. "You're leaving?" There was an edge to how he said that, which she chose to ignore.

"Look, I gotta go. This was—a big mistake."

Before she could take another step, he was next to her. His hand went to her wrist. "How can you say that? Last night proved—"

She started to laugh. She couldn't help it. "Last night proved you are really good at getting me in bed. That's all."

This is how it always worked between them. He turned up the heat with that warm smile and she melted. This was exactly how she'd gotten in trouble in the first place—how she'd lost herself.

He caught her eyes, held them. "I never loved her. You must know that."

Joie covered her ears. "I must not know. I need to reverse time and never know I broke up your marriage."

She'd been living with the ugly fact hovering for far too long. You were either truthful or you weren't, and that defined you. Maybe he needed to justify his actions and tell himself they hadn't crossed a sacred boundary, but she knew the reality of what they'd done. Even if they hadn't actually crossed the line physically.

What was the point of trying to convince him of the truth, anyway? As if anyone could make you see the one thing you didn't want to look at.

She gently pulled her wrist free. "Look, I've got to go."

That's when she saw it in his eyes, how the perpetual brightness had dimmed. She could see how much energy it was taking him just to keep from pulling her against him. The same force threatened to drag her under.

In her senior year of undergrad, she'd surprised everyone by announcing she was going to law school, a decision prompted after hearing a keynote speech by Madeline Crane, a brash and feisty woman attorney who had just won a highly publicized case against a football coach who had been inappropriate with students.

For the first time, Joie no longer felt adrift and unable to decide what she was going to do next. She wanted a career that would make a real difference. She wanted to be Maddy Crane.

After scoring one of the highest LSAT scores in her class, and then passing the bar, she quickly landed a plum job with a large Denver law firm with a regional office in Boise. She was assigned a partner mentor, a highly respected litigator named Andrew Merrill. He taught her the nuanced skills needed to persuade a judge and jury, how to zealously represent a client with a goal to win.

That is how they fell in love, talking about the least sexy things in the world. Interrogatories and motions to suppress. Subpoenas. And billables. And then, everything that mattered.

He now reached and stroked her cheek, no doubt reading her hesitation, a skill every good litigator possessed. "My marriage had been over for a long time. It took falling in love with you to convince me it was time to end it. That's all. You didn't break up my marriage, Joie." And then to close his argument, he added, "I finally did what I should've long ago. I'm here now wanting to make a clean start. Can't we figure all this out? I need you." He paused, like he wanted to say something else, but thought better of it. A good litigator also knew when to rest.

Instead, he caught her eyes, held them, his dark-eyed gaze so intense, she thought it might break her.

She could hear how much he meant it—and felt herself caving. She knew love could be messy, and complicated—she wanted to believe him. Wanted to nestle against his chest and acquiesce to how she felt in his arms.

"Please don't look at me that way," she pleaded, taking a tiny step back.

"What way?" he asked, not so innocently.

Like an addict, she edged closer to that feeling she vowed never to chase again. How could he possibly have this power over her?

"So, can we—"

She cut him off by holding up an open palm—then backed toward the doorway awkwardly, standing there for several seconds, biting at her nails. Her heart pounded in her throat as she dropped her hand and pushed out a fragile response. "I'm not moving back to Boise."

Andrew shot a huge grin in her direction. "You won't have to."

He reached for her but she tapped the face of her watch. "No, sir. I've really got to go." She whipped around and reached for the door, then quickly looked back. "By the way, you might want to wrap a towel around yourself before I open this door."

AT TEN MINUTES TO EIGHT, Karyn raced into the parking lot outside the Sun Valley Lodge and wedged her SUV into her designated spot.

She prided herself on her punctual nature and hated being late. Well, technically she'd be at the meeting on time, but barely.

She grabbed her purse and tote bag from the passenger seat and stepped from her car. After all, it was worth cutting her prep time short in order to spend those few minutes with Grayson.

Not only was he cute with a capital C—blue eyes that constantly twinkled with good humor and those deep dimples —his flirtation made her feel alive again.

In the months following the accident, her world had spun out of control. Life kept marching on all around her, yet she'd been stuck back at the moment Dean left her. No matter how others urged her to push through, she couldn't seem to get to the other side of her sadness.

It was only now that she was learning there was no other side. But rather, an absorption, adjustment, acceptance.

And, there was hope.

She remembered sitting in the pew of Grace Chapel, next to Leigh Ann and Joie and her dad. In spite of being surrounded by family—she'd felt utterly alone. The man she would have had next to her, holding her hand, was the reason they were all there. Never had she felt so isolated—wondering when the quiet terror would leave her.

That is until recently—when a handsome and charming Alaskan pilot appeared on the scene.

For the first time in months, gray skies had fallen away to make room for a little sunshine.

She couldn't be happier.

She locked her car and headed for the front portico, reluctantly forcing her thoughts away from her budding relationship with Grayson and onto the meeting ahead of her. She was in the middle of checking off the agenda items in her head when she noticed something and halted mid-step.

On the far side of the lot, Joie sprinted to her jeep. Her sister glanced back and forth over her shoulders as she unlocked the door. She swung the door open, quickly climbed inside and started the engine.

Seconds later, she sped away.

29

M ark banged on the bedroom door. "Leigh Ann, you've been in there all night. It's time to come out. I mean, you can't just stay locked in our bedroom."

"No!" she hollered. "Go away."

Leigh Ann was furious with Mark and she had a right to be. After nearly twenty years of marriage, did he think he could just toss her aside like an old pair of slippers?

Yes, that's exactly how he thought of her. Despite her high-lighted hair, her bold tattoo and other efforts made, she was nothing more to Mark than a comfortable old worn out piece of footwear he thought he could walk all over.

Despite the sick knot in her gut, she drew a deep breath and pulled back her shoulders. "I have nothing more to say to you, Mark. Go to Boise with whoever that woman is." She thought of Thor Magnum, his sultry brown eyes and the way he'd flirted with her. "If we're on a new playground, I can find me a playmate as well. Maybe I already have."

Mark's muffled voice came through the door. "Leigh Ann,

you're being silly. You've jumped to some mighty crazy conclusions." He raised his voice. "Open this door!"

Tears burned at her lids. She wouldn't give him the satisfaction of seeing the pain he'd caused. "Go away," she repeated.

"I am not having an affair!" he shouted. "Oh, have it your way, Leigh Ann. You always do." With a level of defeat, he added, "I have a big day ahead and I'm not losing any more time over anything so silly."

Every muscle in her torso tightened. So, now he thought she was silly?

She was capable of managing festivals, concerts, fundraisers —while maneuvering her way precipitously through strong personalities and politics, juggling contradicting expectations of the public and the need to be financially viable—all for no pay. Yet, Mark claimed when it came to discerning his faithfulness to their marriage, she was simply being silly.

Hadn't she seen the text? He'd insisted on going to Boise regardless of her suspicions and made it plain she wasn't welcome.

She ripped off her clothes and uncharacteristically tossed them into a wadded pile on the floor before stepping into the shower. A place where the hot streaming water would drown her sobs.

For all her tough talk, the truth of Mark's betrayal smacked her in the face. If he'd hauled off and physically hit her, it couldn't hurt worse.

Truth was, the foundation of her entire being was crumbling beneath her feet. She bit at her bottom lip as she stepped under the streaming water.

She was barely nineteen when they'd met in college and married. While the rest of the girls were going to football games and sorority dances, she was grocery shopping and cleaning toilets—which is hard to do when you are pregnant.

Others with less gumption would have quit school. Mark certainly didn't urge her to press on. But she had. She'd juggled a baby on her hip and a textbook in her hand.

Her high school experience had been much the same with two little sisters to help raise.

She leaned against the shower wall and slowly slid into a puddle at the base. With her head in her hands, she let the emotions flow out of her wounded spirit and down the drain.

Somehow, she'd gotten lost in all of it. She'd given everything, with little in return. Everyone knew her to be smart and ambitious and calculatingly strategic—both at work and in her relationships. Did anyone stop to wonder why she tested every move in her head before she stepped forward?

Did anyone know how heavy her load really was? How many times she'd nearly folded under the weight of all her roles and the need to be perfect in each one?

How could they? She herself didn't entirely understand why she couldn't seem to relax and allow herself to just go with the flow?

The result was no one really knew her—not her family, even her dad and sisters. Not the real her, the one filled with fear and unmet longing.

What did it say that Colby, a boy not known for focusing on academics, elected to attend summer school and remain in Seattle instead of coming home?

Certainly, Mark didn't know what made her ache inside. Even after all these years. Of course, he'd claim she constantly pushed him away with her drive for everyone and everything to conform to her rigid expectations.

Now, her husband had chosen to move on to another, someone no doubt more attractive, physically and otherwise. And if she were really honest, in the secret part of her soul, she had to ask—

Could it be she was to blame?

30

Brightly colored pole banners lined the short stretch of road leading to the Wine and Arts Festival where vendor tents beckoned attendees with unique pieces of artisan work, from glass and metalwork, to pottery and textiles, jewelry and more, along with a wide variety of distinctive fine wine. A large white gazebo stood in the center, with a four-piece jazz band entertaining the crowd.

Karyn turned to Grayson in the car. "Oh, look! There's Dad and Joie. And Nash Billingley—and the Dilworth sisters." This gathering was one of her favorite festivals.

"Geez, where are we supposed to park?" Grayson lifted his eyebrows as they passed a packed shuttle unloading at the gate. "I mean, look at this crowd."

"No worries. Leigh Ann gave me a preferred parking pass." She reached inside her bag and hung a bright turquoise-colored badge from his rearview mirror.

He grinned. "Pays to know people in high places."

Minutes later they were parked and at the entry gate. Karyn looped her hand in the crook of Grayson's arm and pulled him past the ticket taker with a grin and a wave.

"Let me guess," Grayson said. "Another family perk?"

She grinned. "Yup, that's how this Abbott family rolls."

They strolled past a booth displaying earthenware and pottery of all colors and sizes. Grayson slowed. "Man, there's some nice stuff here."

"Yeah, no doubt. And a portion of all the proceeds goes to benefit the Sun Valley Center for the Arts." The lightness in her step reflected the way she felt inside. It was a beautiful day and she was here with a great guy, someone she really enjoyed.

Hopefully, the occasional stares were in appreciation of her blue and white sleeveless dress and matching sandals, and not merely a fixation on the fact Dean Macadam's widow was in public with another man who was not their beloved hero.

The thought prompted her to stiffen and remove her hand, a move that caused Grayson to glance her way. "Anything wrong?"

She innocently lifted her eyebrows. "No—why?"

Before Grayson could follow up, her Dad and Joie stepped from the crowd and approached.

"Hey, you two." Her dad extended his hand, looking extremely gratified to see them together.

Grayson shook his hand. "Hey, Mr. Abbott. Nice seeing you again."

"Please, friends call me Edwin."

The invitation to be less formal seemed to please Grayson. He smiled. "Then Edwin it is."

Her dad looked between them. "You two just get here?"

"Yes, only a few minutes ago," she confirmed. "Traffic is backed up to Dollar Road. Bumper-to-bumper." She turned to Joie, who seemed distracted. "Hey, Sis. What's up?"

"Hey."

Karyn recalled seeing her sister leave the lodge early in the morning and put two-and-two together. "You looking for someone?"

Joie's head instantly flipped around. "Uh, no. Why?"

While her dad and Grayson chatted about steelhead runs up at Redfish Lake, Karyn leaned closer and lowered her voice. "I saw you leaving the lodge the other morning."

When her sister simply stared with no response, Karyn winked and emphasized, "*Very* early."

"Look, I gotta go." Joie turned to their father and Grayson. "Catch you guys later. Nice seeing you again, Grayson." She pivoted and walked away into the crowd, her attention buried in her phone, her fingers working furiously over the face of the device.

"Where's Joie heading off to?" her dad asked.

She shrugged. "She didn't really say."

"Yoo-hoo!"

They all turned in the direction of the female voice. A slightly-built woman with a long, flowing skirt and a peasant top waved. "Oh, Edwin!"

Her dad waved as the woman approached. "Hey, Penny. Good to see you. Grayson, Karyn—this is Penny Baker. She just moved to town."

"Nice to meet everyone," she said, her warm eyes lighting up. She held up her glass of wine. "This pinot noir is delicious. Grown in the Willamette Valley in Oregon—where I'm from."

Grayson nodded. "Great area."

"You've been there?" she asked.

"Oh, yes. Many times."

"Edwin!" Another female voice drew their attention from the opposite direction.

Elda Vaughn hurried toward them, carrying a large piece of yard art.

Karyn fought back a grin and inconspicuously elbowed her dad. "Uh-oh," she whispered.

The look that sprouted on his face clearly indicated he shared her assessment of the situation.

Elda joined them and juggled her art piece to the ground. "Have you ever seen anything so beautiful?" she gushed, caressing the intricate wrought iron. She eyed Penny. "Why, hello. You're new here." She said this as a statement more than a question.

Remembering his manners, Edwin stepped forward and made introductions, adding, "Penny was just telling us she grew up in Oregon."

Elda's icy stare melted into a warm smile. "Oh? I have relatives in Burns."

The two women exchanged stories about their neighboring state, chattering about whales at Depot Bay, the tulip farm in Woodburn and how they both detested driving in downtown Portland.

Karyn finally interrupted. "We need to be moving on. There's a booth I want to hit before his wares are all picked over." She turned to her father's lady friends. "Nice seeing you both. We'll catch up with you later, Dad."

A helpless look crossed her father's face. She laughed and pulled on Grayson's elbow.

When they were far enough away not to be overhead, Grayson gestured with his thumb pointing over his shoulder. "Let me guess. Bo-Peeps?"

A wide grin immediately sprouted on her face. "Yup."

They spent the next minutes wandering past more vendor tents, admiring hand-painted art in unique frames, fired pottery pieces and her all-time favorite—a booth featuring Sun Valley Mustard and food items made with mountain huckleberries.

Her heart picked up a tempo when she looked over at Grayson, felt a tiny thrill when he wove her fingers with his own.

Fresh air caught and held in Karyn's lungs as she thought

about how natural it felt to be with him. How much sweeter life seemed when he was walking beside her. Kind of like how coffee gets better when you added caramel syrup and a dab of cream.

Relationships were complicated matters. Romantic connections, even more so.

She was proud of herself. Instead of remaining in a quagmire of loss, she'd boldly embraced wide-open possibility and the chance for happiness.

That was a big step.

They headed in the direction of the music coming from the gazebo with its white lattice top and hand-carved spindles. The structure looked straight out of a Hallmark movie. Of course, that was likely a result of strategic planning on her sister's part, to give the festival a hometown feel.

Speaking of, where was her older sister?

"Who are you looking for?" Grayson asked as they stopped to enjoy the jazz trio's talents.

"Leigh Ann," she answered. "I expected we might run into her by now."

"In this crowd?"

Grayson was right. More people were showing up. So much so that when they finished listening and moved on down another aisle of booths, her shoulders bumped with someone else's several times.

Karyn looked over at Grayson. "Thank you for agreeing to come with me today."

"Wouldn't have wanted to miss it." His hand tightened around her own, as he paused in front of one of the booths. "Hey, these are nice." He lifted a delicate necklace from a display rack. The piece of jewelry featured a tiny seed pearl charm and a little metal plate with the word *Believe* hanging at the end of a long gold chain.

The artist, a man with brown hair pulled back into a ponytail with a leather strap, stepped forward. "That particular design is hand-faceted."

"May I?" Grayson bent his head in her direction.

The guy nodded. "Sure, go ahead."

Karyn gave them both a bashful smile. She turned and lifted her long hair, allowing Grayson to place the pretty chain around her neck. His fingers brushed her skin as he fastened the chain, sending a tiny shiver across her shoulders.

"There," he said, taking the hand mirror offered by the artist. "Take a look."

She fingered the necklace as she admired the reflection. "It's lovely. Really pretty."

Grayson pulled his wallet from his back pocket. "We'll take it." He offered up his credit card.

"Oh, Grayson. You don't have to do that."

His eyes warmed. "I want to."

As a sign of her gratitude, she lifted on her toes and brushed a light kiss across the surface of his cheek. As she pulled back, she paused—leveled a look at him.

His eyes met her own. They remained that way, staring intently, while the man rang up the sale.

Karyn felt his hands go to her waist. As if in a trance, she reacted and brought her fingers to his face, lightly followed the strong line of his jaw.

She realized he was going to kiss her. And she wanted him to.

He bent, his breath warm against her skin. With a low groan, he cradled her neck to capture her mouth with his own. His lips moved slowly into hers, deliberately, as he pulled her closer until their bodies met . . .

"Karyn?"

The woman's terse voice sucked the breath from her lungs. She whirled.

There stood Dean's parents.

31

Despite appearances, nothing was going right today. While on the surface everything was running smoothly, festival patrons were unaware of the behind-the-scenes chaos plaguing Leigh Ann's organizational sensibilities.

"No, not there!" she barked at the uniformed man as he headed straight into the crowd with his large ice cart. "That area is reserved for attendees only. Read the posted signs. Deliveries are restricted to marked areas only." She pointed to a narrow path between the outer booths.

Don't these people ever stop to think for themselves? Or, at the very least, follow instructions?

First, the electricians had run wires across the designated footpath, which had to be corrected to keep someone from falling and suing. Now she had an idiot ready to bang a cart around in the crowd, running attendees over.

Yes, she was acting like a witch—but she couldn't seem to help it.

She rubbed at her aching brow, wishing she'd gotten more

sleep. These events were trying enough when she was at her best. Today, the effort was grueling.

Truth was, she'd barely been able to concentrate since her blow-up with Mark. How could she be expected to run an important two-day festival when she could barely think of anything but what had transpired between her and her husband, and that her life might soon crumble beneath her feet?

She snapped her clipboard from the top of a stack of water bottles, a tall pile that was obstructing view of a carefully placed container planted with daisies, geraniums and lobelia.

Not bothering to squelch an audible growl, she whipped around to a random passerby. "These people are going to be the death of me!"

"Leigh Ann?"

She glanced up, shocked to see her tattoo artist. "Mr. Magnum?"

"Please, it's Thor." He pulled back and studied her with those intense brown eyes. "You okay?"

Embarrassed, she stared at the anchor etched in ink on his muscular upper arm. She swallowed. "Uh, yes. Sure. I'm just a bit stressed. That's all."

His eyes narrowed. "I imagine this is quite an effort to manage." His vision swept the festival activities. "Takes a lot of juggling, I suppose."

He didn't know the half of it. No one really did.

Her chin tilted slightly and she bit the inside of her lip to keep from showing the sudden emotion that engulfed her entire being.

Her first response was to shrink from his scrutiny, paste on a bright face and paint the situation with brightly-colored representations that would build her up in his eyes and make her feel esteemed. But she was too tired, far too vulnerable to pull it off.

Instead, she caved and admitted her struggle. At least in part.

"I—I haven't been sleeping," she confessed, anger continuing to build as her mind rehearsed the past couple of days.

What she didn't say was why—that Mark had hounded her for a period of days with phone calls and texts that she'd allowed to go unanswered. That she'd kept herself behind a locked bedroom door each time he had the nerve to step inside the house he dared to still call their home. That when his pleas outside that door failed to move her to respond, she'd later returned from a planning meeting to find evidence he'd packed and left for Boise after all, just as he said he was going to. He'd left only a simple note on the counter:

I promise it's not what you think.

Ha, wasn't that what the straying husband always claimed? She was not stupid. She saw the texts on his phone from that woman.

Leigh Ann looked over at Thor, remembered the afternoon in his studio—the way he'd acted toward her, flirting even. While flattering, she'd been too focused on reigniting her marriage at the time to give the handsome stranger any consideration.

That was before Mark refused to cooperate and change his mind, before he'd moved ahead with his plan to decimate her life.

Unexpectedly, the stopper that held back her emotions came unplugged. Tears filled her eyes.

She tried to smile, to assure the man standing before her that she was doing fine, but it was too late. Her distress flowed openly.

Thor reached in his back pocket and pulled out a folded napkin. He handed it to her. "You're not a very good liar."

She stood up straight, nodded and wiped her tears.

"Want me to leave you alone?" he offered, no doubt sensing her reluctance to let him see her fall apart.

"No. I want you to invite me to get out of here with you." This time, she managed a weak smile.

Thor hesitated briefly, then finally nodded. "Sure. Let's go."

After letting one of her staff know she'd be gone for a bit, she ignored the confused look on the gal's face and followed Thor to his car, not caring who might see. Or, that the entire festival might leave the tracks without her carefully steering the course of things.

When they arrived at his vehicle, Leigh Ann was surprised to find he drove a vintage red and white Corvette. Today he had the top down on the rare, and expensive convertible.

"Nice," she remarked. "Needles and ink must be lucrative."

He helped her inside. "Pays the power bill," he said, closing the door. He moved to the other side of the car and got in, stopping first to retrieve two cans from a cooler in the trunk.

She couldn't help but notice that he'd freshly showered. She could still smell the soap. It was also impossible not to notice Thor's tightly muscled body beneath the gray t-shirt.

She averted her eyes uneasily, before remembering why she was with him in the first place. She relented and shed her nagging reservations. Instead, she purposely cast a provocative smile in his direction.

"Thirsty?" he asked, handing her a can of beer.

She took the offered drink, wondering if he intended to drive after drinking alcohol—another thought she had to force from her already cluttered mind. His drinking habits were the least dangerous aspect of this whole thing. Somehow, that excited her.

Everyone else got to act crazy on occasion. Why shouldn't she? She was tired of making sense, always doing the right thing. Her whole life she'd acted appropriately. Likely, she was the only girl in all of Sun Valley who'd never had a one-night stand before she married.

Her conscience pricked.

That's a bad thing?

Ha! How would she know? She'd never let herself find out. Now she was getting tossed aside like a half-eaten cookie.

What was that popular quote? What was good for the goose was also good for the gander!

Thor popped the top of his beer, turned up the can and drank deeply of it, then looked around at the crowded parking area, the people mingling in the distance, the full-leafed maple trees silhouetted against a cloudless blue sky. "You gonna drink that?"

She squelched her nerves, nodded and popped her can— tipped it and drank. The ice-cold beer burned on the way down her throat. Even so, the alcohol eased her tension almost immediately.

"Pretty out here, huh?" She casually let her finger glide over his jeans, dangerously close to forbidden territory. It was as if her hand, and her mind, belonged to another. To someone who wasn't a wife, a mother, a pillar of the community. Deep inside, she wished to shed all those well-practiced roles and trade for a carefree identity, even if only for a little while. Maybe then she wouldn't hurt so bad.

She only hoped he wouldn't notice that her hands were trembling.

A small voice inside warned this was a big mistake. It occurred to her she was now trying to do the hurting. But that was stupid. How could she possibly erase her own pain by inflicting the same on—who, Mark?

He was likely in a hotel room in the arms of that woman at this very moment, or would be very soon.

Thor's eyes followed the trail of her fingers. As if he could read her conflicted mind, he clutched her hand before she reached the danger zone. "Your husband know you're here?"

His question was like an electric charge, unexpected and unwelcome. Leigh Ann pulled her hand back from his grasp. She pushed her head back against the leather of the seat and stared up at the sky. "Not sure he'd care if he did."

Thor nearly snorted. He finished his beer and tossed the can. "Hope not. I'm not into getting my ass kicked when he finds out."

Her eyes stung with humiliation. She blinked, biting at her lip. After several long seconds, she dared to look at him.

Thor took her shoulder. "Look, Leigh Ann—don't get me wrong. I want to, but somehow I think you're going to regret this." Then he added, "A life of regret isn't worth living."

At that moment, she heard a noise. The car door flew open and Mark stood there, glaring.

Her husband grabbed Thor's shoulders and yanked him from the seat and onto the ground. She stared open-mouthed as Mark jabbed his finger at the tattoo artist's surprised face.

"You put one more move on my wife, Big Guy, and I'll make you wish *you* weren't living."

32

"Karyn?"

Her former mother-in-law's voice caused her to pull back from Grayson's embrace. "Aggie?"

"What are you doing?" Aggie puffed up, a marshmallow roasted over a hot flame.

Karyn's resolve melted in response. "Uh, I'm not sure." It was a stupid thing to say, she knew.

Grayson blinked and pulled back from her, looking as unsettled as she felt. He quickly discarded his confusion and stepped forward, extended a hand. "I'm Grayson Chandler. Karyn's—uh, I'm Karyn's friend."

Aggie eyed them with suspicion. Her eyebrows came together in a deep frown. "Looks like a bit more than friends," she huffed, tears already pooling.

Bert placed his hand on his wife's shoulder. In an unspoken message, he let his palm remain there as he took Grayson's hand and shook. "I'm Bertrand Macadam. This is my wife, Agatha. We're her in-laws. Actually, former in-laws."

"Dean's parents," Karyn unnecessarily added for clarification, trying to make her voice light. She forced a smile. "Are you enjoying the festival?"

Aggie wasn't having any of it. She wiped at her eyes. "Yes, we were." The past tense remark hung in the air like rotting bananas, so heavy the comment bent her spirit under its weight.

Dean's mother's eyes dropped to her bare ring finger. Anyone standing within fifty feet could hear the air leave her lungs.

Karyn could almost imagine Dean looking down on the scene. No doubt he'd find humor in the situation and chuckle at what he deemed humorous.

But none of this was funny.

She'd been cruel. Unforgivably so.

Dean's dad restrained himself from showing the scar she'd just carved in his heart, while his mother was a bit more candid with the blow she'd suffered. Without meaning to, she'd hurt his parents deeply.

She could just shake herself for the insensitivity she'd shown these people. How could she not have given them a heads up about her decision to begin dating again and allow them to stumble onto their son's wife kissing another man?

"I'm sorry," she said solemnly. And she meant it. "I should have told you."

"Yes, yes—I think you should have." Tears sprouted yet again in Aggie's eyes. "I know you have every right to move on," Dean's mother conceded, her voice trembling. "It's just—well, I —" Her voice faded. She turned to her husband. "Bert, please. Let's just go."

He took his wife's elbow. "I'm sorry. Yes, I think that's best."

Karyn didn't have any option but to watch as her former in-laws walked away and disappeared into the crowd.

Grayson rubbed at the back of his neck. "Well, that was—"

"—awful," she finished, fingering the chain at her neck.

"So, what do you want to do now?"

"I need to—" She looked at him miserably. "Oh, I'm not even sure what I need to do. But I think you'd better take me home. I need to make this up to them. The sooner, the better."

~

GRAYSON LEFT Karyn at her door with a heavy heart. Crestfallen, he dragged himself to his car, pondering all that had just transpired.

Certainly, that was not how he'd imagined their first kiss.

And he hadn't imagined driving Karyn home from their date in near silence.

"Are you mad at me?" he'd finally asked.

She'd let out a tired, grown-up sigh. "Of course not, Grayson. I'm mad at myself."

"I don't get it." He shook his head. "You're trying to be happy again. That's a bad thing?"

That's when she'd looked at him like he had three heads. His only response—the only reaction that wouldn't be open to the possibility for him to step in it further—was to quietly reach across the seat for her hand.

On the way to her front door, he took another chance and turned to her. "Don't be so hard on yourself, Karyn. You're young and life didn't end when your husband died. Surely Dean's parents didn't think you would remain single."

She stared back at him with a blank expression. "I'm not sure you understand."

He moved to her, took her in his arms. She didn't hug him back, but she didn't pull away either. When he let her go, she wiped at her eyes and looked at him. "I'm all they have left, Grayson."

He wasn't sure he agreed with her. While losing a son was

indeed tragic, turning his widow into a human memorial wasn't in anyone's best interest. Most especially hers.

The burden to carry their sorrow didn't rest at Karyn's feet.

He paused, his hand on the car door handle, the occasional trill of wild birds nestled in the rocky bluffs bordering the golf course the only sound to disturb the late-afternoon stillness.

He inhaled fragrant, fresh air and tried to let go of the rigid tension suddenly building between his shoulders, knowing one major question remained.

Would he be enough for her to come to that realization?

33

Joie stood in front of Room 23, staring nervously at the patterned carpet while waiting for the door to open.

Following the bar convention, Andrew elected to stay in Sun Valley for a few days to spend time with her. But that time had come to an end and he would be leaving later tonight.

She'd spent every available moment with him, reconnecting and forging this new relationship. One free of the notion he was married, and the guilt that had choked the life out of their chance at a genuine relationship.

They'd spent nearly all their time within the confines of this room, taking special care not to be seen by Karyn.

While she was anxious to introduce him to her family, she'd been a bit nervous about the notion. They'd have questions, Leigh Ann especially. It was her intent to keep a tight lid on how they'd first connected and the circumstances that initially drove them apart. The judgment would be too much to bear.

That was why, in the end, she'd elected to make a quick solo appearance at the Wine and Arts Festival and wait to introduce

Andrew at a more opportune time, maybe to her dad first and then her sisters.

Sound came from behind the hotel door. A smile slowly pulled at the corners of her lips as she waited for Andrew to unlock the latch.

"Hey, where've you been?" he asked, as he pulled her inside.

She flung her purse on a chair. "I extricated myself as early as possible, but traffic has Sun Valley Road clogged."

He pulled her into his arms and pressed his lips against her own, sending an electric charge pulsing through her body. He smelled of Creed cologne, his signature brand he'd discovered on a trip to Paris.

Trembling, she pushed him back. "If we keep this up, I'm bound to miss Crusty's birthday party."

"And that's a problem?"

She laughed off his comment. "He's one of my dearest friends."

Andrew looked her directly in the eye. "I want to go with you."

"I don't think that's a good idea."

She could sense Andrew's mind at work as he lifted her chin. "We're a real couple now. We no longer have to hide the fact we're in love."

"Easy for you to say," she said, attempting a light-hearted tone. "This is a small town. Besides, I think you'd best meet my family first, don't you?"

"Well in that case—" He tilted his head toward the bed. "I can think of a nice way we can say goodbye. Let's call it a parting gift."

JOIE SHOWED up at Crusty's forty minutes late.

"Hey, Chill—where you been?"

She patted Dick Cloudt on the back as she passed by him on the way to the bar. "Had some business I had to take care of."

She nestled up to the counter next to Terrance where he sat parked on his favorite stool. "Hey, Terrance. Where's the birthday boy?" She looked him up and down, raised her eyebrows. "And what's up with the spiffy clothes, Mr. Cameron? You're looking rather dapper."

The old professor gave her a wide smile and clasped the lapels of a dated tweed suit jacket. "I bring this bad boy out for special occasions."

She nodded her approval. "Well, very nice."

Crusty appeared out of the back room, his hands carrying a large platter piled high with BBQ chicken wings.

Joie moved to join him. He placed the platter on the counter and she gave his bony structure a big hug. "Hey, my friend. Happy birthday."

He hugged her back. "They tell me I'm turning sixty, but I don't feel a day over fifty-nine."

"Well, of course!" She laughed and waved at her skydiving buddies, Phil and Mike.

Crusty grabbed the bar towel he had tucked in the loop of his pants and playfully smacked at her bottom. "Or, maybe thirty-five."

"Hey, now!" she warned, with a big grin. "Hate to pop your birthday balloons, but you best watch yourself, Mister."

If anyone else had tried that trick, she'd have reacted with a bit more reprisal. Today was Crusty's big celebration. Seemed her normally harmless friend had set aside his rule about never drinking while working. She knew alcohol could alter a person's conduct. That earned him a pass.

Besides, she was in a great mood. The weight of guilt had been lifted. She was free to be with Andrew—to have a real relationship without constantly looking over her shoulder to see who was watching.

He would return next weekend and that's when she'd introduce him to her family. She'd let Leigh Ann go all out and cook one of her over-the-top dinners with all those courses that took forever to eat. No doubt their dad would insist on a roasted leg of lamb for the main course, basted with her sister's signature marinate of rosemary, garlic, olive oil and red wine. They'd have Spanish rice made with Basque chorizo, homemade sourdough bread and mashed red potatoes, with gravy made from the meat drippings. Dad would pour his finest red wine and they'd sit around the table, chatting and laughing.

Funny, she'd never expected to imagine herself in such a scene.

Then again, she'd never imagined herself feeling like this, never expected Andrew to show up again—with his masculine elegance and long, lean-muscled body, his cocky confidence and relentless pursuit of her that had barely left her heart intact the first time, let alone now.

She was finally free to come out of the shadows. While she couldn't be open with the entire truth of how their relationship began, she'd simply explain to everyone that she'd connected with a recently divorced partner at her former law firm and had fallen for him.

A satisfied smile took over her expression as she poured herself a glass of beer from the pitcher on the bar.

That's when she noticed Clint leaning against the wall near the pool table, watching her with his arms folded and a slight grin on his face. She headed that way.

"What are you looking at?"

Amused, he pulled a cue from the wall rack. "Not sure what you mean."

She rolled her eyes. Why did her new boss have to be so —smug?

"Never mind. You up for a re-challenge?" Joie nodded toward the pool table.

Clint ran his hand through the top of his careless hair. "You up for getting your butt kicked?"

She grabbed a cue from the wall and chalked the tip. "Not likely. Or did you forget who swept the table last time we played?"

"You might need to work on that lack of confidence." Clint slipped a quarter from his jeans pocket. "Heads, or tails?"

Joie knotted her hair at the nape of her neck. "Goodness, you're almost charming. Heads."

He grinned and flipped the coin. "Heads it is."

"And so the big take-down begins," she taunted, before lining up her shot. She could feel him watching her as she pulled back her cue and cracked the ball, sending the break scattering across the felt-covered table. She straightened with a satisfied look. "Appears I'm stripes," she said over the noise coming from the bar.

Phil and Mike, and the others up at the counter, were playing a rowdy game of quarters, a contest that required bouncing a coin off the table and into a tiny glass. Missing meant downing a shot. None of them were any good at it, which was exactly the point.

She bent over the felt-covered table for her second shot.

"So, how's your new friend?"

Her gaze shot up at him. "What friend?"

He slowly chalked the tip of his cue stick. "That lawyer friend of yours. Andrew, wasn't it?"

Her body stiffened. She rose and spoke with grave deliberation. "Yes, his name is Andrew Merrell. He's a partner at the law firm where I used to work. Not that it's any of your business really. And I'm sure he's back in Boise, because that's where he lives."

"You sure?"

She pulled herself up even straighter and lifted her chin. His arrogance was getting on her nerves. "What do you mean, am I sure?"

He nodded toward the door. "Because I think your attorney friend just showed up."

34

Leigh Ann scrambled from the parked car. "Mark, stop! What are you doing?" she screamed, and raced to where her husband was tumbling on the ground with Thor. She grabbed his arm, trying to pull him back. "Stop!"

With one full-force shove, Thor sent Mark rolling across the grass, circumventing the attack. He stood and held up his hands in surrender. "Hey, man. We're cool."

Leigh Ann quickly positioned herself between them. "Mark, are you crazy?"

Her husband grabbed her arm, still glaring at Thor. "C'mon, Leigh Ann. You're coming with me." He pulled at her, forcing her to follow him.

"Where are we going?" she demanded.

"To put some rumors to bed!"

Leigh Ann glanced over her shoulders. Thor stood smiling after them. He nodded, as if their foray into the forbidden had ended exactly as it should.

She, on the other hand, was furious. And, extremely embarrassed. And, admittedly a little bit thrilled that she'd finally captured her husband's attention—that he'd been that upset to see her with another man.

"Mark, talk to me. Where are we going?"

His grip loosened the tiniest bit. "I took time away from work and came to this whole thing because I want you to meet someone."

Her eyes widened. "Oh no! If you think you are going to parade me in front of your new—"

He stopped and whirled to face her. "My what, Leigh Ann? I keep trying to explain—you're way off base. As usual, you won't listen. You've made up your mind that I'm having some silly—I don't know—affair, or something. Well, I'm not."

He slid a pocket comb from his pants pocket and handed it to her. "You might want to straighten your hair."

She frowned, grabbed the comb and did as suggested before handing it back. "There—better?"

He brushed grass from his pants. "Yes. Now, c'mon." He took her hand, more gently this time, and guided her toward a woman standing at a vendor booth, where she examined a copper sculpture.

Leigh Ann nearly groaned inside as she noted the woman's casual elegance—the way her khaki slacks were carefully creased above loafers that looked as though they'd never before been worn. Her crisp white button-down shirt accentuated the deep red of her thirty-seven-dollar-a-tube lipstick.

The gold hoops dangling at her ears were real gold, she could tell. And her hair—goodness, she'd kill for that hair. The sandy-colored and beautifully highlighted strands fell fortuitously in place just above her shoulders.

The entire look was very Ralph Lauren. Were she and Ralph possibly friends? Because, she looked like someone who would be chummy with the famous designer.

Any man alive and walking would be attracted.

"Mark!" The woman's voice was soft, yet filled with confidence. She leaned and accepted an air kiss on the cheek from Leigh Ann's husband. "There you are!"

Mark characterized the relationship as improvident, but their connection was anything but casual.

"Andrea, I want you to meet my wife." She felt her husband's hand at her back. "Leigh Ann and I have been happily married for—" He looked her way. "How long has it been, Babe?"

"A long time," she parroted, disregarding the urge to comment on the term *happily*. "Nice to meet you, Andrea—what did you say your last name was?" Even the pronunciation of her name was elegant—with an "ah" instead of a typical "a."

She smiled and extended her hand draped with gold bangles. "Andrea DuPont."

Leigh Ann nodded and looked between the two of them, trying to assess what was really going on here. Were these two trying to pull something over on her? Or, was Mark indeed being candid when he assured her they were not at all romantically involved?

It was worth noting that Mark had failed to even mention his association with this woman until after Leigh Ann learned about her while in the grocery aisle. If it weren't for the Dilworth sisters, she might have still remained in the dark.

"Leigh Ann, in some ways, I feel like we're already friends."

Oh, she's good. Now *they* were friends as well. Just like that.

Leigh Ann cleared her throat, seeing an opportunity to learn more, and she took it. "I don't think Mark mentioned how the two of you met?"

"Andrea and I are business associates, Leigh Ann." His words were a bit clipped, reiterating he'd disclosed the fact earlier, without actually saying so.

She forced a cordial response. "Oh yes, that's right. I believe you mentioned that."

"We're working on a project," Mark added. He took her

elbow and motioned for Andrea to follow as he maneuvered them to a spot out of earshot of the crowd. He never liked talking about his business ventures in public until it was time to begin promotion.

This moved her to consider the two of them might be telling the truth. If so, she'd been acting like a complete idiot.

Of course, in some ways she'd been set up to believe the worst. Mark had been moody and terribly preoccupied. That, coupled with the rumors, and well, she'd jumped to conclusions that were understandable.

To her credit, this time he'd taken concealing his business concerns too far. She was his wife, for goodness sake.

As if reading her mind, Andrea straightened her tortoise-shell eyeglasses and stepped forward to explain. "I'm president of Equity Capital Group, a finance conglomerate headquartered in San Francisco. My company has partnered with your husband to make a very lucrative acquisition."

Mark and Andrea exchanged glances. She remembered the text then, the cryptic message that had sent her imagination into orbit, the one about not wanting to raise suspicion. She scowled at her husband. "What property are you looking to—"

His phone buzzed and he looked down, raised his forefinger. "I've got to take this." He glanced over at Andrea. "It's the appraisers."

She nodded, looking like she never felt pressure.

While Mark turned away to take the call, Leigh Ann folded her arms across her chest and posed her question again, this time to Andrea. Leigh Ann's hand casually rubbed at her chest. "What is this business venture?"

She noticed for the first time Andrea was a bit older than she'd first realized, evidenced by tiny signs at the corners of her eyes and mouth that expensive face treatments had failed to erase.

Before Andrea had a chance to respond, Mark clicked off

his phone. "Good news. The values are right in line with what we'd hoped."

Andrea clasped her manicured hands and broke into a smile. "That's wonderful."

Leigh Ann looked at her husband, her mouth agape as understanding dawned. "Mark, it's time to come clean. Are you the developer for the Triumph project? The enterprise everyone in town is flapping about?" She actually sighed out loud. "Is that why you've been so secretive?"

He pocketed his phone. "No, you know there's a building moratorium up at the mining site."

"Well, then what is this about?"

Mark looked to Andrea and nodded. She smiled before answering. "This should answer your questions." She handed over her own phone, which was opened to an email. "It's all there."

Leigh Ann took the phone and quickly read the email. She let out a mighty sigh, puzzled. "You're buying stock in Preston, USA? I don't understand."

They both turned to her, just in time to notice Ruby Dilworth standing only feet away. Andrea's smile disappeared. Mark's eyes went wide.

Ruby's own expression nearly glittered. Without a word, she whipped around and moved as fast as she could. Toward the exit.

35

Morning sun broke unusually warm over the mountain peaks surrounding Sun Valley, sending the late June morning temperature soaring, while at the same time ominous black thunderclouds rumbled in the distance to the north. The contradictory weather front left everyone edgy, tense, waiting for the storm to hit.

Leigh Ann's emotions were especially strained as she raced across the church parking lot.

It wasn't like her to be late to services, but she hadn't gotten to bed until hours after midnight. Her duties at the Wine and Arts Festival had eliminated any possibility to talk privately with Mark. She'd arrived home still reeling with the information she'd learned and had woken him up from a deep sleep.

"Mark, we need to talk."

Her husband lifted his head from the pillow, his eyelids drooping sleepily. "Leigh Ann, I'm sleeping. Can't this wait until morning?"

She'd thrust a steaming cup of coffee his way and told him to get up. "No, sir. You have some explaining to do."

He groaned. "I already told you everything."

"How much have we invested?" she demanded. Normally, she didn't get mixed up in Mark's business dealings. He'd always provided for them in a more-than-ample manner. But something in his eyes—the way he'd exchanged glances with his new business partner, that Andrea DuPont woman—sent her antennae up. And then there was that declined credit card. She needed to understand more.

Reluctantly, Mark rose from their bed. He rubbed at his neck and yawned before donning his monogrammed robe, the one she'd gotten him for Christmas last year. No doubt he wanted to remain in bed, but knew she was like a dog with a bone and wouldn't quit chewing away at him until he gave in and told her what she wanted to know.

In a discussion over the kitchen table, she learned Preston USA had fallen into a slump over the past five years or so. Stock prices had been dropping and the shareholders were unhappy. They'd threatened to oust the Chairman of the Board, a fellow named Paul Preston who was the grandson of the founder.

Back in the fifties, the elder Mr. Preston invented a ski pole made of aluminum, which became in high demand and sent the success of the company soaring. On the basis of this success, the company expanded to include many kinds of sporting goods and moved the headquarters to Sun Valley.

Preston USA was the second largest employer in the area following closely behind Sun Valley Company, which owned the ski resort, the Sun Valley Lodge and many ancillary enterprises.

Leigh Ann rubbed at her temples. "I guess I'm surprised is all. Your focus has always been real estate. Why something like this? And why would you buy into a company where the stock prices are falling? That makes no sense."

He stood and placed his empty cup in the sink. "It's complex, but you're going to have to trust me on this." He turned to her, seeking support. "We're positioned to leverage our investment in a mighty way. This is our chance, Leigh Ann."

"Our chance?"

"To be rich—not just well off, but to file our financial statements in the same drawer as—I dunno, maybe even someone like Rupert Murdock, or Jeff Bezos."

She looked at him like he was crazy. "Earth to Mark Blackburn. Could you bring your satellite back down to reality a bit? You're insane to believe I'd want to ever be in the same financial sphere as the founder of Amazon, for goodness sakes!"

He rushed to where she sat and knelt, folded her hands into his own. "You think that now, but consider that Colby will marry and start a family soon. He'll have children and we'll be able to leave our grandchildren a legacy few ever know."

He gave her hands a reassuring squeeze. "Things will be a little tight until we get this deal put to bed. I've had to leverage our assets pretty heavily to pull this off. Oh, but Babe. This is a deal of a lifetime."

Leigh Ann climbed the church steps and pulled on the heavy wooden church door. Before entering, she glanced back at the approaching dark sky. Thunder boomed in the distance.

In the end, she'd done exactly what any good wife would do —especially one who had nearly toppled into forbidden territory because she'd jumped to wrong conclusions—she gave in and joined in his enthusiasm, with one slight reservation. "Just so you know. No matter how much money you pile in our accounts, I still plan to do my own yard work."

KARYN TURNED and surveyed the people spilling into the sanctuary. It was typical for Joie to slide into the pew minutes before the service started, but she couldn't remember the last time Leigh Ann had been this late.

Her dad patted her knee. "Quit worrying. Your sisters will be here."

She straightened. "I'm not worried."

His eyebrows lifted. "Oh? Is that why you keep watching the back of the church?"

The first strains of music started playing. She reached for her hymnal. "Okay, busted. Maybe Leigh Ann decided to sleep in, which would be completely understandable. She certainly had a big day yesterday."

Or, perhaps the situation with Mark had blown up.

Her dad grinned and stood as the worship minister took his place at the front of the church. "Sis sure can pull off those big events. She makes juggling all that work look so easy. I know I had a good time. Even bought a hand woven rug for my office." He opened his own hymnal, his eyes twinkling as he leaned and lowered his voice. "I take it you had a good time with your friend, Grayson?"

She gave him a less than committed answer in the affirmative. Not exactly as enthusiastic as he'd expected, she could tell —but she'd barely sorted out the events of yesterday enough to understand her feelings, let alone explain her conflicted emotions to someone else. Especially to her father, who was a master at detecting imitation sentiment offered in place of authentic emotion.

No doubt, she could easily close her eyes and get lost in the memory of that kiss—the way Grayson's lips felt against her own. The little thrill she'd felt in the pit of her belly, the dawning of a hope she thought she'd buried forever, along with her dreams the day Dean died.

Yet, the betrayal in Dean's parents' eyes caused her to have doubts. Maybe she was moving a little too fast.

His dad's eyes turned thoughtful as he looked her way. He leaned and whispered, "It's okay to love again. You know that, right?" He wrapped his arm around her shoulder and gave a squeeze.

She nodded, even if a bit weakly. She had a lot to sort out, and none of it would be easy.

"Excuse me. I'm sorry." Leigh Ann jostled past people sitting at the end of the pew, making her way toward them. When she reached the spot where she normally sat, Karyn leaned and whispered, "Where've you been? Everything okay?"

Leigh Ann nodded. "Everything's fine. Sorry I'm late."

Karyn shared her hymnal with her sister and joined the congregation singing, when another noise caught her attention. She turned and quickly elbowed her older sister. "Who is that?"

With a frown, Leigh Ann shook her head and whispered, "I don't know."

They both watched as Joie made her way up the aisle with a dark-haired man wearing a suit and a confident smile.

36

Along with the arriving storm outside Grace Chapel, Joie's heart thundered inside her chest as she made her way through the doors and up the aisle. People stared as she made her way forward, her hand clutching Andrew's as she bravely slipped into the pew next to her family.

Above the strains of music, she leaned over and whispered, "Hey, sorry I'm late. This is my friend, Andrew."

She steeled herself against what she saw in their eyes, knowing she'd just poked a beehive of inquiry. No doubt her family, and many of the people sitting in this church, were buzzing with questions.

Leigh Ann and Karyn were so caught off guard they failed to hold onto the hymnal they shared and it dropped to the floor. They simultaneously bent to pick it up, butting heads like in some lame television comedy.

"Ouch!" Leigh Ann rubbed at her forehead.

"Sorry," Karyn apologized and grabbed the hard-backed volume off the floor, with its worn spine now worse off.

"Shhh..." their dad muttered, like when they were much younger and got caught talking in church. That didn't negate the fact he couldn't quit staring at the man next to her, his eyes wide with surprise.

Trudy Dilworth pointed and leaned to whisper in her sister, Ruby's ear. And despite her severe cataracts, old Mrs. Carter stared at them from across the aisle with a bit more intensity than seemed necessary. Even Father John appeared a bit bewildered as he moved to the podium.

And that was that. Typical.

Their reaction was not a surprise, really—and no less shocking than Andrew standing in the doorway at Crusty's yesterday.

Seeing him poised there grinning, she'd handed her pool cue off to Clint and made her way to the door. "Andrew, what are you doing here?"

He looked like a little boy caught dangling a pole in his neighbor's fish tank. "Sorry, I texted but you didn't answer."

"I don't understand—"

"After we said goodbye and you left, the notion dawned on me that I don't know any of your friends." He gave a pointed look in Clint's direction.

"So you thought you'd just show up?"

He kissed the top of her head. "Forgive me?"

Did she have a choice? The damage was done. Not that she particularly cared what others thought. She simply wanted to introduce him to her family first, like planned.

She shrugged. "Well, let's get you a beer." She took his arm and pulled him toward the bar. "Hey everybody, I'd like you to meet a friend. This is Andrew Merrill. We worked together when I lived in Boise." The remark danced dangerously close to another truth she wanted to keep tucked safely away, but there wasn't a room big enough to hold all their baggage. Better off to unpack a bit and get in front of any questions.

Crusty quickly extended a hand across the bar. "Well, any friend of Joie's is a friend of mine."

Terrance Cameron laid his pipe in the ashtray before him. "In poverty and other misfortunes of life, true friends are a sure refuge. The young they keep out of mischief; to the old they are a comfort and aid in their weakness, and those in the prime of life they incite to noble deeds." He nodded with satisfaction as he shook hands with Andrew. "Aristotle."

Mike drained his beer mug and hollered over at Crusty. "Get this man a beer and put it on my tab."

Crusty grabbed a frosted mug from the mini-fridge behind the bar.

"Uh, could you make that a gin martini? Up and shaken. Dirty with two olives." He reached for his wallet. "And I'm paying. In fact, I hear we're celebrating a birthday, so get the house a round. On me."

Joie knew the gesture was meant to be generous, but she caught the look on Mike's face. One that told her he didn't really care for her new guy and his grandstanding. She'd remember to gently explain the bar etiquette at Crusty's to Andrew later.

Out of the corner of her eye, she noticed Clint leaning against the wall watching with interest. She shrugged off his scrutiny and decided to challenge his unwarranted judgment directly. "C'mon Andrew, there's someone else I want to introduce you to."

She grabbed his hand and he followed her, martini in hand.

"Clint, this is Andrew Merrill. Andrew, Clint manages the stables where I work."

A sly smile nipped at the corners of Clint's mouth as he leaned against the pool table and crossed his arms. "Yeah, we've met. Andy came by the stables looking for you."

Joie let out a nervous laugh. "Oh, yes. That's right."

"Andrew." Her companion stared down Clint's amused gaze. "The name is Andrew."

"Andrew. Got it." Clint lifted from the table and waved at Crusty. "Next round's on me."

Joie stared between the two men, realizing with surprise that she'd made a grave mistake. Normally, Andrew was a complete charmer. But right now, it was as if she were a fire hydrant standing between two dogs marking their territory.

To end their pissing match and avoid potential battle, she took Andrew's arm. "Look, we gotta go." She hurried over and gave Crusty a hug. "Happy birthday, buddy."

"You're not leaving so soon?"

Ignoring the hurt on her old friend's face, she tried to explain. "I hate to take off, but some unexpected things came up. And—well, you understand."

The sage bartender nodded and gave her a kiss on the cheek. "Sure. I know how things go sometimes."

As soon as they were out the door, she whirled to face Andrew on the sidewalk. "What was all that?"

He feigned confusion. "What do you mean?"

"That." She pointed to the door.

"I don't like that guy."

"Apparently not." She dug in her purse for her keys. "Like it or not, he's my boss. You just placed me in a very uncomfortable situation."

Andrew reached for her. "Oh, baby. I'm sorry. But trust me when I say that guy's got an agenda." When he saw the look on her face, he quickly added, "Look, let me make it up to you."

"I thought you had to get back to Boise."

"I decided to stay over and head back tomorrow. Can you blame me for wanting one more night with you?" He traced his finger along her jawline.

Her irritation melted. "Well, that may well be, but your little change of mind just fanned a rumor that will spread faster than a fire in the Sawtooth National Forest. There's no choice now but for you to meet my family before they hear." At the car, she turned to him. "We're going to church in the morning," she announced.

Andrew scowled. "Church?"

"Yes, because God help us if Leigh Ann first learns about our relationship from the Dilworth sisters."

37

Karyn poured a cup of coffee from the silver urn on the banquette in the conference room and took her place at the table. Before her was a stack of financials for last month.

Jon Sebring, the resort director, cleared his throat. "Okay, let's get started everyone. As you know, we've had a busy June." He turned to Karyn. "Second quarter P&Ls are strong which reflects the hard work of you and the lodge staff. The bar association convention proved to be very lucrative."

"Thank you, Jon." She smiled. They'd successfully dodged a bullet with that leak in the kitchen.

"We're now heading into the height of our summer season," he continued. "We're fully booked at both the lodge and the inn over the Fourth of July holiday and the weeks following. Even the condos have completely sold out, thanks to the headliners scheduled for the upcoming ice show."

Over the next hour, Jon went through his agenda items. When they adjourned, Karyn headed back to her office. Her cell phone was filled with messages, including voicemails left by Grayson and Leigh Ann.

She clicked through until she heard Grayson's voice. "Hey, Karyn. Sorry I missed you. I'm still up at Stanley until tomorrow with the group conducting the salmon supplementary study. Right now, I'm expecting to be home late afternoon. Let's do dinner." There was a long pause. "I—I miss you."

Karyn held the phone to her ear several seconds without moving. Not knowing what to think, she drew a deep breath before clicking off the phone and laying it down on her desk.

She missed him too. Terribly. Which is why she had to get the situation with Dean's parents sorted out as quickly as possible. She'd handled this entire dating thing badly and needed to set things right for everyone concerned.

Her office phone rang, pulling her from her thoughts. She reached and picked up. "Karyn, here."

"Hey, Karyn—it's Melissa at the front desk. Your sister's on the line—Leigh Ann. She sounded a bit anxious."

Karyn scowled, thanked her and pressed the call button on her phone. "Leigh Ann?"

"Oh, thank goodness! Where have you been? I've left messages."

"I know. I've been in a meeting and just got back to my desk."

"Well, we need to talk. You gave no clue what you thought of Joie's new friend at Daddy's last night. He's definitely a player, don't you think?"

"Oh, I don't know. I thought he was nice."

"Nice?" Leigh Ann paused briefly. "Well, I suppose so. Of course, a good litigator has to develop a certain skill set to be successful. I bet he's good at influencing a jury. Still, I can't imagine our Joie falling for a suit. I always expected she'd tumble for a flannel. Someone like that boss of hers."

Karyn leaned back in her chair and swiveled so she could enjoy the view out the window. "Joie's a big girl. She's perfectly capable of choosing a boyfriend."

Her sister huffed. "I'm not so sure. Something tells me this guy is more than a boyfriend. I think she's serious about this Andrew—what was his last name?"

"Merrill."

"Merrill. Yes, that's right. Mark my words—these two are getting serious." She let out a chuckle. "But they're sure cute together, don't you think? Ha—Joie is in love with a lawyer—and a partner at that. Maybe she'll decide to practice again. Oh, wouldn't that be wonderful? She has so much potential."

"So, you really think they are that serious?"

"Of course! She brought him to church, didn't she?"

Her sister definitely had a point, but as interesting as she found this conversation, time was ticking and she had a lot to get done today. "Leigh Ann, can we talk about this later? I'm at work right now."

"Oh, that's right. Sorry. Oh, I know—why don't you meet me at the Sun Valley Club when you get off work? It's been forever since we've played Trail Creek."

"Okay, but I'll have to run home for my clubs. Make it four-thirty."

"Great! See you then."

Minutes after hanging up, Joie called. "Hey, Sis. Got a minute?"

Karyn glanced at the wall clock. "A very short one."

"What did you think of him?"

"Of Andrew?" This is a bit out-of-character for Joie, openly asking others to weigh in on her choices. Especially any decision related to her love life.

"Yeah. Do you think Dad liked him?"

Karyn fought back a tiny grin. "We all thought he was—very attentive. Obviously, he's smitten with you."

Her little sister laughed. "*Smitten?* You watch far too many Hallmark movies. C'mon, what did you really think?"

Karyn weighed her words carefully. "I liked him—truly. We're just a little surprised—"

"We? You and Leigh Ann have been discussing me?"

"Oh course we discussed you," she responded. "It's what we do."

She knew Joie was rolling her eyes at that. It didn't matter. Think what she may, her little sister was well aware they'd formed a clique long ago, forged out of long nights too numerous to count, all filled with gossiping and giggling—the three of them tightly bound as though knitted together with unseen but indestructible threads.

While their temperments varied as widely as the slope ratings on Baldy, she and her sisters had each other's backs. Always.

"Joie, I'm a bit surprised. You don't often care what others think."

There was a pause on the other end of the line. "I— Andrew's different."

The admission took Karyn aback. "This is a new color for you—vulnerable."

"Well, take a picture because you're not likely going to see this shade again any time soon."

The retort made Karyn chuckle. Now, this was Joie. "Okay. Well, here's the thing little sister—despite that brave sass of yours, and the crazy ways you try to shelter yourself from pain, I think you're a very smart and thoughtful woman who understands there are no guarantees in matters of the heart. So, if you think this Andrew guy is possibly the one—go for it. It's a rare mistake that can't be reversed."

"Now you sound just like Dad. Seriously though, while I wish a few chapters in my life hadn't been published, I'm still hoping for a happy ending."

"You'll get one," Karyn assured. "I promise."

"Hey, Karyn?"

"Yeah?"

"I love you."

She smiled. "I know."

It wasn't until she got off the phone with Joie that she realized her sage words were not only meant for her sister, but could've been her sub-conscience trying to also bolster her own morale.

She had to find a way to move bravely ahead with her relationship with Grayson, but without stepping on the feelings of Dean's parents. With any luck at all, she'd figure out how to maneuver this mess and get her own happily ever after.

"Where have you been?" Leigh Ann demanded, moving toward Karyn as she entered the clubhouse.

"Sorry I'm late," she offered, with an apologetic shrug. "My afternoon completely got away with me. I'd no more got off the phone with you and Joie called, which put me late and then—"

"Joie called you?" Distracted, Leigh Ann waved over the caddy. "I've already got us a cart." She turned to the caddy. "Can you get my sister's clubs from her car and we'll meet you at the first tee box?"

Karyn handed over her car keys to the young kid and followed her sister across the plush carpet.

"What did Joie want?"

Karyn waved to a guest she'd seen at the lodge earlier. "She wondered what we thought of Andrew."

Leigh Ann raised her eyebrows. "That doesn't sound like Joie. What did you tell her?"

"I told her our opinions didn't matter really, that only she would know if this guy is worth getting serious about."

"Well, that's silly!" She waved for Karyn to follow as she ducked into the pro shop. "Do you have enough extra balls?"

"Yeah."

"How about tees?"

"Got it covered."

"Well, at least grab some bottles of water."

Karyn dutifully opened the cooler door and retrieved several bottles. "Do we need a cooler?"

Leigh Ann shook her head. "I don't think so. We can always have more delivered out to us."

Minutes later, they teed off. Leigh Ann hit a beautiful shot straight down the fairway, landing only feet from the green. Karyn didn't hit as far, but still landed a nice shot.

They climbed into the golf cart, Leigh Ann on the driver's side. She turned to Karyn. "So, did you find out exactly how they met?"

"Who?"

Her sister rolled her eyes. "Joie and Andrew. How did they meet? Did they know each other at the law firm? I mean, I'm sure they did if Andrew was a partner."

Karyn pulled on her glove and fastened the snap at the wrist. "We didn't exactly play twenty questions."

"I know, but—well, even though she has a law degree, her poor choices created one big mistrial—know what I mean?"

She shrugged. "In some ways, maybe. But Joie is smarter than you give her credit for being."

Leigh Ann parked the cart and climbed out. She grabbed her nine iron from her bag at the back. "And, what about you?"

Karyn climbed from the cart and surveyed the distance to the green. "What do you mean?"

"How are things between you and Grayson?"

"Fine," she answered, a little too quickly. She retrieved her water bottle, unscrewed the cap and took a swig. "Look, there's a deer!" She pointed to a doe standing on the edge of the fairway, near a stand of pines and quaking aspen trees.

Leigh Ann walked toward her ball, calling back over her shoulder. "That's it? Fine?"

Her sister's voice startled the deer, sending it splashing through the creek bed before it vaulted up the opposite hillside.

"You scared Bambi," Karyn scolded, watching the delicate-legged animal sprint up the opposite hillside and over the sagebrush-covered crest. When the deer was no longer in sight, she turned back to her sister. "To answer your question—yes, we're fine." And then, purposely changing the subject, "I've noticed you've been silent on the situation with Mark. But you're smiling again. I take it the hair, the tat, and uh, everything—it worked?"

"I learned my husband wasn't having an affair."

"I think I told you that."

Leigh Ann looked at her like she had two heads. "If I remember correctly, you told me to kick him out!"

"I did not," she argued. "I said *if* he was having an affair, you needed to kick him out. Besides, you weren't exactly looking to follow any advice I might offer. Your feet were cemented in the whole strategy of winning him back thing."

Leigh Ann lined up for her shot with determination. "Well, he wasn't having an affair."

"So, what was that text all about?"

Leigh Ann swung, lobbing the ball in the air. She shaded her eyes and watched as it landed on the edge of the green. "Her name is Andrea DuPont. She's Mark's new business partner."

"Business partner?" Karyn walked the few paces to her own ball, eyed the shot.

Her sister followed her. "Yes, some big venture they're trying to pull off."

Karyn lined up, pulled her club back and swung through, sending her ball into a perfect arc onto the green, just inches from the flag. She pulled her arm in a victory pump. "Yes!"

"Nice one."

Karyn responded with a wide grin. She tucked her club under her arm and followed Leigh Ann to the green. "So, is this the Preston USA deal?

Her sister's expression turned to shock. "How did you know?"

Karyn and Leigh Ann stared at each other, nodded and said in unison, "The Dilworth sisters."

38

Karyn stood before massive wooden doors, flanked with terracotta pots of various sizes, some with bright pink geraniums and blue lobelia, others filled with yellow and orange cosmos and miniature daisies.

Dean's mother loved flowers, hence the bouquet Karyn held in her hand—sweet peas tied with raffia, her former mother-in-law's favorite. She clasped the peace offering tightly and reached for the doorbell, hoping for the best.

Why was she so nervous?

True, these familial lines sometimes blurred after the death of a spouse, with no clear definition of what was expected. Even bloggers couldn't agree. She'd checked. But even though Dean was gone, the Macadams were still family. Weren't they?

She lifted her finger to the button, only to let it drop to her side yet again. She stared at her floral apology.

Maybe she was making a mistake. Showing up unannounced was a bad idea. She should have called first.

Before she could collect her nerves, the door suddenly opened, startling her. She jumped back.

Dean's father's eyes widened. "Karyn? What are you doing here?" He glanced up and down the street.

"I—I'm sorry. You look like you're expecting someone," she stammered. "I should have called first."

"Nonsense. I heard a noise and thought you were the lawn guy, that's all." Bert stepped back and motioned her inside. "Come in."

"Bert? Who is it?" Aggie called.

"It's Karyn, dear," he answered.

"Oh." The frosty word chilled the room as Aggie entered the foyer.

Karyn displayed her warmest smile. "I hope I'm not interrupting your plans or anything." She remembered the flowers and offered them. "I saw these pretty sweet peas at the farmer's market this morning and thought you'd like them."

Aggie took her peace offering, buried her nose in the blossoms. "Ah, they remind me of your wedding." She turned to her husband. "Do you remember all the table vases we filled with sweet peas?"

Bert nodded and placed his arm around his wife's shoulders.

Karyn stared at the large wedding portrait displayed prominently over the Macadam's fireplace. She cleared her throat. "Yes, I remember too. They were lovely."

"Are you hungry?" Bert asked. "We were just about to sit down to brunch."

"I made eggs benedict." Aggie added, her face still creased with distrust.

Without his mother needing to say so, Karyn knew the dish was Dean's favorite breakfast. "Thank you. I'd like that."

She followed the older couple to a table that looked like something plucked from a Williams Sonoma catalog. A pretty blue and white checked tablecloth with light yellow napkins flanking white plates and stemmed goblets filled with orange juice, no doubt freshly squeezed.

As they took their places, Aggie retrieved the vase from the center of the table, replaced the single white daisy with the sweet peas. Her expression softened the tiniest bit. "These are lovely."

Karyn wasn't the first woman to make the mistake of falling short of her in-law's expectations, but not many failed as spectacularly as she had. She double-downed on her effort to repair the damage their relationship had suffered. "I'm so very glad you like them, Aggie. And your table is lovely. You have such pretty things."

After a momentary, yet uncomfortable silence, a weak smile finally stretched across Dean's mother's face. "Thank you, dear." Just as quickly, her smile evaporated. "We'd hoped all this would be yours someday."

She looked like she wanted to say more but her eyes turned wistful. She coughed like a fish bone was stuck in her throat and quickly turned for the kitchen, returning with a tray of fruit compote in petite glass dishes with long-handled silver spoons.

Bert tried to break the tension with small talk. "So, how's your job going? Do you like—uh, working?"

Dean's dad was trying to be pleasant. The Macadams weren't the sort of people to work for someone else.

Karyn struggled through another awkward silence, her mind battling for something to say, something chatty and light. "Oh, yes. I wasn't sure about making such a drastic move into the work force like that. Of course, sitting in the house alone every day wasn't doing me any good." She smiled a big honeyed smile for good measure and enthusiastically scooped a bite of melon and placed it in her mouth.

Aggie grasped her own spoon with rigid measure and lifted

a diced peach toward her mouth, pausing half way. "These past months have been extremely hard on all of us."

Bert dabbed his linen napkin at the corner of his mouth. "Yes, I think losing Dean put all of us a bit off kilter."

Dean's mother gave her husband a pointed look. "We never expected to bury our child—our only son. Now—well, now it's as if we're losing you too." Her eyes suddenly filled with watery emotion.

Karyn's heart stilled.

Not for the first time, she wished Dean were still alive. She wished he hadn't clamped those skis on his feet that day. Wished he hadn't ridden the chairlift up to his favorite run—a gnarly Super G course that spit out any skier who failed to negotiate the steep pitch onto Greyhawk. She wished that call had never come—the one she'd never even known to dread.

She swallowed and reached for her former mother-in-law's hand. "You'll never lose me," she tried to assure. "We'll always be linked by our love of Dean."

Aggie vehemently shook her head. "That may be true at some level. But you're moving on. You've already met someone —and kept it from us."

"I shouldn't have," Karyn admitted. "I just didn't know how to—"

"Be glad you're so young, that you can replace Dean and marry again, have babies."

Karyn couldn't believe what she was hearing. "I—I'm not *replacing* Dean. I'm—oh, it's so hard to explain." She placed her spoon on the table and nervously fidgeted with her wedding ring.

Bert weighed in, his eyes deeply saddened. "We love you, dear. You're the only family we have left. We certainly want you happy." He let out a heavy sigh. "You have to understand how hard it is for us to see you go."

Karyn wanted to scream, "*I'm not going anywhere!*" At the same time, she knew there was little she was going to be able to say to change how they felt. At some deep level, she even understood.

At times, the sounds of mourning still echoed in her mind. The heaving sobs from Dean's mother. His father crying out to the hospital workers blocking his path as he tried to follow the gurney, "That's my son . . . my boy." Her own keening wail when together they learned the news that changed them all forever.

They had wept, together and alone.

Despite having little else in common, she and Dean's parents were woven tightly by profound loss.

An unwanted lump formed in her throat.

Would the Macadams even be her in-laws anymore if she married someone else? I mean, how did all that work anyway?

Yes, she wanted to fall in love again—longed to be happy. But not at Bert and Aggie's expense.

She'd just have to find a way to assure Dean's parents they would remain in her heart and in her life no matter what the future held.

39

The week leading up to the Fourth of July was always one of the busiest times of the summer for Sun Valley Company and its employees. All the accommodations in the area were booked—the Sun Valley Lodge, The Inn, and all the company-owned condominiums, as was most of the other lodging in the area.

Sun Valley Stables was experiencing a similar overload.

"What do you mean you accidently overbooked the nine o'clock?" Chelsea Rae huffed. Joie's co-worker knotted her hair into a bun at her neck before slipping her cowboy hat in place.

From behind the counter, Patty drew herself upright, her spine stiffening. "I can assure you, I didn't put too many guests in the schedule on purpose."

Joie didn't do workplace politics. She'd either pop off with a snarky comment meant to shut the tension down, or she'd simply leave these two to their catfight and head out to the arena to start saddling up the horses.

This morning, she was in a good mood and granted them a measure of patience. "There's an obvious solution," she offered, slipping her hat into place. "Move someone to a later time."

Patty's eyes filled with panic. "Move them where? The slots are all full—the nine, eleven, one, two-thirty and even the four o'clock."

Chelsea Rae unwrapped a stick of gum and put it in her mouth. "Well, figure something out. There's only so many horses and so many guides."

Outside, the parking lot was already beginning to fill with their first riders of the day. Joie pulled her hat low on her forehead. "See if you can move someone to five-thirty. I'll take them out."

Andrew was due to arrive to spend the holiday with her, but he had a hearing scheduled and wouldn't be here until late this evening. She could either sit at home and watch the clock, or stay busy.

"I—I don't' know. Wouldn't Clint have to clear that first?"

"Patty," Joie repeated the girl's name slowly, now rummaging for patience. "This is a wild guess, but I doubt Clint can come up with a better idea."

Chelsea Rae coughed. "Uh—hashtag awkward," she said, pointing.

Joie turned to find Clint approaching the soda machine, an amused smile nipping at the corners of his mouth. Without a word, he slipped a coin into the slot then pressed a button sending a can clanking to the bottom.

She met his gaze. "What?"

"I didn't say anything." He bent and retrieved his Dr. Pepper from behind the clear plastic trapdoor. Still grinning, he opened the tab on the top of the can.

"I offered a fix. What more do you want? I could light up sparklers and jump up and down, but I'm fresh out." She wanted to look away, but she couldn't make herself move.

"I'm a little surprised you're offering to stay late, that's all. It's Friday night. I figured Barbie might be anxious to see Ken."

He smirked. "I suspect he's coming to town for the weekend. Am I right?"

Patty looked completely puzzled. "Who's Ken and Barbie?" She glanced at her schedule. "I don't think we have anyone by that name."

Joie's insides tightened. Unwilling to give in to his judgment, she flipped and headed for the door. "Just let me know what you want to do."

Outside, she tilted her face to the early morning dawn and tried to shake Clint Ladner's attitude toward her, which was one of amusement more than respect—a plight that irritated her more than she wanted to admit.

She tried to imagine why she even cared, when her phone buzzed in her pocket. She fished it out, delighted to see a text from Andrew.

"Hey, babe. My hearing got set over until next week so I'll be heading out early. I booked a room at the lodge and should be in town by early afternoon. Would've stayed at your house, but thought we might get a little noisy. We don't want to wake any coyotes."

A slow smile stretched across her face. She blushed as her fingers worked the keyboard. *"Why sir! I have no idea what you are talking about."*

His response came quickly. *"LOL! You know exactly what I'm suggesting."*

Her fingers tapped across the screen. *"Okay, we'll give the coyotes a pass. But I'm afraid I just agreed to work late. See you about eight?"*

Andrew texted he would order room service so they wouldn't have to bother with going out. In fact, he suggested they might not get dressed the entire holiday. There would be plenty of fireworks right in their room. Then he added, *"I love you."*

Joie stared at those words, finding it hard to breathe. The

sentiment had been a long time coming, given all the obstacles they'd faced. Smiling to herself, she realized there were more important things than having to breathe and typed out her response— words that, for the first time in her life, came out effortlessly. *"I love you too."*

She walked toward the horse pen basking in the elation of the moment.

Since reconciling with Andrew, her life had taken a seismic shift. Like a schoolgirl, she read his flood of texts, waited for his calls and flushed with excitement every time the phone rang. All he had to do was say her name and she'd get a buzzy feeling in her gut.

Joie pocketed her phone, not bothering to hide the silly grin on her face.

That's when she noticed Clint standing only feet away.

She gave him a dirty look.

Her boss held his hands up in surrender, his eyes sparkling with amusement. "Sorry. Didn't mean to interrupt."

She rounded on him and went for the bridle, making a show of rolling her eyes. "What do you need?"

He withdrew a folded envelop from his shirt pocket and offered it. "Your paycheck," he explained. "You ran out of the office before I had a chance to give it to you."

She took a couple of tentative steps in his direction, shifted the bridle over her arm and took the envelope. "Thanks."

He grew serious. "Hey, honestly. I can take that last ride if you need me to. Especially if you have someplace else you need to be."

Joie hesitated. Not even more time with Andrew could make her fold to that smug look on his face. "No, that's okay. I got it."

He shrugged. "Have it your way."

By the end of the day, she stood in the doorway of the tack barn waiting for the final guest to show almost wishing she'd swallowed her pride and accepted Clint's offer. Especially when she sifted through the texts that had come in from Andrew while she was up on the trail.

He'd hit a lot of traffic coming into town, what with the holiday crowd and all. But he'd arrived at the lodge and had a bottle of champagne chilling in a bucket of ice. Their room had a balcony overlooking the ice rink and the firework show. And, one final message: "*Hurry and get here!*"

She checked her watch, wishing she could.

Where was—she checked the schedule attached to the clipboard hanging on a nail—uh, Maddy Crane. A solo.

Wait—she knew that name.

Maddy Crane? *The* Maddy Crane?

At that moment, a baby blue vintage convertible—a Jaguar perhaps?—pulled into the yard. The driver waved and climbed out.

The petite woman unwrapped the scarf from her head. She wore patterned jeans and a ruffled white blouse, with turquoise-colored boots that perfectly matched the shade of chunky jewelry at her collar and wrist. She slipped designer sunglasses from her face and tucked them up in her blonde hair, which was pulled back into a fancy knot at the nape of her neck and headed over.

"Sorry I'm a bit late darlin'. I thought I had time to browse that cute little bookstore in town. Big mistake!" She gave Joie a pink-lipped smile and extended her hand. "I'm Maddy Crane. What's your name, sweet thing?"

Madeline Crane was well known in legal circles. Despite her frilly southern style, opponents had nicknamed her "Mad Dog" for her shrewd litigation skills, which had landed some of the largest damage amounts awarded in the Idaho court system, including a highly-publicized case that involved taking down a predator coach who acted inappropriately with female students.

Joie swallowed, rubbed her palms against the front of her jeans, and took the hand of the woman she so admired. "My name's Joie—Joie Abbott."

"Well, so very nice to meet you Joie Abbott." Maddy glanced at her diamond-encrusted watch. "I hope I didn't' hold you up from anything important, darlin'. Shall we get going?"

Joie's face broke into a wide smile. "Uh—you bet. The horses are all saddled and ready." She motioned her into the barn. "This way."

Within minutes, they were mounted and off, making their way up the trail leading to the top of Dollar Mountain. "Ms. Crane, do you visit Sun Valley often?" Joie asked, trying to make small talk.

"Yes, my firm owns a condo. And, please. Call me Maddy."

A smile sprouted on Joie's face. She forced a deep breath and met the confident blonde's gaze squarely. "Okay, sure. Maddy it is."

"I don't know why, but my surname always makes me feel so old. Not that I'm a spring chick by any means. Maybe it's true that life begins at fifty, but without the help of some very expensive cosmetics, everything starts to wear out, fall out, or spread out. And that's the sad truth darlin'. Of course, like many women of a certain age—" Her eyes sparkled as she coughed lightly into her fist. "--I'm only twenty-eight."

They shared a laugh. Not only was Madeline Crane smart as a whip, she was incredibly funny.

At the crest, Joie reined in her horse. "Here's where we usually take a break. Let the horses rest a minute."

Maddy nodded. "Sounds good to me, darlin'."

Despite the fact those boots were no doubt designed more for looks than function, Maddy dismounted like an expert, then whipped her reins over her shoulders and tightened the cinch on her saddle.

"You've ridden before?" Joie climbed off her own horse.

"Many times. My *thuh'rd* husband owned one of the largest horse farms in Kentucky."

"Yeah?"

Maddy nodded. "Sadly, that 'ole sweet-talker couldn't keep his General Lee from marching on the neighbor lady's battle-field. Especially every time a trial took me out of town."

"I'm sorry to hear that."

Maddy waved her off. "Don't be. After he fired his musket where it didn't belong, I marched my dented pride into a divorce attorney's office, then straight to a jeweler with his checkbook in hand." She held up her hand to show off one of the largest diamonds Joie had ever seen. "Despite how our marriage ended, we're still friends. He even came to my fourth wedding." She shrugged. "Unfortunately, that one died on me and I've never remarried." She patted the gelding's hindquarters. "But don't feel sorry for me. The magnolia still blossoms, if you know what I mean."

Joie offered Maddy Crane a cold bottle of water from her pack filled with ice. *Would Andrew's wife feel as magnanimous when telling her story?*

"Thank you, darlin'.." Maddy took the bottle. She loosened her grip on the reins, allowing her horse freedom to duck his head and eat a tuft of grass at her feet. He nickered his appreciation.

"What a glorious view," she said, taking in the stunning vista below. From up here, a person could see all of Ketchum and Sun Valley, bordered by the jagged Sawtooth and Pioneer mountain ranges.

After taking a drink, she smiled appreciatively and screwed the top back on her bottle. "So, tell me your story."

"My story?"

"Everybody's got a story."

Joie felt instant regret. For one of the first times in her life she wished she had a better opening argument. "I grew up here in Sun Valley. My dad's a sheep rancher. His ranch is just north of here." That, she was proud of. The next part was what gave her pause. "I—uh—left home and went to law school."

Maddy's face brightened. "You're an attorney?"

Joie averted her gaze and stared at the valley below. "Yeah. I practiced for a brief time in Boise."

"At a firm?"

Joie nodded and explained how she'd worked for a firm known for their insurance defense work. "I loved litigation, especially the discovery process. I've been told I have an inquisitive mind, but frankly I think I'm just snoopy." Nothing was more fun than finding the "smoking gun" document or email that changed the course of a case, good or bad. It was one of the few times she'd felt really competent—and respected.

Maddy nodded in solidarity. "I enjoy the fight—every case is like a giant chessboard with moving pieces requiring careful strategy to successfully checkmate the opposing king."

Joie forced a weak smile, while tamping down a familiar pang. Rarely did she admit to herself, let alone to anyone else, how much she missed being a lawyer—the thrill, the affirmation—all of it.

She made a point of looking at her watch. "Well, I suppose we should get you back." She screwed the lid on her bottle and slid it back in her pack.

The prosecution failed to rest. "You don't practice any longer?"

Doing her best to avoid meeting the look in Maddy's eyes, she slipped her foot in the stirrup and mounted her horse. "Not currently. I'm licensed, so maybe I'll activate and practice again someday."

Joie smiled as brightly as she could and eagerly steered the conversation to a safer topic. "Are you planning on going to the ice show tonight? My sister is the director of hospitality for the Sun Valley Lodge. I could get you tickets," she offered, and for the next while they made their way back to the stables chatting about the upcoming fireworks display and the best places to eat.

When they finally reached the stables, Joie's phone buzzed. *Where are you?*

Without bothering to respond, she slipped the phone back in her pocket and tethered the horses before walking Maddy Crane back to her car. "It was a real pleasure to meet you. I didn't say it earlier, but I want you to know I'm a huge fan. I followed many of your cases, especially the one with the coach. That was a remarkable win."

Maddy let a grin form. "Well, technically it wasn't a win. We settled, but not until we'd emptied the plaintiffs' bank accounts."

"I remember. It was on all the news channels."

At her car, Maddy reached into her bag and retrieved a business card. "Look, I'm a pretty good judge of character. Something tells me you are a smart woman, and might want to step back into the fray someday." She pressed the card into Joie's hand. "When you do, give me a call. I have a solo practice, but this twenty-eight-year-old is not getting any younger." She winked. "Perhaps it's time I consider taking on an associate."

Joie felt seared with disappointment, at what could've been. She quickly shook her head. "I—I doubt I'll ever move back to Boise."

Maddy shrugged. "Well, darlin', in that case we may have to think about opening a satellite office here in Sun Valley."

Joie went wide-eyed. "Uh—I don't know what to say!"

"Say you'll consider my offer." Maddy pointed to where

Joie's phone was buzzing in her pocket yet again. "And that guy who keeps texting you? I hope he knows he has a great gal." She grinned and climbed into her car. "I'll be in touch. But not for a few weeks. I'm on vacation, you know."

40

L eigh Ann couldn't breathe. She coughed and pulled her head from the oven door, gasping for air.

Yes, she had a self-cleaning oven, and a woman who came in every week to straighten her house. But neither scrubbed her Thermador entirely to her satisfaction, so every few months, for good measure, she liked to hit the interior with a blast of spray cleaner and a stiff brush.

With determination, she tucked her head back into the oven and scoured the surface with a particularly vigorous action, hoping to remove the remnants of her latest venture, both cooking and otherwise.

What had she been thinking? Even if what she believed about Mark had been true, she'd nearly taken her life over a cliff.

She'd managed to convince Karyn on the golf course that this whole misunderstanding with Mark had been no big deal. The truth was that the entire situation had shaken her to the core.

First, she'd let gossip and her own proclivity toward

looming disaster lead her down a trail where she'd thought the very worst of her husband, that he was having an affair.

And what did she do in response?

She'd decided to fix the situation in the most absurd manner, let her deepest insecurities push her into taking measures that were—well, at best silly and at worst desperate attempts to gain back the control she felt she'd lost. Not all things could be easily fixed, especially on your own.

She circled the scrub brush along the sides of her oven interior.

And then there was Thor Magnum.

God only knew what would have happened had Thor not been a gentleman that day, if he had not had the good sense to stop her from proceeding into the very thing she'd accused Mark of.

Father John would claim the good Lord had protected her from her own foolishness. If that were so, she was extremely grateful. Otherwise, she'd have gone the way of David and Bathsheba and her life would be baked.

Leigh Ann pulled her head out of the oven a second time and wiped her forearm across her sweaty brow.

That's when she saw Mark standing in the doorway of the kitchen, watching her and smiling.

She immediately felt self-conscious. "What?"

Mark cocked his head. "What in the world are you doing?"

She lifted from the floor and pulled the rubber gloves from her hand. "I'm cleaning the oven."

A puzzled look crossed his face. "But, don't we have—," he paused, letting the rest of the sentence hang in the air unspoken as he crossed over to her. He pulled the scarf from her hair and kissed the top of her head.

Instinctively, she pulled back. "I need a shower."

He put his finger to her lips. "Shhh . . . "

His finger trailed along the side of her neck. He lifted her chin. "Listen, there's something I want to say."

"Mark—"

"Shhh," he repeated, this time more insistent. "I want to tell you I'm sorry."

"Sorry?" she whispered.

"I was so wrapped up in my business deal, I neglected to hear you. Without meaning to, I let you think the worst and failed to recognize how afraid you—"

This time she put her fingers on his lips and shook her head. "No, I'm the one who is sorry, Mark. I let my insecurities get out of hand. I thought the worst. I almost made a horrible mistake."

Like some Disney movie, the sun broke from behind a cloud sending light shining through the window.

She let the gloves drop to the floor as his fingers trailed down her neck, to the buttons on her blouse. He unhooked each slowly and pulled back the fabric, revealing bare skin, and her tattoo.

Breathing heavily, Mark bent and kissed the image of the seal on her shoulder.

A tingle ran through her stomach as she clutched his dark hair and moaned.

In a quick movement, he swept her up into his arms and headed for the bedroom, but not before a car door slammed outside. He hesitated.

"Don't stop now," she pleaded, not anxious for this feeling to subside.

"Not on your life," her husband told her.

Unfortunately, the front door swung open. Colby hoisted his duffle on his shoulder. "Hey, I'm home."

Mark and Leigh Ann grinned at each other.

Mark set Leigh Ann's feet on the ground and quickly went for his back pocket and pulled out his wallet. "Hey, kid. Glad you're home. But, here's a hundred. Now take off and grab some pizza and head for your Aunt Karyn's.

Leigh Ann giggled. "Yeah, we'll meet you at the ice show."

Their son looked momentarily puzzled. A slow grin dawned and he winked at his dad. "Whatever you say, old man."

Minutes later, Leigh Ann and Mark were in bed.

He slid over her and pressed his lips to hers with an urgency she hadn't seen from her husband in some time, a passion that matched her own. It'd been a long time since they had connected like this and she wasn't about to waste a moment of this unexpected intimacy.

Mark nibbled at her ear, kissed her neck, her shoulder and then pulled the top sheet over his head as he left a trail of kisses on her stomach.

Suddenly, he lifted from beneath the sheet, his eyes wide. "Leigh Ann! What in the world?"

She giggled and pulled him back to her.

41

J oie hurried through the lobby of the Sun Valley Lodge and climbed on the elevator where she rode up to the second floor. She quickly made her way to the room where Andrew waited, and knocked on the door with a huge grin on her face.

The door opened and Andrew swept her inside and into an embrace. "It's about time you got here," he said, finding his way to her lips. He had changed into comfortable clothes and tasted of champagne.

She threw her head back and laughed seeing a half-eaten plate of chocolate covered strawberries and an open bottle on the coffee table. "I see you waited for me."

His room was much bigger this time. A dividing wall with a gas fireplace separated a sitting area with a lovely sofa and desk from the room with a king-sized bed. A balcony faced Mt. Baldy as well as a fantastic view of the ice-skating rink below, where a crowd was gathering for the ice show and fireworks display.

"What in the world took you so long?" he asked. He poured her a glass of pricey Moet and Chandon. "I've been in town for hours."

She grabbed the remote and turned down the volume on the television before taking the offered drink. "I know. I'm sorry. But just wait until you hear who I took on a trail ride."

She couldn't wait to tell him she'd met Madeline Crane, and that the feisty and highly successful attorney had dangled an offer for her to consider—an opportunity to practice law again. Not that she didn't adore the days she spent on horseback and the hours training Fresca, the new gelding she'd been working for months, as well as the horse she and Clint had rescued. She didn't even mind taking clients on trail rides.

Still, she'd gone to law school and worked hard to pass the bar exam for a reason. Not only did she enjoy the mental challenge the law provided, it was a financially sensible, and highly regarded profession. One she had intended to return to someday.

"Chatting can wait." Andrew quickly lifted his t-shirt over his head and pulled on the drawstring to his lounge pants.

Joie stepped back and held up her hand. "Whoa, Cowboy!"

"What?" He gave her a wicked grin. "I've been waiting for this rodeo all week. Open the gate, I'm ready to get bucked off." He grabbed her hand and pulled her to the bed, pushed her onto the satin duvet and pulled at the buttons to her blouse.

She escaped his embrace and laughed. "Can I at least get undressed?"

By the time they'd finished and fell back against the pillows, the sun had lowered in the sky behind Baldy. Excitement from the crowd that had gathered at the ice arena below drifted through the slightly open doors to the balcony, along with the first strains of music.

Joie placed her empty champagne flute on the bedside table. She nudged Andrew. "C'mon, let's get dressed and head out to the balcony. The show's going to start soon."

Reluctantly, Andrew pulled himself from the rumpled

bedcovers. "I'll call room service. I'm starved. You want a steak?"

She shook her head. "No, thanks. I'm not hungry." She pulled a pair of clean jeans from her overnight bag, tugged them on and threaded her belt in the loops. "But you go ahead."

Joie headed onto the balcony, anxious to catch a glimpse of the opening lineup for this summer's Sun Valley on Ice show, a truly star-studded event with skating champions in amazing costumes, and choreographed performances that left a mesmerized audience swooning and cheering for more.

Andrew stood behind her, his hands on her shoulders. "Honey, they say it's going to be at least an hour. I'm going to run down and pick my order up, since it'll be faster."

"You're not one known for patience, are you?" she teased, brushing his cheek with a kiss.

Before pulling away, his lips met hers with a dominance that suggested he'd prefer to skip the steak altogether, as well as the production unfolding below.

"Oh, no sir!" She playfully pushed him away. "I'm not missing the ice show."

He grinned "Okay, have it your way."

Andrew moved inside to finish getting dressed, but not before popping her on the backside. "Be back in a jiff," he called out before shutting the door.

She smiled, not believing her good fortune.

When she'd been forced into a decision in Boise—not even a decision really, because nothing would have allowed her to continue the relationship with Andrew while he was still married—she'd moved home to recalibrate. A few weeks turned into a month, a month to six, and then over a year. The time since moving back from Boise had been deflating, with life veering off-course and taking a trajectory she hadn't expected, or even wanted.

Now, everything seemed to be moving back in place.

But now Andrew's marriage had ended, leaving them free to pursue the strong feelings that had pulled at them in the first place. On top of that, she had a potential job on the horizon, one that might allow her to return to the practice of law.

No longer did she need to hang her head in shame and beat herself up for falling in love with a man who was already taken, with the heartache that followed.

She was free to love Andrew with wild abandon. And he loved her.

She wasn't one for fairytales, but this relationship definitely had a storybook ending.

Looking out from the balcony, she spotted a few familiar faces in the crowd below—Nash Billingsley sat near the front edge of the ice skating rink flanked by his two little grand-daughters. The Hamiltons were making their way to their seats, not far from where Trudy Dilworth sat with her camera pointed.

Her sisters would be gathered at a special table on the veranda, compliments of the Sun Valley Resort, a perk granted Karyn as the director of hospitality. Normally, she'd be right there with them, but tonight she'd be watching from this vantage point and nestled in Andrew's arms. Not necessarily a bad thing.

A phone rang from inside the room and Joie wandered back to the bedroom and picked it up from the bedside table, only to recognize it was Andrew's phone and not her own.

She hesitated, not recognizing the number. She clicked it off and put the phone back on the table.

Almost immediately, the phone rang again.

Joie scowled, torn about whether to answer it. In the end, she decided not to. Answering someone else's phone just didn't feel right.

When the phone immediately rang a third time, she reconsidered. Perhaps there was an emergency, or maybe Andrew was calling from downstairs and had forgotten her number and didn't have the ability to check the number in his phone, because here it was in her hand.

She made a split decision and slid her finger across the tiny screen. "Hello?"

"Hello," came a woman's voice. "Who is this?"

Joie frowned. "Uh, excuse me?"

There was a brief pause. "Look, I don't know who you are or why you have my husband's phone, but I can only guess he lied to me—again. You can tell that scumbag it's finally over. I don't care how much he begs this time, I'm not staying. Oh, and tell him this divorce is going to cost him—big." The phone went dead.

Joie stood there, stunned.

Her husband?

Her hand trembled as she shut off the phone and laid it back on the table, the impact of what she'd learned slamming against her chest.

He was still married. He'd lied to her!

She'd fallen for his deception and tumbled into his bed like some ninny without a brain or a lick of sense.

Humiliated, she gathered her clothes and shoved them into her bag. How could she have been so gullible? So stupid?

Tears burned at her eyelids as she zipped the bag shut and moved for the door.

Furious that she'd been duped and played for a dummy, she grabbed the costly bottle of Moet and Chandon and heaved it against the wall, sending bubbly liquid spraying across the two-toned gold wall covering and plush carpet.

She'd been a fool—once again, she'd petted a kitten only to learn he was a skunk.

Andrew Merrill had robbed her of so much—her dignity, the practice of law, her dreams.

Well, no more.

42

The days leading up to the Fourth of July holiday had stretched Karyn's abilities and self-confidence to the max.

The lodge had been booked for months, yet phones were still ringing off the hook with tourists making requests for rooms. The concierge staff had been working around the clock booking rounds of golf, horseback rides, and massages in the spa. She couldn't get enough tickets to cover the demand for the annual theatre presentation of Yankee Doodle Dandy held at the Opera House, and the ice show had been sold out for weeks.

On top of that, the laundry service had short-changed them on linen deliveries causing housekeeping delays. Two of their ice machines had gone on the blink. And Melissa Jaccard was battling a bad case of vertigo and had called in sick for the third time this month, leaving her short-handed at the front desk.

When Grayson showed up at her office door and reminded her the ice show was about to start, all she could do was look up at him with desperation.

"I'll be just a minute," she mouthed and pointed him to a chair.

"I'm sorry, ma'am. But we don't allow pets in the rooms, especially micro-pigs." She paused and listened. "No, I understand. But the Sun Valley Resort has a policy against—yes, I know who you are. I'm a huge fan. Love your movies."

She rubbed the spot between her eyebrows. "Could I suggest boarding services at the Sun Valley Animal Center? I'd be happy to make those arrangements."

Karyn smiled in Grayson's direction.

"You would? Great! I'll get that done and we look forward to having you with us."

She hung up and flung herself against the chair back with an exaggerated sigh. "A pig—the woman has a pig!"

Grayson gave her a sympathetic nod. "Wow."

"Wow is right. My entire day—no, my entire week has been like that."

"Sounds like you need some fun. You about ready to head out?" He stood and offered his hand.

One of the perks of her job was a reserved table where she and her invited guests could enjoy the ice show—a spot with an astounding view of the ice rink. Her family was gathered out at her table and no doubt wondering where she was, including Colby who had arrived home from school.

"Yes, more than ready." She reached for Grayson's hand and entwined her fingers with his.

They moved for the door when, in an uncharacteristic move, she suddenly closed her office door and leaned her back against it, grinning. "I've missed you."

Grayson beamed. "Well, I missed you too." He brushed her hair from her cheek. "It's been days."

His touch swept her into a pool of longing, a feeling so strong, the emotion startled her. "Days," she whispered.

"We could—I mean, I suppose we could catch up a bit. But

frankly, I wouldn't mind picking up where we left off—the last time we were together." There was a sparkle in his eyes as he moved so close she could feel his breath.

He was going to kiss her.

She lifted her mouth to his. They'd both waited a long time for this moment.

A knock pulled her attention and the door swung open. Jon Sebring appeared, poking his head through the open door. "Karyn? I thought I saw you—"

He was immediately taken back. "Oh, goodness. I'm so sorry." His expression turned apologetic. "I didn't know you weren't alone."

Karyn scrambled out of Grayson's embrace. "No—no, that's fine. I—uh, is there something you need?"

Grayson hung back, rubbed the back of his neck.

Jon glanced between them. "I don't want to interrupt, but I'm afraid there's a man at the front desk asking for you."

Karyn glanced at Grayson. "Oh, okay—"

"He's rather insistent," Jon said. "I told him I'd do what I could to find you."

She patted Grayson's chest. "Don't go anywhere. I'll be right back."

She followed her boss out to the lobby.

"Over there, that's him." Jon pointed to a man pacing the plush carpet in jeans and stocking feet. "He seemed very upset and insisted you were the only one who could help."

Despite his appearance, she recognized Andrew Merrill instantly. "He's a friend. I'll take care of things," she assured Jon.

Her boss nodded. "Great. See you out at the show."

Karyn wandered over. "Andrew?"

Her sister's boyfriend looked up, rushed over. "Have you seen Joie? Do you know where she is?"

"My sister? No, why?" Concern sprouted in her gut. "I thought she was with you."

Andrew seemed to deflate before her eyes. He brushed his hand through his precise hair, a move which left a couple of strands sticking up. "She was. But—" He suddenly grabbed her wrist. "Could you text her? Ask her to meet you here in the lobby?"

She heard the desperation in his voice, saw it in his eyes. "I don't understand—why don't you text her?"

Andrew heaved an intense sigh. "We had a—I think we had a misunderstanding."

"You think? You mean you don't know? What did she say?"

"She said nothing," he admitted. "I came out of the bathroom and she'd already gone."

Karyn tried to process what she was learning. Joie was one of the most direct people she knew. Rarely would she sugarcoat a thing—even if confrontation were involved. Despite how happy her sister had recently seemed, it was obvious something had gone terribly awry.

She held up open palms. "I think I need to stay out of the middle of this."

Andrew stepped back. His eyes turned dark and resolute. "I see. Well, then there's not much use in taking more of your valuable time."

She swallowed and mirrored his determined tone. "I hope you enjoy your stay at the Sun Valley Lodge."

JOIE WALKED into the dark barn and turned on the lights. The horses immediately became restless, whinnying and snorting. She passed the stalls slowly and made her way directly to the end, to the stall where they'd housed the rescue horse.

She eased the stall door open, taking care not to spook the gelding who was now on the mend, thanks to good care and strong antibiotics. "Shhh—whoa, boy."

Despite her quiet assurance, the horse's nostrils flared and he became skittish, pushing back against the wall, the scars from his injuries—both physical and emotional— still visible.

Joie reached in her jeans pocket and pulled out a sugar cube. She placed the treat in her open palm and advanced slowly, offering it up to the gelding.

At first, he wouldn't take it. Joie wasn't swayed. She patiently held out her palm. "It's okay. It's all right."

She couldn't blame the horse for its reluctance to trust after the neglect suffered at the hands of people who were supposed to care for its welfare. Turns out, trust had to be earned.

She'd learned that the hard way.

Once again, she'd clung to something that wasn't solid. Andrew Merrill had trampled on her ability to trust her own judgment. A few short years ago, she'd been poised to soar. That was before she'd tangled with a habitual sweet-talking liar.

She carefully reached out to the frightened horse again. This time the gelding took a cautious step forward, nickered and nibbled the offered sugar cube. Joie scratched the horse's ears before stepping back.

Andrew Merrill robbed her of her self-respect and made her question her own innate goodness. Then, just like that, he showed up and dangled restoration in front of her—only to rip another wound into her heart.

How could he do that to her? To his wife?

There might be fifty shades of gray, but commitment was black and white. And honor was a color Andrew Merrill would never wear.

Joie retreated against the wall, sliding down into the cedar shavings and openly wept, emptiness spreading inside her.

"Hey, you okay?"

Startled, she looked up to see Clint. Inside, she groaned. "Oh, please. Not now."

"You okay?" he repeated, moving inside the stall with her. "Because, you don't look okay."

She swiped the back of her hand across her nose. "Wow. Take me now, sailor."

He stood there for several seconds before he simply joined her on the floor. He leaned his head against the wall. "Want to talk about it?"

She sniffed and tried to sound strong, despite the tears that still rimmed her lashes. "With you? Not likely."

Clint didn't try to argue, didn't try to cheer her up. Instead, he sat there, chewing on a piece of straw. Quiet.

After a length of time, he finally broke the silence. "See that horse? Some idiots didn't recognize its value. Didn't properly care for it. But the resulting deep wounds did heal—in time, and with the proper nurturing." He paused and let his words sink in before going on. "Scars are durable, tougher than delicate flesh. You are a woman of great strength, Joie Abbott. You'll survive this hurt."

He gently placed his arm around her shoulders, pulled her close and rested his cheek against the top of her head.

And she let him.

43

Back in Karyn's office, Grayson took one look at her face and immediately knew something was up. "Hey, what's the matter?"

She shook her head. "Looks like something has happened between Joie and Andrew. I suspect it's not good."

"Something happened?"

"Yeah," she said, gathering her purse. "That was Andrew in the lobby. He asked me to help him find her."

"He lost her?"

Karyn rolled her eyes. "No, silly. She took off—like she does whenever she's hurt. C'mon, we've got to go."

"Where are we going?"

"I need to let Leigh Ann know. From there, I'm not sure." She didn't leave him any choice but to follow as she made her way back down the hall.

Grayson scrambled to catch up. "Wait!" He took hold of her wrist, stopping her midway through the lobby. "Joie knows how to reach you. I know you love her and all, but maybe she just wants to be alone to process things."

She realized with a start that he might be right. Reluctantly, she nodded. "Okay, yeah. I suppose there could be some truth in what you're saying. I just—"

He pulled her close. "No, I get it. You love your sister and what happens to her matters."

She took a deep breath, thankful he understood. "The three of us are—well, we're very close. I mean, we're different as night and day but we're like a cord of three strands, tightly woven."

Grayson lifted her knuckles to his lips and kissed them. "Even so, it's okay to unwind from them on occasion."

"Hey, there you are!" Leigh Ann appeared in the doorway leading out to the portico and waved them outside. "Hurry up, you're going to miss the show. Dad, Mark and me—we've all been waiting for you."

"What about Colby?"

Leigh Ann shrugged. "He's hanging with friends. Said he'd join up with us later." Her sister turned to Grayson. "You spend years raising them and then they never want to spend a minute with you. This morning I gave him some socks, told him I found them at the dollar store. You know what he said to me?"

Grayson shook his head. "What's that?"

"He told me I got ripped off!"

They laughed and made their way onto the portico and through the crowd.

"Hey, everybody," Grayson said as they approached the table.

Her dad stood and patted his shoulder. "Good to see you again, Grayson. This is quite the crowd, huh?"

Grayson pushed his hand through the top of his shortly-cropped hair. "Man, you're not kidding. I ended up parking at Karyn's place and I just jogged over."

She raised her eyebrows. "You jogged? All the way from my place?"

Leigh Ann slid in next to her husband. His arm went

around her shoulders and a look passed between them, one Karyn hadn't seen in a while.

Their dad seemed to notice too, and smiled. "Remember when I used to bring you girls to this show every summer?" he asked.

Karyn took a seat next to Grayson. "I sure do. One year, Leigh Ann sewed us matching outfits to wear to the show—all in red, white and blue. If I recall correctly, Joie threw a fit and refused to wear hers."

Their dad laughed. "Ah, yes. I remember. Only I'm not sure if it was the costume or the fact we wouldn't let her wear her skates."

"Yeah, just try to convince a stubborn six-year-old that blades won't work on grass," Leigh Ann murmured.

"She became quite the skater though," their dad reminded. "Every winter, Joie practiced for hours and hours on the pond out at the ranch."

"Yes, and despite her being a little pistol at every turn, I stayed out there on the ice with her, coaxing her on."

Mark squeezed her shoulders. "Always the big sister."

"Hello, hello." Trudy Dilworth swept up to their table, wearing hot pink leggings and a flowing white sleeveless top. Her ample arms were decorated with stacks of gold bracelets, that bangled as she fanned herself. "Goodness, it's warm this evening."

She glanced at Mark and Leigh Ann, raised her eyebrows. "Well, well! Just look at you two love birds—holding hands and all."

"Hi, Miss Trudy." Leigh Ann greeted her with a satisfied smile. "Where's Ruby?"

"Oh, she's been at the Opera House for days, shepherding the final touches on the Yankee Doodle Dandy production. You're all going tomorrow night, aren't you?"

"We wouldn't miss it," their dad assured her. All of them nodded in agreement.

"Well, I can't chat long. I'm joining some of my art students and they're waiting." She fingered the side of her hair. "Oh, but aren't these ice shows wonderful? Next to the symphony series, these productions are my very favorite of the summer. I especially adore the synchronized skating. Such loveliness. Did you know every big name figure skater in history has starred in this show at some point? It's true—from the 1956 Olympic champs Tenley Albright and Dick Button, all the way through to today's stars."

Miss Trudy leaned down and shielded the side of her mouth with her hand so as not to be overheard. "It's a shame the men must now wear trousers. I miss the good 'ole days when leotards were still allowed." She winked and dropped her hand. "Oh, how I wanted to be Peggy Fleming or Dorothy Hamill gliding on the ice next to all that *manliness*."

Karyn ignored the inuendo. "My favorite was Tara Lipinski."

Leigh Ann perked up, frowned. "I thought Kristi Yamaguchi was your favorite? Remember when she made that ridiculous fitness video with the California Raisins?"

"Hey now." Karyn gave her sister a look of mock horror. "What's wrong with the California Raisins?"

"Apparently not much," Leigh Ann teased. She pulled a bottle of wine from a basket she'd brought and passed out wine glasses. "Especially since you had dozens of their posters on your bedroom wall growing up. It was a toss-up who you loved more—those California Raisins or The New Kids on the Block."

That little tidbit seemed to tickle Grayson. "Is that so?"

"Don't listen to Leigh Ann," Karyn handed a corkscrew to Grayson, who took it and opened the bottle. "I think I remember my oldest sister meditating, sitting cross-legged in her bath robe for weeks after the Dalai Lama visited the Community School."

Leigh Ann rolled her eyes. "Wrong sister. That was Joie."

"Where is Joie?" Mark asked.

"We're not sure." Leigh Ann pulled out a second bottle. "She's spending time with Andrew."

Miss Trudy lifted her eyebrows "Who is this Andrew?"

"Her new boyfriend," Leigh Ann reported. "Andrew Merrill is an attorney Joie worked with in Boise."

"Oh? Well, that's wonderful!" Miss Trudy's smile was rich and genuine. "Wouldn't it be nice if she decided to practice law again. She's such a smart girl, that one."

Leigh Ann nodded. "We're all hoping."

Miss Trudy waggled her fingers in a little wave. "Well, I'd better move along. We'll see you at the Opera House tomorrow night, if not before."

Everyone bid her goodbye.

Karyn waited until the wine had been poured before she couldn't stand it any longer. "Leigh Ann, maybe we shouldn't have told Miss Trudy about Joie and Andrew."

Mark picked up his glass. "Yeah, if your sister finds out, she's going to hunt you down like a pair of Jimmy Choos on clearance."

Leigh Ann playfully punched at his gut. "What? Joie has nothing to hide. And, I can't think of anyone who cares less about brand name shoes."

Karyn glanced over at Grayson. Perhaps this problem wasn't hers to untie, but she couldn't bear to keep what she knew a secret one more minute. "I'm afraid there might be more to the story."

That got Leigh Ann's attention. "What do you mean?"

Karyn took a deep breath and recounted what had happened earlier in the lobby, how Andrew Merrill had been

frantic to find Joie. "I hope I'm wrong, but looks like the relationship has already turned sour."

Both her dad and Leigh Ann's faces showed immediate
dismay. "Oh no, I hate hearing that," her dad said.

Mark shook his head. "That's tough. We were all hopeful
she'd finally found someone."

Her sister shook her head. "Truthfully though, I was afraid
that might happen. Joie doesn't have the best track record with
men. And Andrew looked like a player. Don't you think he
looked like a player?" She took a sip of her wine.

Karyn didn't know whether to defend her sister, or agree.
"Regardless, if true, Joie's likely hurting. And that's typically
when she goes into hiding."

She wanted to say more, suggest they possibly go try and
find her, but the announcer introduced the first production
number. The crowd quieted and the music began.

Leigh Ann leaned and lowered her voice. "I just hope she
isn't at Crusty's with her friend, Jack Daniels."

Karyn nodded, took a deep breath and forced her attention on the ice, taking in the graceful movements of the
skaters as they entered the rink, the way they moved in
perfect unison, the stunning costumes and the electrifying
music.

She slipped her hand into Grayson's, knowing he was right.
Joie likely needed time to process this turn in things. There'd
be time to console her when she was ready to talk about it.

On the ice, four skaters were performing an amazing barrel
jumping routine. Karyn tucked away her concern and let the
grandness of the ice show carry her away.

At intermission, Colby showed up with two of his buddies
from high school. "Hey, everybody. Any spare room at this
table?"

"We'll make space. Sit down, boys." Leigh Ann quickly
stood and motioned for Mark to scoot over.

"Hey, Aunt Karyn. Grandpa." Colby pointed to his friends. "You remember Nick and Jimmy?"

Karyn greeted the guys and then turned to Grayson. "This is Colby, my nephew. He's an engineering major at the University of Washington and is home for the rest of the summer."

"Engineering, huh? Impressive."

Instinctively, Karyn looked to her sister. This is where Leigh Ann would often jump into a conversation and explain how she and Mark were steering their son toward a biomedical engineering specialty, and what could potentially become a very lucrative career.

Surprisingly, her sister was barely paying attention to the discussion around the table. Her head leaned close to Mark's and she whispered something in her husband's ear. They both laughed, enjoying their private exchange.

Soon, it was time for the grand finale—an amazing performance with skaters in red, white and blue costumes making their way across the ice to the tune of Lee Greenwood's patriotic song *God Bless the U.S.A.* Overhead, fireworks crackled and burst into color-filled lights sprinkled from above the crowd.

Karyn glanced sidelong at the neighboring table where a small girl perched on her father's shoulders clapped with joy. Her sister laid her head against her husband's shoulder. Colby stared at his parents with a wide grin on his face.

Grayson squeezed her hand.

She looked up into the dazzling sky, grateful. Despite a myriad of stresses, what had started out as a day filled with pressure had magically morphed into a wonderful night spent with people she loved. Most especially Grayson.

She told him so as he walked her out to her car after the ice show. "Grayson, this was a perfect evening." She wove her fingers with his. "Even though I nearly derailed the entire experience before it even started by giving in to interruptions."

He squeezed back. "Yeah, there were a few of those." He

looked at her thoughtfully, stopped and cupped her chin, lifting her face to his. "Speaking of, I believe you owe me a long overdue kiss."

"Here? In the parking lot?" She tilted her head playfully. "How would it look if some of the lodge guests were to see us?"

He grinned and lightly brushed her hair from her face. "Wouldn't be the first fireworks they'd witnessed this evening."

Grayson leaned into Karyn, so close he could smell the shampoo she'd used. They were finally alone and without interruption. He'd waited a long time for this kiss, and he wasn't about to let another second pass without feeling her lips against his own.

He reached and nested his fingers in her long silky hair—pressed his lips against hers, tenderly at first and then with growing intensity. From the moment their mouths touched, he was a man hopelessly lost, bewitched by the heady experience.

He kissed her full on the mouth, his body stilled against hers. This felt so right, so natural.

All he could hear was the roar of blood in his ears. It had been too long since he'd felt like this—far too long. He'd wanted her for months—well, from that first day when he'd stumbled upon her at the Hemingway Memorial.

Her breathing became shallow and warm on his skin as she returned his kiss with an insistence that surprised him. A groan trapped in his throat as she locked herself against his chest. "Karyn," he whispered, paralyzed by the heat of her body.

"Woo hoo—there you are!"

Their heads bolted up in unison to find the Macadams crossing the parking lot, only paces away.

His heat immediately simmered to a slow boil. He groaned in frustration. What were *they* doing here? And, why now?

Karyn raced to straighten her blouse, her hair. "Bert, Aggie —um—well, hello."

Shock crossed Aggie's face. "Oh, dear. Bert, I think we interrupted—"

"No, no," Karyn quickly assured. "No interruption. Really." She quickly glanced back at Grayson before continuing, "Did you enjoy the ice show?"

Bert nodded enthusiastically. "We had seats in the VIP box. The fireworks were stunning."

Grayson's hand went to Karyn's back. "We loved them as well. But hey, we were just about to head out. So, maybe we can catch you later?"

Karyn stepped forward and gave her former mother-in-law a hug. "Yes, I'm afraid that's true. But I'm so glad we ran into each other."

Bert and Aggie exchanged cagey glances.

"We were kind of hoping you might join us for a bite of dessert at Konditorei," Aggie said, not bothering to conceal her disappointment. "It's just a short walk. We wanted to treat you to a sampling of their sachertorte, which is simply to die for."

Amazed, he watched as Karyn's resolve melted. She looked back at him. "I suppose—I mean, maybe we have time for one little piece of chocolate cake. Don't we, Grayson?"

What was he going to say? He looked at the three of them staring at him and reluctantly nodded. "Yeah, I guess. One small piece of cake."

He wasn't sure they even heard him. Karyn had already linked her arm with Aggie's and they were three paces ahead, leaving him to walk with Bert, a situation that was uncomfortable at best, and completely awkward at worst.

Bert felt it too. They followed the women and walked the short distance in silence.

Inside the café, the women parked them at an open table

near the window and sent Bert to the counter to place their order.

Aggie set her bag on the floor next to her chair and lifted her nose in the air. "I love the way it smells in here." She turned to Grayson. "So, our girl tells us you moved here from Alaska?"

"Yes," he confirmed, joining in her attempt at small talk. "I'm a backcountry pilot." He slipped his hand over top of Karyn's.

"Goodness. That sounds . . . very adventurous." Aggie fingered her collar. "And a little dangerous."

"Well, no. Not really."

"You should see the house Tessa McCreary found for Grayson," Karyn's voice was so sparkly, it dang near glittered. "Gorgeous property up Warm Springs nestled against the river."

Bert returned to the table followed by a girl carrying a tray loaded with their desserts. He slid into his chair, lifted the napkin and placed it over his lap. "Did you just mention Tessa McCreary? She did a marvelous job finding our place, and we couldn't have asked for a more shrewd negotiator when we were vying for that house for you and Dean."

Their server placed their dessert plates. "Would anyone like coffee this evening? We are featuring a wonderfully rich European blend. Fresh roasted this morning."

Bert and Aggie nodded enthusiastically. "Oh yes," Aggie said. "Cups all around."

Bert slid a piece of dark chocolate cake onto his fork and into his mouth. He chewed with appreciation and swallowed. "Oh, this *is* delicious," he quickly reported.

Aggie's face broke into a smug smile. "Like a little piece of Vienna on a dessert plate." She turned to Karyn. "By the way dear, Bert and I are so glad we ran into you. Our talk the other day spurred us to buy you a little something." She turned to her husband. "Isn't that so, Bert?"

"Yes, we thought a lot about what you said. About how we'd always remain family, no matter what your future holds." He and Aggie exchanged wide smiles.

She pulled a blue envelope from her purse and slid it across the table. "Don't open it now. Wait to open it until later, when you're alone."

Grayson fought to keep from scowling. He stole a glance at Karyn, who seemed reluctant to meet his gaze.

She reached for the envelope. "What is it?"

Aggie waved her off. "You'll see. It's something special." She looked to her husband. "A little gift from two people who love you very much."

Perhaps he'd missed something, but there was a glimmer of challenge in the woman's eyes. Which is why later back out at her car, he urged Karyn to open the envelope.

"Aren't you curious?" he prompted. "Of course, if you'd rather open it in private, I'd understand."

"No, that's not it."

"Then what?" He knew he was being pushy. The contents of that envelope were none of his business. Still, he couldn't seem to back off from urging her to reveal what was inside.

She shrugged and pulled the blue envelope from her bag. "I warn you, the Macadams lean toward extravagance. I mean, from our earlier conversation you likely guessed they bought Dean and me a house for a wedding present. On the morning I turned thirty-two, a brand new Buick Enclave sat in our driveway wrapped in a huge red ribbon."

He raised his eyebrows and patted the top of her car. "This one?"

She nodded reluctantly. "Uh-hum. The Macadams are very affluent, and they lavished much of that wealth on Dean. When I walked down the aisle with their son, they extended that generosity my way."

He let his gaze drop to her hand. "Is that why you put the ring back on?"

A spasm of guilt crossed Karyn's face. "It's complicated," she said, with a thread of pain in her voice.

He drew a deep breath. Did he even have the right to push her to start over? Maybe she wasn't as ready as that kiss had suggested. "Look, I know it's hard to let go. I've learned that lesson from experience."

She shook her head. "This is different. His parents have been so good to me. While they can be a bit officious, and often intrusive, their hearts are in the right place. I simply can't bear to wound them in any way." The look in her eyes begged him to understand. "I'm all they have left. They need time to adjust to the idea of you and me, that's all. It's the least I can do."

How could he argue that? Still, he felt like a new puppy forced to wear the prior pet's collar.

He pointed to the envelope. "So, you going to open that?"

"Of course." As if to make a point, she donned a bright smile and ripped the end open, then pulled out a folded paper that appeared to be an official document of some sort. A frown quickly sprouted on her face.

"What is it?"

"I—I'm not sure." She curiously fingered the gold seal at the bottom.

He held out his hand. "Do you mind?"

She slid the document into his hand and fixed her eyes on him, blinking nervously.

After scanning the contents, his head shot up, confused. "The Macadams bought you a pair of cemetery plots?"

Karyn chewed her nail and slowly nodded. "Next to theirs."

"I don't get it."

She reluctantly stared at him. "They're for me—and Dean."

He rubbed at his jawline. "You mean, Dean isn't already—" He didn't finish his sentence.

"Dean once mentioned he wanted his ashes spread at the Hemingway Memorial," she explained. "So, I never—I put things off for a while. Until I felt ready."

Understanding suddenly dawned. So, that's what she was doing that day when he first saw her. The revelation pushed the air from his lungs. "Oh."

Karyn gently pulled the cemetery deed from his hand. "The Hemingway Memorial—it was a bit of a private joke between the two of us."

Grayson rubbed at the back of his neck. "So, you want to be buried next to your dead husband, and his parents?"

Flustered, she refolded the certificate. "I—I don't know. I mean, no—Dean and I both wanted to be cremated."

His whole body felt odd, like an engine idling too fast. What was he supposed to do with this news?

He paced the pavement, trying to find the right words.

She grabbed his wrist. "Grayson, talk to me."

It felt for a moment like time had stopped. Finally, he flipped around and stared at her. "Karyn, what is it you want?" He motioned between them. "From this?"

"What do you mean?"

"I need you to know that I'm not pushing you. I get that you lost your husband a relatively short time ago, and I can only imagine the pain you still carry at some level. That in a way, you'll always have a spot in your heart for Dean. I understand. Really, I do."

"But . . . ?"

He looked right at her. "I need to know what you want?"

"You asked me that already, and I don't know what you're getting at?" She looked in a near panic. Even so, he wouldn't retreat. This was too important.

He took both her hands in his. "I don't date." Seeing the confusion on her face, he hurried to clarify. "I acknowledge we are still very early in this relationship, but I need you to know I moved into this with full understanding of what I hoped for. I looked ahead—months, years—I don't know how long, but I knew that somewhere out there I wanted you in my life."

"Like in marriage?" she asked, her eyes wide.

Obviously, all this was coming at her far too fast. He forced himself to slow down and explain. "Perhaps." He fingered one of her shoulders. "Of course, that would be down the road a ways."

He took a deep breath and leaned back against her SUV, looking up into the starry black sky. "The entire time I was married to Robin, I had to compete—with her schedule, her ambition, her job. Finally, I lost out to another man, one I didn't even realize was in the picture until it was too late."

She reached for his arm. "Grayson—"

He hesitated, but was unwilling to pull back. "I want you in my life, Karyn. But I won't compete with Dean." He swallowed and looked her directly in the eyes. "I just can't."

44

"Oh my, and what did you say back?"

Karyn laid her head against the back of the rocking chair on her dad's porch, filled with misery. "That's the trouble, Leigh Ann. I didn't say anything."

Her sister sighed, reached out for her hand. "Oh honey, I'm so sorry."

In the distance, Joie's truck barreled down the lane, a plume of dust trailing behind.

Leigh Ann shook her head. "I wish she'd learn to slow down."

Karyn bent and petted Riley, curled up at her feet. "Not going to happen."

Minutes later, Joie climbed the porch steps with a bright look on her face. "Hey, you two."

Leigh Ann exchanged a confused look with Karyn. "Hey to you too."

"You okay?" Karyn ventured.

"I'm fine. Why shouldn't I be?" Joie's worn cowboy boots scuffed against the wood on the porch as she made her way to the third rocking chair and sat.

Leigh Ann wasn't one to dance around the bush. "Karyn met up with Andrew at the lodge."

"Oh," she shrugged and picked something off her jeans. "That."

"Yes, that." Leigh Ann countered. "What happened? Karyn suspected you two might have had a blow up. Are you still together?"

Their younger sister shrugged. "Well, that would be a negative." She turned somber. "Look, there's something I need to tell you. That I probably should have told you guys a long time ago."

Joie took a deep breath, and spilled.

She told her sisters all about her history with Andrew, how closely they'd worked together at the firm, creating a situation where they'd spent many late nights at the office, just the two of them. She revealed how she'd come to admire Andrew and how she'd felt when he singled her out for special projects, and then when he heaped on accolades and praised her efforts in front of others.

"Before long, I was hopelessly infatuated. Of course, it didn't take a lot of nudging on his part for me to believe it was love." She shook her head. "No, I can't sugarcoat any aspect of this story. I did love him."

Confusion creased Leigh Ann's forehead. "I don't understand. Then why in the world did you leave him and the firm and return to Sun Valley?"

Karyn reached and gently touched her sister's arm. "Let her tell the story."

"Of course. I'm sorry." Leigh Ann sighed. "Go on."

Joie wistfully looked out from the front porch as if the rest of the story might be found in the grass out in the meadow. After a long pause, she opened her mouth and made a simple comment. "I mucked up—big."

Leigh Ann scowled. "Messed up how?"

"He was married."

The implication of what her sister had just admitted hit. Karyn's heart thudded painfully in her chest for several long seconds. She exchanged glances with Leigh Ann, who seemed unable to respond.

"Go on," Karyn urged, forcing sympathy in her voice.

Joie looked over at them miserably. "I ended it all as soon as I learned. That's why I ran home."

"And you hid out here," Leigh Ann said, comprehension flooding her expression.

Karyn leaned forward from her chair. "But I don't get it. Then why did you start everything back up again if you knew he was married? Especially after you took such a bold step and left him behind."

Leigh Ann looked heartbroken. "Karyn makes a good point, Joie—yes, why?"

Uncharacteristic tears rimmed Joie's lashes. "Yeah, that's deserved. Like an idiot, I believed him when he said he was divorced."

"He lied to you?" Leigh Ann popped up from her chair, her eyes flashing anger. "That rotten puke!"

Understanding dawned. "So, you ended it," Karyn said. "That's why Andrew was so distraught and looking for you last night."

Joie nodded.

Leigh Ann knelt and took Joie's hands in her own. "I'm sorry I wasn't there for you."

Joie's thumb caressed her big sister's hand. "I knew you and Karyn were here. I didn't want you to think less of me for falling for Andrew in the first place. It was a stupid thing to do. Like something out of a bad movie, or something."

Leigh Ann held up a palm, silencing her. "Oh, honey. Stupid runs in this family, I guess." She stood. "I suppose it's time I come clean as well."

Over the next minutes, Leigh Ann choked out her own admission—that in her recent hurt and confusion over Mark's suspected adultery, she'd stupidly sought retribution with Thor Magnum. "While nothing happened, it could have. I was lucky and Mark showed up."

"God, what did Mark do?" Joie asked, voicing Karyn's exact thought.

Leigh Ann's face broke into an impish smile. "Well, he pulled that six-foot-tall hunk of a man out of that car and threatened to beat the crap out of him, that's what!"

Joie grinned. "Way to go, Mark!"

"Yeah, that's very romantic, if you ask me," Karyn added.

Leigh Ann's face turned somber. "Moral of the story, I have a great man and we love each other very much. I will never doubt him again."

She turned to Karyn. "What about you? What are you going to do about Grayson Chandler? Seems you have a good man too." She paused. "That is, unless you blow it and let him walk away."

KARYN SAT IN HER SUV, gathering her nerve. Several seconds passed before she finally drew a deep breath and opened the door, focused on the task ahead.

She walked up the sidewalk leading to Grayson's house, remembering a day not so long ago when she'd persuaded him to make the purchase, how she'd convinced him the house would be perfect.

Secretly, she'd wanted to spend time with him here—even then, secretly hoping their friendship might blossom into something more, even if she hadn't been able to admit it to herself at that time.

Karyn stepped up to the front door, her mouth turning to

cotton and her palms sweating. Would he even want to hear what she had to say?

She raised a shaking hand to knock, then realized the doorbell was a better option and pushed the button. It felt like an eternity before she heard movement beyond the door and it swung open.

Grayson stood there looking surprised. "Karyn?" He wore jeans and a light blue shirt, with the bottom buttons left open. He was barefooted.

"I need to talk to you." She didn't wait for him to answer. She brushed past him and quickly glanced around the foyer and his living room, appreciating all he'd done since moving in. "I like it," she said.

Looking confused, he brushed his hand through the top of his hair. "You hungry? I was just about to fix a sandwich."

"What kind?"

He shook his head, still puzzled. "Uh, meat." He headed for the kitchen.

She followed, lagging behind several paces. "What kind?"

Grayson tilted his head back in her direction. "Depends. What kind do you want?"

She approached him achingly slow. "Are you asking me what I want? Because I've done a lot of thinking and I know what I want."

Grayson's face lit up. He pivoted, strolled to meet her. "You do?"

"Oh, yes. I do." She held up her hand, showing off her naked finger. "No longer any question about it."

He pulled her into his arms and nestled his face against her hair. "I'm really glad to hear that."

Her heart pounded, she lifted and touched his chin, traced the edge. "I was lucky to have loved Dean, but he's gone. I'll do anything I have to in order to have a new life—with you."

"And the plots?"

"I thanked Bert and Aggie and returned their gift."

The news that she'd declined their largesse seemed to make him extremely happy. Even so, he pulled back, looked at her intently. He regarded her a long moment, then reminded her softly, "I don't date."

She grinned back at him. "No need to worry, Grayson. Neither do I."

He wouldn't let her break eye contact. "Good, because I plan to give you one hundred percent of me every single day I have the chance, and with any luck, I'll get to do that for a very long time."

45

Gravel crunched beneath her feet as Karyn traversed the walkway leading to the Hemingway Memorial. Overhead, the sun dazzled against a clear blue sky. A pair of yellow-and-black butterflies flitted from a wild poppy, glided across the path in front of her to a clump of blue flax.

In the distance, the sound of water bubbling across the rocky streambed pulled her toward the monument. A stand of aspen trees shaded the area, their tiny dollar-shaped leaves barely moving in the still air.

She tucked the tiny box against her chest, moving forward with determination. At the creek bed, she stopped and knelt, sinking her knees into the rich, brown dirt.

"Well, Dean. I'm back." Her hands trembled as she stared down at the box, ran her fingers across the crossed skiis. "I'm finally ready."

A gentle breeze blew through the aspen leaves, sending them dancing in the air.

"But before I do, I need you to know that I'll always love our story, that I'll often pull the pages of our life together from the recesses of my mind and read them again and again. Ours was such a beautiful story—and in many ways, you were the one who gave me the strength to start a new one."

She took a deep breath, appreciating the clean, crisp air. "You see, I've found someone who is willing to hold the pieces of my heart, the fragments that formed the night you died, and put them back together. I want to be whole again."

She lifted and removed the lid from the box.

Through misty eyes, she carefully held the wooden container over the stream. "I will always love you, Dean Macadam."

She scattered the contents across the rippling water.

Deeply satisfied, she stood on the bank with her hands folded in reverent silence, watching the contents float down the stream. She remained that way, taking in the moment, until finally the dusty film on top of the water was no longer in sight.

She drew a deep breath, knowing this hour, this minute— she would tuck inside her heart and remember forever.

When she turned, she smiled broadly—and waved at her sisters who stood waiting for her at the car.

EPILOGUE

Hey, everybody—Miss Trudy here. Kellie and I are so glad you joined us for the debut story in the Sun Valley Series. Don't you just love these three sisters? I hope you'll continue to read on.

I'm not one to spread gossip, but rumor has it there is a lot in store for readers. Take Leigh Ann's husband for instance. Both Ruby and I believe something is up with that new business venture. You can count on it.

And Joie is on the brink of some very good things. Not only will she partner with that sassy southern attorney and start a law practice in Sun Valley, but there's a budding relationship with a certain stable manager that we're all wanting to see unfold. Am I right?

And, Lordy! I'm afraid there are some real surprises on the horizon for sweet Karyn—not all of them good—and just when she and Grayson have committed to a pursue their new relationship.

Anyway, sweet things, Kellie is writing as fast as she can. Make sure and sign up for her **newsletter** by clicking HERE so you get notices when future books in the series are available.

Don't forget to check out all the information on Sun Valley she has on her **website** at www.kelliecoatesgilbert.com (PS—that's her hometown area!)

You might also enjoy Kellie's new **LOVE ON VACATION** stories. These shorter length romances invite readers to come on vacation with characters who travel to Sun Valley and stay at the iconic Sun Valley Lodge. This groundbreaking series is packed with tales of dating and mating, love and marriage and promises to keep your emotions and your funny bone on high alert. You'll also see a few recognized characters from the SISTERS book show up on occasion. Click HERE to check out the first story, *Otherwise Engaged.*

Well, I've got to scoot. I have an art class to teach. But, we'll see each other again soon!

~Miss Trudy

ALSO BY KELLIE COATES GILBERT

THE MAUI ISLAND SERIES

Under The Maui Sky

Silver Island Moon

Tides of Paradise

The Last Aloha

Ohana Sunrise

Sweet Plumeria Dawn

Songs of the Rainbow

Hibiscus Christmas

-

THE PACIFIC BAY SERIES

Chances Are

Remember Us

Chasing Wind

Between Rains

-

THE SUN VALLEY SERIES

Sisters

Heartbeats

Changes

Promises

-

LOVE ON VACATION SERIES

Otherwise Engaged

All Fore Love

-

TEXAS GOLD SERIES

A Woman of Fortune

Where Rivers Part

A Reason to Stay

What Matters Most

-

STAND ALONE NOVELS

Mother of Pearl

* * *

Available at all retailers

www.kelliecoatesgilbert.com

ABOUT THE AUTHOR

USA Today Bestselling Author Kellie Coates Gilbert has won readers' hearts with her compelling and highly emotional stories about women and the relationships that define their lives. A former legal investigator, she is especially known for keeping readers turning pages and creating nuanced characters who seem real.

In addition to garnering hundreds of five-star reviews, Kellie has been described by RT Book Reviews as a "deft, crisp storyteller." Her books were featured as Barnes & Noble Top Shelf Picks and were included on Library Journal's Best Book List.

Born and raised near Sun Valley, Idaho, Kellie now lives with her husband of over thirty-five years in Dallas, where she spends most days by her pool drinking sweet tea and writing the stories of her heart.

For a complete listing of books and to connect with Kellie, visit her website:

www.kelliecoatesgilbert.com